...**HER**

"...US
The nighting... to have
c...use to expect... ...racters,
a... ...ings ...at are tough to predict, won't be disappointed."   —*Publishers Weekly*

"Andrews's smooth and erudite style, realistic snappy
dialogue, and subtle humor create an intriguing and
entertaining romp."   —*New York Journal of Books*

DUCK THE HALLS

"Andrews leavens the action with her trademark
humor, including dueling Christmas dinners and an
extravagant—and extravagantly funny—live Nativity
scene."

—*Publishers Weekly*

"*Duck the Halls* offers a wealth of yuletide yuks amid
the Christmas carnage, and Andrews' faithful fans will
flock to greet the birth of her latest funfest."

—*Richmond Times-Dispatch*

"Meg, as well as her quirky extended family, makes this
humorous cozy a holiday treat."   —*Booklist*

THE HEN OF THE BASKERVILLES

"The 15th novel in this bird-themed popular cozy
mystery series offers more fine-feathered foibles
to chuckle over. Andrews' ever-present humor and
detailed animal lore will be familiar pleasures, and
the grounded and endearing heroine offers the perfect
balance to the silly shenanigans in this neatly plotted
potboiler."   —*RT Book Reviews*

"Diverting . . . Enjoyable."   —*Publishers Weekly*

SOME LIKE IT HAWK
"Uproarious."   —*Criminal Element*

"[This] series gets better all the time."   —*Booklist*

THE REAL MACAW
"As always, Andrews laces this entertaining whodunit with wit, a fine storyline, and characters we've come to know and love."   —*Richmond Times-Dispatch*

STORK RAVING MAD
"Meg grows more endearing with each book, and her fans will enjoy seeing her take to motherhood."
        —*Richmond Times-Dispatch*

SWAN FOR THE MONEY
"As usual in this hilarious series . . . a good time is guaranteed for everyone except Meg."
        —*Kirkus Reviews*

"The Meg Langslow series just keeps getting better. Lots of cozy writers use punny titles, but Andrews backs them up with consistently hilarious story lines."
        —*Booklist*

SIX GEESE A-SLAYING
"Fans will enjoy [this] entry in Andrews's fine-feathered series."   —*Publishers Weekly*

"Fans of comic cozies who have never read Andrews' Meg Langslow mysteries have a real treat in store. . . . Lots of silly but infectious humor and just enough mystery."   —*Booklist*

Also by Donna Andrews

The Nightingale Before Christmas

A Meg Langslow Mystery

Donna Andrews

St. Martin's Paperbacks

This is a work of fiction. All of the characters, organizations, and events portrayed in this novel are either products of the author's imagination or are used fictitiously.

THE NIGHTINGALE BEFORE CHRISTMAS

Copyright © 2014 by Donna Andrews.
Excerpt from *Lord of the Wings* copyright © 2015 by Donna Andrews.

All rights reserved.

For information address St. Martin's Press, 175 Fifth Avenue, New York, NY 10010.

ISBN: 978-1-250-04959-9

Printed in the United States of America

Minotaur hardcover edition / October 2014
St. Martin's Paperbacks edition / October 2015

St. Martin's Paperbacks are published by St. Martin's Press, 175 Fifth Avenue, New York, NY 10010.

10 9 8 7 6 5 4 3 2 1

Acknowledgments

Thanks, as always, to everyone at St. Martin's/Minotaur, including (but not limited to) Matt Baldacci, Anne Brewer, Hector DeJean, Melissa Hastings, Paul Hochman, Andrew Martin, Sarah Melnyk, Talia Sherer, Mary Willems, and my editor, Pete Wolverton. And thanks again to David Rotstein, Stanley Martucci, and the art department for the glorious Christmas cover. One of these days I hope to give them a bird of paradise to work with.

More thanks to my agent, Ellen Geiger, and the staff at the Frances Goldin Literary Agency for handling the boring (to me) practical stuff so I can focus on writing.

Many thanks to the friends—writers and readers alike—who brainstorm and critique with me, give me good ideas, or help keep me sane while I'm writing: Stuart, Elke, Aidan, and Liam Andrews, Renee Brown, Erin Bush, Carla Coupe, Chris Cowan, Meriah Crawford, Ellen Crosby, Kathy Deligianis, Laura Durham, Suzanne Frisbee, John Gilstrap, Barb Goffman, Peggy Hansen, C. Ellett Logan, David Niemi, Alan Orloff, Valerie Patterson, Shelley Shearer, Art Taylor, Robin Templeton, Dina Willner, and Sandi Wilson. Thanks for all kinds of moral support and practical help to my blog sisters and brothers at the Femmes Fatales: Dana Cameron, Charlaine Harris, Dean James, Toni L.P. Kelner, Catriona McPherson, Kris Neri, Hank Phillipi Ryan, Mary Saums, Marcia Talley, and Elaine Viets. And thanks to all the TeaBuds for years of friendship.

Thanks to Sarah Byrne, who gave generously at the Bouchercon Albany charity auction to have a character named after her. I hope the Art Deco room pleases. Melissa Banks also donated generously to the Malice Domestic auction to enable her daughter Kate to appear as Sarah's business partner. And, of course, thanks, as always, to Dina Willner for allowing me to name Dr. Blake's frequent co-conspirator after her late mother.

Much gratitude to Regan Billingsley of Interiors and Sandra Beveridge for answering my questions about show houses and the design world. Any mistakes in the text are obviously ones I made in spite of their patient and generous assistance. Mark Stevens provided invaluable answers to my questions about Virginia's criminal code. If this book contains any legal errors, they are obviously things I also should have asked him about.

And above all, thanks to the readers who continue to read Meg's adventures.

Chapter 1

December 20

"Passementerie."

Mother was standing in the evergreen-trimmed archway between the living room and the foyer, directly beneath the red-and-gold "Merry Christmas" banner, frowning at something she was holding.

Since I had no idea who or what "passementerie" was, I just sat there in the foyer of the Caerphilly Designer Show House with my pen poised over my notebook-that-tells-me-when-to-breathe, waiting for Mother to elaborate. For a few moments I heard nothing but the soothing strains of an orchestra playing "Silent Night" from a radio somewhere behind Mother.

Evidently Jessica, the reporter from the Caerphilly College student newspaper, wasn't as patient as I was. After all, she was here to interview the dozen interior designers who were decorating rooms in the show house, not to play guessing games with them.

"What's 'passementerie'?" she asked.

"Elegant, elaborate edgings or trimmings"—Mother stepped closer and showed us the little bit of black-and-purple braid she held in her hand—"with braid, cord, embroidery, or beads. The right passementerie can absolutely make or break an upholstery project."

"I see," Jessica said, although I could tell she didn't really. Nor was it clear to me why Mother had interrupted my interview with the reporter to display bits of upholstery trimming to us. But before answering, I glanced around and let the Christmas decorations surrounding me temper my mood. The holly and red velvet ribbons wrapping the stair rails. The gold mobile of stars and angels hanging from the ceiling light in the upper hallway. The fact that Mother had a few strands of gold tinsel snagged in her hair.

"Today's new word, then," I said aloud. "Passementerie. Do you want me to use it in a sentence?"

"That would be nice, dear," Mother said. "Particularly if the sentence is something like, 'Hello, Mother. The UPS man just delivered a package from the Braid Emporium containing the passementerie you ordered.'"

"Alas," I said. "The UPS man only delivered two packages, and neither of them contained passementerie." There. That was also a sentence.

"The Braid Emporium was supposed to overnight it," Mother said. "The day before yesterday."

I lifted my hands and eyebrows in a gesture meant to convey the utmost sympathy along with a complete refusal to take responsibility for the shortcomings of either the United Parcel Service or the Braid Emporium.

"Maybe it's hidden under all the snow," Jessica said. "The drifts are two feet high in some places."

"I've checked the drifts," I said. "And packages began disappearing long before the first snowstorm."

"Perhaps one of the other decorators took it by mistake?" Mother gestured as if tucking a stray lock of her beautiful if implausible blond hair back into her chignon. I hadn't actually seen any strands out of place, so I assumed she was trying to suggest that she had been working so hard that she was in danger of becoming disheveled.

"Always possible that someone else picked it up by mistake," I said. "That's why I asked everyone yesterday to please stop having stuff shipped here to the show house—to avoid such misunderstandings." And to avoid the possibility that one of the more competitive decorators would try to sabotage the competition by diverting important packages. "But I assume your passa-whatzit had already been sent before then. I'll ask them all."

Mother closed her eyes and allowed one faint, long-suffering sigh to escape. The reporter didn't sigh, but she was clearly impatient. Or maybe just hyperactive, from the manic way she was tapping her feet on the floor and drumming her fingers on her knees. And upstairs someone's radio came on, tuned to a very different Christmas station. I liked both "Run, Run Rudolph" and "Silent Night," but not simultaneously.

"I'll be in my room when you find my package," Mother said.

She sailed back through the archway, head held even higher than usual. Her head brushed the evergreens framing the doorway, making all the tiny little bells attached to the branches tinkle merrily. The bells lifted my mood, and I glanced over to see if Jessica was impressed. Most people were when they met Mother, who in her seventies still had the slender elegance and regal blond looks of someone decades younger.

Jessica didn't look impressed. Just impatient.

"In her room?" Jessica asked. "I didn't realize anyone lived here."

"She doesn't," I said. "She's decorating the great room. Which is decorator-speak for what we normal humans call the living room. Or maybe the family room."

Jessica had stopped tapping, thank goodness, but now she was nervously twisting one lock of her copper-red hair around a finger.

"I thought the old guy with the beard and the Georgia accent was the decorator," she said.

"That's Eustace Goodwin," I said. "He's decorating the kitchen and the breakfast room." And would probably have a fit if he heard himself described as "the old guy with the beard." Eustace was a dapper if slightly plump fifty-something.

"You need a different decorator for each room?"

I managed to stop myself from responding with my own version of Mother's long-suffering sigh. Clearly Jessica hadn't read any of the material we'd sent over to the student paper before showing up here to do her story. I needed to start at the beginning, which meant the interview would probably take a lot more time. Not even ten o'clock, and I could already see my plan for the day going down the drain.

But instead of snapping at Jessica, I closed my eyes and took a deep breath. At any other time of year, I'd have counted to ten, but this close to Christmas, all it took was the holiday scents to calm me: spruce, pine, cinnamon, and clove. And upstairs, someone had changed the "Run, Run, Rudolph" radio to the same channel Mother was on, so now I could hear "The First Noel," in stereo. I reminded myself that I'd finished all my Christmas shopping and most of the wrapping. I could do anything.

"This is a decorator show house," I said, opening my eyes and focusing back on Jessica.

She had pulled out a small digital camera and was craning her neck around, taking pictures of random things while she listened to me. At least I assumed she was listening.

"The house is sponsored by the Caerphilly Historical Society. In a show house, you get a different designer for each room, and they all show off their best possible work. When the show house opens—in three days, on Christmas Eve—people will pay to tour it, and the historical society gets half of the money."

"If there's any left after paying the decorators," she said.

"No, the decorators don't get paid," I replied. "They're doing this for free."

"For free? All of it?" Jessica looked up at the holly-decked crystal chandelier over our heads, which would not have been out of place in a small palace, and snapped a few pictures of it.

"They do it for the exposure," I said. "If you're someone with a big house and enough money to hire a decorator, what better way to check out the local talent than to come to a show house, where a whole bunch of designers are demonstrating their talent?"

"That really works?" Jessica sounded dubious. "I mean, have you actually gotten any clients for *your* decorating business that way?"

"I'm not a decorator," I said.

"You're not? Then what are you doing here?"

A question I asked myself at least once a day. What was I doing here when I could be home with my family, enjoying the holiday season? Maybe even spending a little time at my anvil since Caerphilly College was on winter break and my husband Michael would be home to watch our five-year-old twins. Ever since the boys had arrived, my once-thriving blacksmithing career had taken a backseat to sippy cups, naps, and lately T-ball.

I glanced up to see that Jessica was still waiting for an answer. And frowning as if I'd been trying to pull a fast one on her by impersonating a decorator. Well, I probably could if I wanted to. I couldn't tell a finial from a mullion, but after the last few weeks I could toss off the jargon like a real pro.

"I'm the on-site coordinator," I said. "Here to keep everyone organized."

"Sounds like a thankless job," she said. "How'd they rope you into that?"

"They threatened to turn my house into the show house," I said. "I agreed to organize it if they'd hold it somewhere else. Anywhere else."

"Yeah, that'd be worth it. So, the people who come to see this are mostly rich people, right?"

"Or people who want to see what the pros do to help them get some ideas for their own do-it-yourself projects," I said. I actually wanted to ask why she was taking so many pictures of the banister and the stair treads. "Some people come to get holiday inspiration—since this is a Christmas show house, after the designers finish doing their rooms, they get to decorate them for Christmas." Should I remind them again about the holiday part of their marching orders? Some of them, like Mother, had gone overboard, but others had yet to hang a single strand of tinsel.

"And every room decorated in a different style?" she asked.

"By a different decorator," I said. "And so probably in a different style. For example, as you can see, Ivy Vernier, the decorator in charge here in the foyer, is an expert in trompe l'oeil. Painting stuff so it looks real," I added, seeing her blank look at the French phrase. A few weeks ago I might not have known it myself. I pointed downward. "That floor's not really marble."

"It's not?" Jessica bent over, and then plopped down on the floor, the better to study it at close range. She began tapping on the floor, as if testing to see if it really was wood. "Wow. Can I talk to the painter?"

"She's not here at the moment." Ivy had gone home with another headache. She'd been doing that a lot lately. Was it, as she claimed, a combination of paint fumes and eyestrain from so much close work? Or was the pressure of our deadline getting to her? Or was she reacting to the stress of dealing with the other designers? Dealing with one in particular—

"She'll be around a lot in the next two days," I said aloud. "To finish up her work before our opening. She might even come back before you leave today, and if she doesn't, I can give you her contact information."

Jessica nodded, and took several pictures of the faux marble floor. And then several of the faux oriental carpet in the center of the marble.

"And on the walls she's illustrating Christmas carols and the fairy tales of Hans Christian Andersen," I added. To one side of the door, the Little Match Girl already sat shivering in sparkling painted snow. The three kings processed majestically up the wall beside the stairs, bearing the richest, most bejeweled gifts I'd ever seen. But the seascape of "I Saw Three Ships A-Sailing In" was only three quarters finished, and the painting of "The Steadfast Tin Soldier" barely begun—how could Ivy possibly find time to finish?

I banished those thoughts and concentrated on the reporter, who was staring at the three kings. And reaching out to tap them.

"Careful," I said, grabbing her arm. "Some of the paint might still be wet."

"Yeah," she said. "Wow. So what's in here?"

She scrambled up and headed for the double French doors at the right side of the foyer.

"The study," I said. "Done in a modern interpretation of the Art Deco style by Sarah Byrne from the decorating firm of Byrne, Banks, and Bailey."

"Wow!" She was peering through the glass panes. And probably leaving a nose print. For a reporter, she hadn't yet displayed a very impressive vocabulary. I hoped she'd find a few more varied expressions for her article. But I had to admit that, like Ivy's painting, Sarah's black, red-and-gold Deco-themed fantasy was worth a few wows. I coveted it, just a little. A good thing Michael and I were very happy with our Arts and Crafts style interior—decorated, naturally, by Mother.

Of course, if seeing Sarah's room inspired Mother to do a little Art Deco experimentation, I could find a room in our oversized Victorian house for it. Michael's office, perhaps? Or one of the guest rooms?

"This designer's not around either?" Jessica stepped into the room and ran her finger over the dramatically curved arm of the closest of a pair of Art Deco armchairs upholstered in red velvet.

"She was here a minute ago," I said. "Probably had to fetch something." I was disappointed not to find Sarah around. If Jessica was going to interview some of the decorators, Sarah was one of the ones I wanted to steer her toward, and not just because I found her congenial. She was also articulate, upbeat, and funny. She usually wore a streak of some bright color in her blond hair—green, purple, red; whatever fit her mood—and dressed in odd but interesting clothes.

I was hoping Jessica would illustrate her article not only with pictures of the rooms but also a few of the more presentable designers. Mother's cool blond elegance. Eustace's dapper charm. Sarah's puckish grin and funky retro style.

Yes, definitely a good idea to keep Jessica here till Sarah came back. I nodded with approval as the reporter drifted around the room, taking pictures.

"Try out the chair," I suggested. "You'd be amazed how comfortable it is."

She perched tentatively on the edge of the red-velvet seat and then smiled and relaxed back into it.

"Wonderful," she said. "I would love to have a chair this comfy for studying back at my dorm room. Why do I suspect it might cost a little more than I want to pay?"

"It probably costs as much as your annual tuition," I said. "And my husband's on the faculty at Caerphilly College, so yes, I know how high tuition is. Those chairs are Sarah's pride and joy. Authentic something-or-others."

"If I ever get filthy rich, I'll buy one," she said, wriggling a little deeper into the chair. "But what happens to the chairs when the show is over? The owner of the house doesn't get to keep them, surely?"

"The owner of the house is the First Bank of Caerphilly," I said, "which has been trying to sell it ever since they foreclosed on it six years ago. They very graciously agreed to let us use it for the Christmas show house. They're putting it up for sale as soon as the show is over, so of course they're hoping that someone will fall in love with it and want to buy it."

"Weird that it wouldn't sell before," she said. "It's a nice house. Or did it need a lot of fixing up after being empty for six years?"

"The Shiffley Construction Company did a little fixing up, as their donation to the project."

"That's the company Mayor Shiffley owns?"

"Yes. Randall Shiffley's a big supporter of the historical society." And luckily, not here to hear me call thousands of dollars in major repairs "a little fixing up."

"So if all the decorators—" Jessica began.

"I am going to kill that man," came a voice from the doorway.

Chapter 2

Jessica and I looked up to see a tall ash-blond woman standing in the doorway. Martha Blaine, another designer. The one Mother and I called "the other Martha"—though not, of course, to her face, because we'd figured out she wasn't a big Martha Stewart fan. Like Mother, she was tall enough that her head brushed the trailing evergreens, and she whacked them aside with a vicious swipe.

A loud hammering began upstairs.

"I said—" Martha began, raising her voice to be heard over the hammering.

"You're going to kill him," I said. "I get it. You'll have to take a number, though. What's he done now?"

I didn't have to ask who she wanted to kill. There were only two male decorators in the house, and everyone loved Eustace Goodwin.

"What hasn't he done?" She paused as if briefly overcome by the weight of Clay Spottiswood's transgressions. I heard the whir of Jessica's camera as she took a few pictures of Martha in the doorway.

I wondered, not for the first time, if Martha had stage experience. Not only did she carry herself with a certain dramatic flair, she also had the trick of speaking from the diaphragm so her voice could easily be heard in the last row of the theater. Or, in this case, in the farthest corners of the house. Outside the study the hammering stopped, and everything suddenly seemed very still, as if all the other designers on the premises were pausing to eavesdrop.

"What's he done today?" I asked.

"He's been rinsing paintbrushes and rollers in my bathroom again," Martha said. "And bloody carelessly. Oh, and he's dripped paint all over Violet's room on his way to mine."

Inhaling the evergreen scent wouldn't help with this. I closed my eyes to count to ten. Martha, who'd had several occasions to watch me perform this temper-calming ritual over the last few weeks, waited patiently. I hadn't even made it to five before Jessica piped up.

"Who's this you're going to kill?" she asked.

I frowned at Martha and shook my head to suggest that perhaps we should not be having this conversation in front of a reporter. Either she didn't get my signals or she ignored them.

"Claiborne Spottiswood," she said. "If he doesn't stop messing up other people's rooms— I don't know why Clay was allowed to participate in the show house to begin with."

"He's a local decorator, and he turned in his application before the deadline, and the committee approved him," I responded.

Martha scowled at that, but didn't say anything. I didn't have to remind her that she had waited until two weeks after the deadline to apply, and wouldn't have gotten in, despite her impressive reputation, if the committee hadn't been short on applicants and eager not to offend her. I thought she should be happy with what the committee had given her—two bathrooms and the laundry room. Not the most glamorous rooms in the house, but still, rooms that could be fabulous when done by a designer with her talent. In the five years since she'd moved from Richmond to set up shop here in Caerphilly, she'd quickly become one of the town's leading decorators.

But even though she was well on her way to making her rooms fabulous, I knew she was still angry that the committee had accepted Clay. Not just because they'd given him the master suite, which she thought should have been hers. There was bad blood between the two of them. I'd figured out that much. Maybe I should find someone who could tell me why.

But not right now, with Jessica drinking in every word and occasionally snapping off a few shots with the little camera, whose whirring and clicking was starting to get on my nerves.

"You can't let Clay keep ruining our work like this," Martha said. "Unless you want a half-finished, paint-spattered mess on opening day."

"Agreed," I said. "I'll go inspect the damage, and then I'll talk to him."

I strode out into the foyer and started up the stairs, walking as calmly and deliberately as I could. Martha and Jessica followed. Upstairs, to my relief, the hammering had stopped.

At the top of the stairs, to my right, I could see the open double doors to the master suite. When I was a few steps from the top, Clay Spottiswood stuck his head out.

"Where's my package?" he asked. "I'm expecting a package."

"Not happy with all the packages you've stolen from the rest of us?" Martha snapped.

"Stop blaming me for the packages," Clay said. "I've lost packages just like the rest of you."

He had—or at least claimed he had—and he'd probably spent more time complaining to me than all the rest of the designers put together.

I ignored both Martha and Clay and turned left. I could see spots of blood-red paint on the tarp covering the hall floor. And a few spots on the walls, where Ivy, the trompe l'oeil artist, was painting an elaborate mural of the Twelve Days of Christmas.

Had this, rather than paint fumes, stress, and eyestrain, caused the headache Ivy had gone home with?

I heard the whirring and clicking of Jessica's camera. Well, okay. Document the damage.

I entered Violet's room, which she was decorating in what Mother called "Early Disney Princess." Her room was so over-the-top that Mother and I sometimes called her "Princess Violet," though the name was a bit incongruous for a small and rather mousy-looking woman of around thirty. Everything in her room was in pink, white, and lavender. White-painted furniture. Wallpaper with pink and lavender floral garlands on a white background. Matching fabric on the twin bed and the half canopy over it. Pink and lavender decorations on the white-painted built-in bookshelves. A cluster of pink, white, and lavender stuffed animals and pillows on the bed.

The drops of red paint stood out like a trail of blood on the pink, white, and lavender petit-point rug.

I carefully avoided stepping on the drops, in case they were still wet, and entered the bathroom.

A good thing I knew it was only red paint. The room looked like a crime scene from a slasher movie, with not just drops but splashes, sprays, and even a few puddles of red. They stood out dramatically against the white-on-white spa look Martha had chosen for her design. The tile could probably be scrubbed clean and the walls repainted, but many of the towels and accessories would have to be replaced.

Behind me, in the Princess Room, I heard a shriek. I winced. Apparently Violet had come back and discovered the damage. I stuck my head back into the room and saw the hem of her frilly ruffled dress disappearing through the doorway to the hall. The wailing faded into the distance, and I suspected she had fled downstairs to seek comfort from Mother.

I grabbed one of the hand towels, its soft white terry cloth surface smeared with red. Then I turned, almost bumping into Martha and the reporter. Martha smiled, no doubt because she was pleased with the frown on my face. Jessica was clicking away with her camera.

I strode through the Princess Room and the hall and stopped in the double doorway of the master bedroom suite. The hammering had started up again and seemed to be coming from somewhere nearby—either the master bath or the huge walk-in closet.

"Clay!" I shouted.

Two heads popped up in the far corner of the room. Clay's workmen, Tomás and Mateo. Neither of them spoke more than a few words of English. They looked alarmed.

"*Que nada*," I said, giving them as much of a smile as I could manage. I thought *que nada* meant something like "it's nothing to worry about." They didn't look reassured. I wished my Spanish was good enough to say, "Don't worry, I'm not mad at you, I'm mad at your pig of a boss, and by the way, I could find you better jobs in about five minutes if you'd like to stop working for him."

Clay didn't answer. Tomás and Mateo went back to whatever they were doing behind the giant four-poster bed. Whirring and clicking noises at my elbow warned me that Jessica was here.

If one of the other designers had been causing a problem,

I'd have postponed dealing with it until after Jessica left. But Clay had already used up his last chance and then some.

"Claiborne Spottiswood!" I yelled. "Get out here before—"

"Where's that package I asked you for?" The hammering stopped, and Clay reappeared from the master bath, evidently attempting to deflect me with a counterattack.

"I don't know and I don't care." In fact, I didn't even believe he was missing a package. More likely he was pretending to have lost one. He'd probably overheard some of the designers speculating that he was behind the disappearances. "You've splashed red paint all over Ivy's hallway, Violet's rug, and Martha's bathroom."

"How do you know it's my paint?" he said. "There are eleven other decorators in this house—"

"But only one of them is using this particular shade of red." I held the hand towel up against the wall. The blood-red stains on it matched the walls perfectly. "All paintbrushes are supposed to be cleaned downstairs in the garage. And if you couldn't be bothered with going downstairs, why not mess up your own bathroom?"

"Wasn't me," Clay said. "I'll speak to my painters."

"You can't blame Tomás and Mateo," Martha said. "I was still here last night when they left. And my bathroom was fine then. You were here, doing some touch-up painting."

Clay scowled at her. He was probably considered tall, dark, and handsome by those who'd only seen him in a good mood, but it had been a while since I'd been able to see past his personality. And when he scowled, his thick black eyebrows and neatly trimmed goatee made him look almost diabolical.

Jessica was staring around the room in openmouthed surprise, even forgetting to use her camera.

"Martha's right," I said. "The bathroom was fine when I

left last night, and the only ones here were her, Clay, and Eustace."

I felt a pang of guilt—usually I was the last one to leave the house, and made sure everything was locked up and in good condition. But the closer we got to opening day, the longer the designers seemed to work, and I had a family to think of and Christmas preparations of my own. I wouldn't have left workmen unsupervised, but I thought—silly me—that the designers could be trusted.

"Martha, Violet, and Ivy will be giving me invoices this afternoon for the time and materials required to repair the damage to their rooms," I said aloud. "Clay, I'll expect reimbursement from you by tomorrow morning, or you're out of the show house."

I heard a gasp from behind me. I glanced over to see Mother, Violet, and Eustace standing in the doorway, peering over the reporter's shoulders. Violet was the one who had gasped. She was looking shocked, wrapping her fluffy pink embroidered cardigan around her as if to protect herself from my wrath. Mother and Eustace were beaming with delight.

"Oh, so you're going to have a show house with no master suite?" Clay leaned against one of the garish red walls and folded his arms. He made a dramatic picture, and Jessica obligingly captured it with her camera.

"I imagine several of the other designers would be happy to pitch in and help out," I replied.

"I've already got a design for the space," Martha volunteered.

"And I'd be happy to help out," Mother said.

"Same here," Eustace added.

"If you think you can use my stuff—" Clay began.

"Of course, not, Claiborne," Mother said. "I'm sure

Randall Shiffley can get a crew over here anytime to haul all your materials back to your shop."

She gave him what Clay probably thought was a sweet smile if he didn't know Mother very well. Eustace's expression was a lot more noncommittal, and Martha looked like a leopard about to pounce. The clicking from Jessica's camera had started up again, so I assumed she was enjoying the scene. Of course, the photos she was getting right now weren't very flattering. Perhaps I should start planning a way to mug her for her camera and delete any photos I didn't want to see on the front page of the student paper.

"I'm losing money on this gig as it is," Clay grumbled.

I decided to accept this as a capitulation.

"Then be careful how—and where—you clean your equipment from now on," I said. "Okay, everybody. Back to work."

"Yes, dear," Mother said. "Oh, Claiborne—as long as I'm here, I'll take my vase back."

She smiled and pointed to a Chinese urn sitting on top of the chest of drawers. Its elegant shape and cool blue-and-white color were completely at odds with the red-and-black color scheme and aggressively modern furniture that filled the rest of the room.

"Your vase? I'm afraid you must be mistaken." Clay stepped between Mother and the vase and crossed his arms as if prepared to fight her for it. Which took a lot of nerve—I recognized the urn as one that, ever since I could remember, had stood on the mantel of the house I'd grown up in, down in Yorktown.

"I'm sure you saw it downstairs in my room yesterday," Mother said. "Someone must have brought it up here by mistake. Silly, isn't it? The color's all wrong for your room."

"You're right, about the color," Clay said. "I thought it might make an interesting contrast, but—well, not my best idea. I'll be taking it back to my shop tomorrow."

"You're quite sure it's yours to take?" Mother's tone was deceptively gentle. Any sane person with a normal instinct for self-preservation would be leaping to hand her the vase.

An idea struck me.

"Well, if he's positive it's his vase, that's that," I said.

Mother frowned at me. Clay smirked with premature triumph. Jessica frowned and lowered her camera, as if resenting me for preventing another dramatic confrontation for her to photograph.

"But I'm curious, Clay," I went on. "Who do you keep in yours?"

"Who do I what?"

"Mother keeps her great-aunt Sophy in hers." I walked over, lifted the vase, and shook it. I was relieved to hear the familiar rattle of the cremains inside.

"You're decorating your room with someone's ashes?" Clay backed away from me as if afraid Great-Aunt Sophy might have died of something contagious.

"She was so fond of beautiful design," Mother said. "I always like to bring her along if possible and make her a part of my projects. And the vase has always been one of my favorites. That's why I recognized it so easily."

"What a coincidence," Clay said. He was visibly recovering from his initial shock. "My urn—"

Was the jerk about to invent his own great-aunt? I took the top off the urn and peeked inside.

"Yes, looks like Great-Aunt Sophy," I said. "And look!"

I gritted my teeth, stuck my hand into the urn, and then pulled it out, brandishing a small object in triumph. "Her onyx ring!"

Jessica's camera captured my dramatic revelation with a burst of whirs and clicks.

"Dear Sophy!" Mother had pulled out a handkerchief and was pretending to blink back tears. "How she loved her little trinkets."

"Yes." I brushed the ring off and handed it to Mother, who closed her fingers around it and clutched her hand sentimentally to her heart.

"So you see," I said to Clay, "you must be mistaken. I'd recognize this urn out of a million."

"I do hope yours turns up soon," Mother added. "Bring it along, Meg."

She sailed out of the room. I popped the top back on the urn and followed her. When I got out into the hall, I handed it to her.

"Onyx ring?" she murmured. "Looks more like a dime-store trinket to me."

"It is," I said. "I had it in my pocket—I brought it in to give to Eustace for his wise man costume in the living nativity scene."

"Thank you, dear." She beamed at me, and then began carefully descending the staircase with the urn in hand.

Eustace stepped out of the room.

"Your great-aunt's ashes?" He shook his head and made a face.

"Actually, Sophy's ashes got dumped in the York River years ago by a sneaky criminal," I said. "But Mother liked the urn, so she reused it for the ashes of one of our favorite cats. I thought human cremains were more likely to put off Clay."

Eustace chuckled at that.

"Oh, Mother has your wise man's ring," I said. "And don't worry," I added, seeing his grimace. "It was never actually in the urn—I palmed it."

Violet slipped past Eustace into the hall and fled back to her own room with a flash of pink and ruffles. Jessica followed her out but stopped near me in the hall, camera ready. I glanced through the master bedroom door. Mateo and Tomás, who had been peering over the bed to watch our confrontation, smiled nervously and ducked back down to work on whatever they were doing.

"Sorry about that," I said to Jessica. "Just give me a minute to wash my hands, and then I can show you some more of the rooms. Martha, mind if I use your bathroom?"

"Be my guest, doll." Martha could be touchy, but clearly browbeating Clay had put me in her good graces for the time being.

"Is it always this . . . dramatic?" Jessica asked, as she followed me across the hall.

"Darlin', we're decorators," Eustace said. "We all have egos and pinking shears, and tempers usually get a little short this close to an opening. It'll all turn out okay. Don't worry."

Was he reassuring Jessica or me? He smiled, lifted one forefinger to his temple in ironic salute, and went back downstairs.

"He's not far off," I said.

Jessica followed me through the Princess Room, where Violet was making little squeaking noises of dismay while rolling up the paint-stained petit-point rug. Jessica stopped to take a few shots of the damage.

In the bathroom, I washed my hands with a generous dollop of Martha's imported geranium-scented liquid soap and dried them on the least stained of her white towels. Martha was muttering to herself as she stuffed the ruined towels and accessories into a black plastic garbage bag.

"First the packages and now this," she said. "He'll do

anything to sabotage the rest of us. You need to keep an eye on him."

"We don't know that he's the one taking the packages," I said. "But yes, I'm keeping an eye on him." And on all of them. Clay wasn't the only one whose competitive instincts were working overtime.

I tried for a moment to think of something I could say to cheer her up. Then, when Jessica appeared at my shoulder and began snapping pictures, I gave up the notion as impossible.

"Come on," I said to Jessica, and I led her back out into the hall.

"Everyone seems to come to you with their problems," she said. "So this on-site coordinator gig—you're like the boss or something?"

"Or something," I said. "I'm the one responsible for making sure everything turns out okay. Settling any disputes. Enforcing the committee's guidelines—for example, that the designers are not allowed by make any structural changes to the house without prior approval. And if—"

"Oh, my God!"

I recognized Sarah Byrne's voice, coming from downstairs in the study, and turned to sprint down the stairs to see what new disaster had struck.

Chapter 3

I ran into the study and found Sarah frantically trying to push one of the beautiful red-velvet armchairs out from under a stream of water that was coming through the ceiling.

"Help!" she shrieked. "That bastard's trying to flood me out!"

Jessica and I leaped to the rescue. The three of us managed to shove one of the chairs out into the hall. As we were turning to go back in for the second chair, Eustace appeared in the hallway. Instead of helping, he galloped up the stairway, shouting in rapid-fire Spanish along the way. Tomás and Mateo appeared at the top of the stairs. More machine-gun Spanish. Tomás disappeared back into the master bedroom. Mateo raced down the stairs after Eustace. The two of them dashed into the study and quickly rescued the second chair. Meanwhile, Martha, Violet, and even Mother showed up and helped carry out all the other smaller—and, I hoped, less valuable—objects.

The water slowed and then stopped. Tomás called out something in Spanish from upstairs. Mateo answered.

By this time we'd hauled everything out of the room that wasn't nailed down. Sarah sat down in the hall, with her head between her hands, curled in an almost fetal position.

"My beautiful room," she muttered. "My beautiful room. It's ruined."

Mother and Martha stood on either side of her, patting

her on the back. Usually it was Mother or Eustace to whom the younger designers like Sarah and Violet turned for moral support. Was Martha just trying to look good in front of the reporter? Or was she feeling a sense of kinship with Sarah because Clay was responsible for both of their woes?

Tomás had come downstairs, and he and Mateo and Eustace were discussing something in Spanish. Much pointing toward the ceiling. Now that the water had stopped, I could see, to my relief, that there was only a little damage visible, right around the ceiling light fixture. Still, there wouldn't be any damage at all if Clay hadn't done whatever he'd done.

Speaking of Clay, what had he done? I hurried up the stairs and into the master suite. Clay was standing there, sopping wet and toweling himself off with some ratty paint-smeared rags.

"I need a towel," he said.

"What the hell were you doing?" I asked.

"Removing the wall between the bathroom and the closet," he said. "I wanted to open up the space."

I stepped into the bathroom. The wall was half demolished, and I could see the broken end of a pipe. There were puddles all over, with chunks of wallboard soaking in them, and a sledgehammer leaning against the wall.

For a moment, I contemplated picking up the sledgehammer and decking Clay with it. I closed my eyes and took deep breaths until the urge passed. Then I pulled out my phone and called Randall Shiffley.

"Meg? I'm already on my way over there. What's up?"

"We need some help out here," I said. "Clay Spottiswood was removing a wall—"

"The load-bearing wall between the master bath and

the big closet? The one I told him not to touch under any circumstances?"

"That's the one," I said. "Apparently, in addition to being load-bearing, it also contains some of the pipes for the bathroom. He's flooded the study downstairs. We're going to need some workmen to repair the damage. Tomás and Mateo can't do it all themselves."

"I have work I need Tomás and Mateo to be doing," Clay protested.

"Too bad," I said. "For the time being, Tomás and Mateo will be fixing all the damage you've done—here and downstairs in Sarah's room."

"But—"

My temper boiled over.

"Get out of here right now!" I stamped my foot as I said it, for good measure.

"I need to finish—"

"You're finished for the day!" I said. "And maybe for good. I'll call later to tell you if you'll be allowed to continue or if we're kicking you out of the house completely."

Clay opened his mouth to argue, but looking at my face must have made him think better of it. He disappeared for a moment into the walk-in closet, then reappeared, putting on his coat as he stormed out.

I was still taking my deep, calming breaths when I heard the front door slam downstairs.

"Meg?" I'd almost forgotten that I had Randall on the phone. "You really kicking him out?"

"I think I should let the committee make that decision," I said. "Things would certainly be a lot more peaceful around here if he was gone. And Martha would kill for a chance to do this room. She already has a set of plans, you know—she really expected to get it."

"Then she should have applied before the deadline like everyone else, instead of assuming the rules didn't apply to her and we'd come begging."

"No argument from me," I said. "But right now I'd rather have her doing the master bedroom than Clay. Do you want to bring this up with the committee, or shall I?"

"I'll take care of it," he said. "I'll tell the rest of the committee we need to hold an emergency meeting this afternoon or this evening. You hold down the fort there at the house. I'll send over some guys."

I was reassured. Not just that help was on the way, but also that Randall, who was on the committee, would support me if I decided we had to kick out Clay. I suspected without Randall's influence the committee might have caved when Martha pitched her hissy fit. Of course, they probably wouldn't have taken the master suite away from Clay— they'd have demoted one of the lesser designers. Princess Violet of the Many Ruffles. Or the designer Mother and I called Goth Girl, who was turning the third bedroom into a black-and-red pseudo-medieval lair. Or Our Lady of Chintz, who was running amok with too many different prints in the dining room, causing Mother, at regular intervals, to mutter thanks for the pocket doors separating it from her living room.

Or maybe the Quilt Ladies, the cheerful pair of designers who were turning the bonus room over the garage into a quilt and craft room. We all forgot the Quilt Ladies were there half the time, since their room was a little apart from the main body of the house. You could reach it from the garage via the back stairway. Or you could go through the now-paint-smeared back bathroom. Not my favorite feature of the house, that bathroom. From the main part of the house, you couldn't reach it from the hall, only from one or the other of the two smaller bedrooms. And yet it had a back door leading to the bonus room. If Michael and I had bought this house, the first thing I'd have changed would be to remove that back door. I wasn't sure what would worry me the most about that door—that it would let burglars sneak in through my sons' rooms, or that it would give the boys such an easy way to sneak out when they got old enough to think of doing so.

But however dysfunctional the house's floor plan might seem to me, the two stairways were going to make traffic flow easier once we opened up the house to visitors. We could send people up one set of stairs and down and out through the other.

I made a mental note to drop by to see the Quilt Ladies later in the day. Just because they weren't squeaky wheels didn't mean I should ignore them.

I was still standing in the master bedroom, surveying the damage. Tomás and Mateo returned, followed by Eustace. The two workmen disappeared into the ruined bathroom.

"The *muchachos* can fix everything Clay ruined," Eustace said. "But it's going to take time. And that's not something we have a whole lot of."

Did he have to remind me? Today was Saturday, December 20. The show house's main run would be from December 26 through January 5, but we'd given in to the historical society's request to have a special preview day—with wine and cheese to justify higher prices—on December 24. And just to make sure all the rooms were ready for the sneak preview, we'd arranged for the judges for the best room contest to make their tour of inspection at 9:00 P.M. on December 23. So we had today, tomorrow, Monday, and most of Tuesday to get everything done. I hoped Clay hadn't just ruined our chances of making our deadline.

Of course, our secret weapon was Randall Shiffley. As the town mayor, he had the strongest possible motive for making the show house successful. And as a leading member of the family that had a virtual monopoly on the building trades in Caerphilly County, he could draft an almost unlimited supply of skilled labor to get projects like this done.

"Randall's sending over some workers," I said aloud. "It would help if you and the guys can figure out what materials we'll need and call him."

"Will do."

I was turning to go. I had the feeling I should make sure Sarah was okay.

"One more thing," Eustace said. "Tomás and Mateo understood enough of what happened just now to figure out that Clay might not be coming back."

"I'm leaving that up to the committee," I said.

"Fair enough," Eustace said. "But they're a little worried, because he hasn't paid them."

"You mean for today?"

"At all."

"But they've been working here for weeks."

Eustace raised one eyebrow as if to say "what do you expect?"

"What a jerk," I said. "I'll mention it to Randall. Maybe the committee can work something out. Put pressure on him."

"Or the committee could pay them and force Clay to reimburse them as a condition of being in the house."

"And if he refuses?"

Eustace leaned back, put his hands on his hips, and made a slow, deliberate survey of the décor in Clay's room. The enormous four-poster mahogany bed, with its black sheets and red curtains. The oversized matching bureau and dresser. The black leather recliner. He wrinkled his nose slightly, as if detecting a faint but foul odor.

"We've got his stuff," he said. "Not to my taste, but it should be worth something."

He had a point.

"I'll mention it to Randall," I said. "Right now I need to go down and check on Sarah."

I found her standing in her room, looking shell-shocked. The red-and-gold oriental rug was gone, and Tomás was using handfuls of rags to dry off the floor. The brass ceiling fixture was sitting in one of the red-velvet chairs, and Mateo was atop a ladder doing something to the damaged section of ceiling.

"How are you holding up?" I asked Sarah.

"I'm lucky, I guess." She didn't sound as if she felt lucky. "They stopped the water before it ruined everything."

The streak in her hair was bright blue today, and from the way she was anxiously twisting the strands around her finger, I was afraid she'd pull out all the blue before too long.

"Stop that," I said, pretending to slap her hand gently. "Bald would not be a good look for you. Where's the rug, anyway?"

"In the garage, with fans drying it out," she said. "Is that okay?"

"It's fine," I said. "If you need a nicer space, you can always spread it out in the master bedroom. Clay's not around to complain."

"Is he out for good, or just for the day?" she asked.

"Up to the committee," I said. "I know how I'd vote, and if they ask me I'll tell them."

She smiled a little at that.

"You're sure it's okay for Tomás and Mateo to work on my room?" she asked. "I know there must be a lot to do in Clay's room."

"Yours comes first," I said. "And Randall's sending reinforcements. If you need anything, just ask."

"Just keep the reporter away for a while," she said. "Neither I nor my room are ready for our close-ups."

"Oh, my God," I said. "The reporter. Where has she gone?"

Sarah shook her head and went back to work—inspecting every inch of the red-velvet chairs to make sure they'd taken no damage. I went in search of Jessica.

I found her in the third bedroom, the one being decorated by Goth Girl. Whose real name was Vermillion, although come to think of it, I wasn't sure that actually counted as a real name. I was pretty sure she hadn't been born with it, and heaven knows where she'd left her last name.

Jessica was sitting on the very edge of a black-and-red sofa shaped like an open coffin, and she and Vermillion were sipping tea out of black Wedgwood cups. At least I hoped it was tea. A black Wedgwood plate containing black cookies with red sprinkles on them sat on the coffee table, which had been formed by placing a thick rectangle of black glass on the wing tips of two black-painted faux stone gargoyles. Vermillion had added a few small touches to meet the requirement that the designers decorate their rooms for Christmas—but the sprigs of holly around the windows had been painted glossy black, to match the walls, and her Christmas wreath was made of thorns.

Jessica and Vermillion weren't actually having much of a conversation. Vermillion was staring over her teacup at Jessica, who was gazing around the room with a deep frown on her face, as if daring the various bats, spiders, and gargoyles to come alive and attack her.

"There you are," I said. "Ready to continue the tour?"

Jessica leaped up without a word, slammed her teacup down on the coffee table, and ran out of the room.

I winced at the clink of delicate china on glass.

"Sorry," I said to Vermillion. "She didn't break anything, did she?"

"No." Vermillion was holding the teacup close to her eyes to inspect it. "But I don't think she likes my room much."

Obviously the proper response was to reassure her that Jessica was nuts and the room was beautiful, but I didn't think I could sell that one. And I wasn't sure if she'd be pleased with Michael's comment that if he ever directed a production of *Dracula* at the college he'd ask her to design the set.

"I think people are either going to love it or hate it," I said finally. "I guess we know where Jessica stands."

Vermillion smiled slightly at that, so I guess it must have been the right thing to say. And come to think of it, maybe shocking non-Goths was partly what she was after. She was only in her twenties. Ten or fifteen years ago I'd done much the same thing. Not turning Goth, of course, but doing things just to shock my more conservative relatives and neighbors. Some of my choices in wardrobe and boyfriends still came back to haunt me when we pulled out the family photo albums at reunions, but at least one of my rebellious decisions had turned out pretty well if you asked me: the decision to apprentice myself to a blacksmith instead of going to grad school as expected.

I went back into the hall and found Jessica gripping the

railing that divided the upper hallway from Mother's great room below.

"Horrible," she was muttering. "My—oh, my God. That room. That poor room. Look what she's doing to it."

She was almost in tears.

"What's wrong with it?" I glanced down at Mother's room as if pretending to think Jessica was talking about that. Mother had gone in for a cozy, homey Victorian style, with overstuffed tufted red-velvet sofas and chairs, a lot of dark carved wood, and blue-and-white china. It wasn't my taste, but it was handsome.

"Not the living room," she said. "That's okay. Rather nice really. But the bedroom—Morticia or Elvira or whoever she is has painted the walls glossy black. It's hideous."

"We'll be painting them a normal color when the show's over," I said. "Along with the blood-red walls in the master bedroom."

"It was a perfectly nice, normal bedroom," she said. "And now it's like something out of a horror movie."

"Not my taste, I have to admit," I said. "But apparently some people are very keen on her work."

Although the only person I'd ever heard of hiring her was an aging heavy metal drummer who'd bought a farm outside town and built a honking big mansion whose thirty or forty rooms were all decorated by Vermillion.

"Sorry," Jessica said, shaking herself as if to throw off some residual effects of being in the Goth bedroom. "But that room just creeps me out."

"You're probably not alone," I said. "I don't think Vermillion's room will be a front-runner for the prize."

"Prize? I thought you said the designers were donating all this?"

"They are," I said. "Half the profits go to the Caerphilly

Historical Society. And each decorator has designated a charity. On the twenty-third, the members of the County Board will go through the house and decide which room they like the best. The winning designer's charity gets the other half of the proceeds."

"I guess that's why they're all so keyed up and snapping at each other," Jessica said.

I winced, and hoped the image of designers snapping at each other didn't make it into her article. And I wondered, not for the first time, if it really had been a good idea making the County Board members the judges. Most of them were male, all were over fifty, and I suspected there wasn't a one in the bunch who could define "passementerie." I doubted Vermillion's room would stand a chance with them. But would Clay's?

I glanced down at Mother's room. Which was definitely going to be a contender. She was supervising several helper bees who were decorating the two-story Christmas tree that filled one corner of the room.

Wait a minute. The helper bees seemed to be undecorating the tree.

"I think you've got that backwards," I called down. "Shouldn't the ornaments be going onto the tree?"

"I'm rearranging things," Mother said. "Having the tree here spoils the look of the fireplace. I'm going to put it there—in the archway to the dining room."

Where it would completely block any possible view of what Our Lady of Chintz was doing to the dining room. I could understand why she was doing it. And it wasn't as if we needed the archway for traffic flow.

"Fine," I said. "Carry on."

"Meg?" Our Lady of Chintz appeared behind us. "May I talk to you for a moment?"

Perhaps she wasn't completely thrilled with Mother's plan to block off the archway between their rooms with tinsel and spruce.

"Señora?" Tomás was also waiting to talk with me. Or, more probably, pantomime with me, since his English was about as good as my Spanish.

"Meg?" Princess Violet was standing behind Tomás, clutching her purse with both hands and looking anxious.

"Look, you're busy," Jessica said. "May I just wander around? Talk to the designers, take pictures?"

"Wander all you like," I said. "Just don't bother the designers if they tell you they're busy, and always ask permission before taking pictures of their work. Some of them are fussy about work-in-progress shots."

"Will do." She turned and scampered down the stairs. I breathed a sigh of relief when she had disappeared without taking any pictures of Violet or Our Lady of Chintz. Who were looking particularly . . . themselves at the moment. Or maybe it was because they were standing side by side, both, even to my unfashionable eyes, seriously in need of a wardrobe makeover. Someone should tell Violet that at thirty-something she should leave the pastel prints, ruffles, and lace to her rooms and find a more sophisticated style. And while I was relieved that Our Lady of Chintz didn't dress with the same wild explosion of colors and prints that she stuffed into her room, I didn't think the shapeless brown and gray garments she wore were a good alternative.

Not my problem, I reminded myself, and put on my helpful face to see what they wanted from me.

Luckily, Our Lady of Chintz didn't object to the location of the Christmas tree, as long as she was allowed to decorate the bits visible in her room to match her design scheme. I gave her my blessing.

Tomás handed me a note from Eustace saying that effective immediately, Tomás and Mateo were on Randall's payroll, and unless I had any objection he'd have them get started repairing the wall Clay had destroyed.

"*Sí*," I said to Tomás. "*Gracias.*"

He flashed me a quick smile and hurried back to the master bedroom.

Princess Violet had lost her key to the house. Again. I'd deduced as much when I saw her holding her frilly pink purse.

"I'm so sorry," she said. "I could have sworn I left it on the dresser in my room."

"Why don't you just keep it on your key ring?" I asked. I was already headed downstairs to the locked cabinet in the coat closet that served as my on-site desk. I'd learned to keep a few spare keys there.

"I have one on my key ring," she said. "My main key ring. But I can't find that today. I'm using my spare key ring. And it's really a nuisance, because the car key I have on my spare key ring is a valet key that doesn't open my trunk and—"

"Here you are." I handed her a key. "Twenty dollars deposit."

She continued babbling about her key rings—apparently she had three or four, each containing a slightly different assortment of keys. I waited until she'd rummaged around in her purse and found two fives and a ten—none of them in her wallet. I wrote out a receipt, handed her the top copy, and put the money and the carbon in my locked cash box.

Randall Shiffley strolled in while I was completing this transaction.

"I'm soooo sorry," Violet said, as she tucked the key into her purse. "I'll try to hang on to this one."

She scurried back upstairs.

"Can you get a few more keys made?" I asked Randall.

"*More* keys? We must have enough keys floating around for half the town to have one."

"I suspect we could find most of them if we searched Violet's house, her car, and her purse," I said. "Let's just make sure the place is rekeyed as soon as the show house closes."

"Already on my punch list."

That was one of the things I liked about Randall. His punch list was the equivalent of my notebook, and I knew that anything on it was going to get done, and on time.

"The bank had a lot of problems with squatters and vandals before we started working here," he went on, "so they're pretty hyper about security. Speaking of vandals, is Clay still here?"

"I chased him out."

"Sorry, Stanley," Randall called. "Not here."

I turned to see Stanley Denton, Caerphilly's leading (and only) private investigator, standing in the foyer.

"I'll check on that damaged wall," Randall said as he headed upstairs.

"Hey, Stanley," I said. "What do you need Clay for?"

"Got some papers to serve on him."

"I didn't know you did process serving," I said.

"Not my favorite kind of work," he said. "But it pays the bills."

"What's Clay getting served for, or are you allowed to say?"

"No big secret," he said. "Clay and one of his former clients are suing and countersuing and filing charges against each other like crazy. Almost a full-time job lately, serving papers on the two of them. She says he didn't finish her house and what he did was all wrong; he says she rejected work that was done according to her orders and hasn't paid him."

"He's a jerk," I said.

"Well, she's no prize either, but I have to admit, the whole downstairs of her house is a sorry mess." He shrugged. "It's for the courts to decide. All I need to worry about is finding him for the latest set of papers. He wasn't at home last night, and his office hadn't seen him but said to come over here."

"He left here maybe half an hour ago," I said. "Not voluntarily. I'd offer to call him, but he might misinterpret it as me backing down from kicking him out. Maybe you could get Randall to call him."

"Thanks," he said. "I've got his number."

"By the way," I said. "Any chance you could get Randall to hire you to do a little detecting here at the show house?"

"Detecting what?"

"Someone's been stealing packages," I said. "Stuff the decorators have ordered. None of the packages have been fabulously valuable, but there have been so many of them that it probably adds up to hundreds of dollars by now. And the whole thing's got some of the decorators at each other's throats."

"Not that I'd mind investigating, but have the police done what they can?"

"Now that's a good question," I said. "I keep telling the designers to make a police report about it, but who knows if any of them have done so. I'll talk to the chief tomorrow."

"Good," he said. "And I'll talk to Randall about hiring me to supplement their efforts."

He headed upstairs after Randall.

I looked at my watch. Almost time for me to leave, to meet Michael and the twins for an afternoon of caroling, Christmas shopping, and eventually dinner. But with so much going on, I couldn't leave my post unguarded. I'd asked my cousin Rose Noire to fill in for me this afternoon. Where was she?

Probably out delivering more of the customized, organic herbal gift baskets that she sold by the hundreds over the holiday season. I was still getting used to the notion of my flakey, New-Age cousin as the owner of a thriving small business. I'd have felt guilty, asking her to take the time away from her work, if I hadn't been sacrificing so much anvil time myself.

"Meg?" I looked up to see Martha standing nearby. "Any chance I could go up and take a few measurements in the master bedroom?"

"Technically that's still Clay's room," I said.

"Understood. And if the committee decides to let him stay, I'll just have wasted a few minutes of my time. No problem. But if they decide to kick him out, I want to be able to say that yes, I absolutely can get the room ready by opening day."

I thought about it for a few moments. Mother and Eustace still had a lot to do in their rooms. Sarah would be fighting the clock to undo what Clay had done to her room. And I couldn't see handing the master bedroom over to any of the others. If we kicked Clay out, Martha would be the logical person to take over the master bedroom.

"I feel responsible," she said.

"For everything Clay has done?"

"Well, not exactly," she said. "But I am to blame for getting him into the decorating business in the first place. He used to work for me—*briefly*. Till he got too big for his britches and struck out on his own. Taking half my clients with him. The female half," she added, with a bitter laugh. "A few of them started crawling back when they figured out they'd made a mistake, but by that time it was too late. My business was folding."

No wonder Martha felt so miffed at Clay getting the room she'd wanted. If only I'd known from the start how much hostility there was between them.

"Take your measurements," I said. "But be discreet."

She smiled a small, tight, triumphant smile and turned to go upstairs.

"And if you're thinking of searching his room for the missing packages, don't bother," I called up the stairs after her. "Already done that myself. Several times."

She chuckled mirthlessly at that.

With my luck, Clay would come barging back in and catch her at it. I really wanted to be gone before that happened. Where was Rose Noire?

As if my thoughts had summoned her, the front door opened very slowly and Rose Noire peeked into the foyer. Her wild mane of hair frizzed out from beneath a purple knitted hat, and her expression was anxious.

"Meg?"

"There you are," I said. "Just in time. Come in."

"I can feel the negative energy trying to push me away when I try to cross the threshold." She stepped inside, as if with an effort, and planted herself solidly, obviously expecting the negative forces to attack. "There's something evil in this house."

"Not at the moment. I chased him out for the rest of the day." Rose Noire had taken an almost instant dislike to Clay, claiming he had a very negative aura. I didn't share her faith in auras, mantras, energy work, and whatever other New Age concepts currently fascinated her. But I had to admit she was spot-on when it came to sniffing out a bad egg like Clay. "Close the door—you're letting the cold air in."

"Cold but clean air," she said. But she closed the door as she said it. She was wearing a deep-purple dress instead of her typical pastels, and a lot more charms and amulets than usual hung from her neck and wrists. "It's not just him," she said. "There's a lot of dark energy in this house. Is it okay if I do a cleansing while I'm here?"

"As long as you keep the decorators happy and busy and don't let them break anything else, you can do anything you want." I wasn't sure I believed in Rose Noire's smudging and herb sprinkling, but at worst it did no harm. And most of the time, it actually made me feel better. Anything that could improve the atmosphere here in the house was fine with me.

"By the way," I said. "Clay isn't allowed back until either Randall or I say so. If he tries to get in—"

"He shall not pass!" Rose Noire exclaimed, drawing herself up to her full height and lifting her chin in defiance.

"We'll be fine, dear." Mother appeared in the archway. "If Clay comes back, Eustace and I can help Rose Noire handle him."

"And I'll be here to help, too." Randall was coming down the stairway, with his phone to his ear. "I'm calling him now to lay down the law. Clay? When you get this, give me a call. We need to talk."

"And there's a reporter here somewhere," I went on to Rose Noire. "Student. Long red hair. Name of Jessica."

"Right here." Jessica appeared on the stairway.

"This is Rose Noire," I said. "She's taking over for me. She can answer any questions you have. Feel free to roam around, but please remember that the designers have a tight deadline. Oh, Rose Noire—when Ivy gets back—"

"I'm back." Ivy looked up from the rear of the foyer, where

she was sitting cross-legged on the floor, dabbing paint on the unfinished mural.

"Sorry, I didn't see you come in." No one ever did. Ivy was ethereally thin and painfully shy, and appeared to have mastered the art of fading into the woodwork. "This is Jessica. She's a reporter from the student paper. She's very impressed with your work, and would like take pictures of your paintings *if* you're okay with that, and interview you *if* you have time."

Ivy nodded uncertainly.

"But give her a chance to settle in and get a little work done right now," I said to Jessica.

"Yes, let me fix you some tea," Rose Noire said. "And show you Eustace's kitchen."

She led Jessica off before I could warn the reporter about Rose Noire's teas, which were always organic and healthy but rarely delicious.

"Don't talk to her unless you want to," I said to Ivy. "Mother and Rose Noire can handle her if you don't."

"Thanks," she said, with a quick smile.

The house was in good hands. I waved to everyone, stepped outside and took a deep breath.

Rose Noire was right. The air out here was cleaner. And it wasn't just getting away from the construction smells of paint, glue, and sawdust. All the hostility between Clay and the other designers hung over the whole house like some kind of psychic air pollution. I had the feeling he'd be causing more trouble before the show house was over.

But not right now.

I stopped to take a few more breaths and study the sky. It was obviously cold, since all the snow already on the ground showed no signs of melting, and the dull gray sky suggested more snow was on its way, but maybe I was getting used to snow and cold. Instead of cold and gray, I decided the weather was bracing.

My enjoyment of the out-of-doors was interrupted by voices coming from somewhere to my left, on the other side of the tall snow-covered bushes that flanked the front porch.

"Just keep it," said one woman's voice, hot and angry.

"I don't want it." Sarah, who I'd thought was still in the study, inspecting the damage. And the other voice belonged to Kate Banks, one of Sarah's partners in Byrne, Banks, and Bailey. I'd never actually met Bailey, whoever he or she was. "I don't even want it around me."

"And what if he tries something? Something worse than trying to ruin your room."

"Pretty sure that was an accident."

"After all he's done to us before?" Kate went on. "You don't think he's mean enough—?"

"Oh, I think he's mean enough," Sarah said. "I just don't think he's smart enough. I think he was totally astonished when the water started gushing out of that wall, and only worried about what it was doing to his room."

"You never should have taken this on," Kate said. "You should have—"

"Maybe I should have listened to you," Sarah said. "But I didn't. We just have to get through this. *I* just have to get through this. Don't worry about it."

"I should give him a piece of my mind," Kate said.

"Don't give him the satisfaction. Don't worry about me. I'll handle it."

Kate made an inarticulate noise and I saw her dashing across the lawn. I pretended to have just come out of the front door.

"Hey, Sarah," I said. "Was that Kate I saw? She should come in and get a preview of the house."

"I think she wants to wait and be surprised by the finished product." She was smiling, but I could tell it was an effort. Her hand went up as if to torment her blue lock again, but she stopped it halfway with a glance at me.

I liked Sarah. She was in her early thirties, a little younger than me, and in the past few weeks we'd discovered any number of shared tastes and interests. We usually saw eye to eye about what went on in the house.

But I could tell that right now wasn't the time to presume on our developing friendship by asking her about the argument she'd had with her partner.

"Well, I'm off," I said. "Tomás and Mateo will be helping with the repairs, and Randall's sending some more guys over. Call me if there's anything you need."

She nodded and went back into the house, looking preoccupied.

Nothing I could do now. I'd check on how she was doing after Tomás and Mateo and Randall's crew had worked their magic.

Chapter 4

"There's Mommy!"

"Mommy!"

Michael and our five-year-old twins, Josh and Jamie, were standing on the sidewalk in front of Caerphilly Assisted Living, waving frantically as I strode across the parking lot.

"Where are the rest of the carolers?" I asked.

"Inside, warming up." Michael gave me a quick kiss. "The boys wanted to wait outside for you."

"Mommy, it's going to snow, isn't it?" Jamie asked.

"Is not," Josh said. "Can we sing 'God Rest Ye Merry'?"

" 'We Three Kings,' " Jamie said.

"We can sing them both," I said. "Let's go inside and warm up."

Inside we found Robyn Smith, the Episcopalian pastor, and Minerva Burke, leader of the New Life Baptist Choir, with an ecumenically diverse group of about thirty carolers, ranging in age from senior citizens to a few kids almost as young as the boys.

"That's everyone," Robyn said, handing us four small carol books. "Let's go."

She and Minerva led the way down the hall toward the building's main lounge. Some seventy or eighty seniors were gathered in several rows of chairs, with a line of wheelchairs along the back. Everyone seemed delighted with our arrival—I wasn't sure whether it was the prospect of our caroling or the joy of seeing half a dozen small children.

We did indeed sing both "God Rest Ye Merry, Gentlemen" and "We Three Kings." And also "Joy to the World," "Silent Night," "O Little Town of Bethlehem," and several other old favorites. The boys knew all the words—or thought they did—and could at least approximate the tunes. It was a stroke of genius on Robyn and Minerva's part to include the children. We grown-ups were providing most of the volume and almost all of the on-key notes, but the children were the main focus for our audience. I loved the fact that we were bringing a measure of holiday cheer to townspeople who weren't able to get out and enjoy all of the events of the season.

We closed with "We Wish You a Merry Christmas," and then Robyn introduced all the carolers and thanked the audience for allowing us to share the holiday season with them. Most of the grown-up carolers went to help the staff wheel the residents back into the sun room for the upcoming bingo game. The children gravitated toward the Christmas tree, and amused themselves with shaking and poking the wrapped presents heaped around it and checking for tags, in case Santa had delivered a few of their presents here by mistake.

I spotted a familiar face and went over to greet Alice, one of the two Quilt Ladies decorating the bonus room at the show house.

"Shirking your post at the house, I see," she said, with a grin.

"Said the pot to the kettle," I replied.

"Oh, we're nearly finished," she said. "I came over for the weekly quilting bee. Want to see what we're up to?"

I followed her across the hall to a recreation room where half a dozen seniors were either gathered around a long table, arranging bits of fabric into patterns, or sitting at sewing machines stitching more bits of fabric together. Brightly colored quilts, ranging from crib size to queen size, hung on the walls or were draped, unfinished, over the tables and a couple of racks.

"We started the quilting program as art therapy for the residents," she said. "But then we realized we could do a lot of good with the quilts. Sometimes we give them to poor people or sick people, and other times we auction them off for good causes. When the New Life Baptist Church had that problem last year with the skunks in the choir loft, we auctioned off a black-and-white quilt with a theme of skunks and musical notes. Made over five hundred dollars toward the renovations."

"Lovely," I said, meaning both the quilts and what they did with them.

"We call ourselves Quilters for Good," she said. "It's the charity we've designated in case our room wins the prize at the show house. Unless someone decides to disallow us."

"Why would they?" I asked.

"We don't have any kind of formal organization," she said. "Clay Spottiswood seemed to think you wouldn't be allowed to give it to us. He was saying—"

"Clay Spottiswood says a lot of things that nobody listens to," I said. "Don't worry about it. If you win the prize, we'll find a way for Quilters for Good to get the money."

"Thank you!" She seemed limp with relief.

I spent a few minutes praising the quilts—easy to figure out which quilters belonged to which quilt by seeing who beamed when I exclaimed over each one.

Then I headed back to collect Michael and the boys.

But halfway there I paused in the hall, pulled out my cell phone, and called Randall.

"What's wrong?" Randall asked.

"Nothing's wrong," I said. "I was just wondering about something. What charity has Clay designated in the unlikely event that his room wins the competition?"

"Designers of the Future. Provides scholarships for deserving low-income students who want to study art, architecture, or interior design."

"Sounds worthwhile," I said.

"And legit," Randall said. "He gave us a copy of the paperwork for making it an approved 501(c)(3) tax-exempt organization."

"The Quilt Ladies' charity isn't," I said. "It's just them and a bunch of seniors here at Caerphilly Assisted Living making quilts for good causes."

"And doing a hell of a lot of good, especially this time of year," he said. "I figured if they win, we can set up something through one of the churches to get them the funds. Not a church in town they haven't helped."

"Good. I was just wondering. Do you need me, or can I carry on with my plan of finishing my Christmas shopping this afternoon?"

"I'll call if anything comes up that we need you for."

And Randall did call a couple of times during the afternoon, but only with questions I could easily answer without returning to the house. Michael and I split the boys up, and I took Josh shopping to get presents for his daddy and brother, while Michael and Jamie shopped for presents for Josh and me.

I'd have been overjoyed to be doing almost anything that got me away from the show house, but strolling around

Caerphilly with Josh was perfect. I wasn't sure which I enjoyed more—seeing familiar holiday sights through his eyes, or having him point out Christmas details I hadn't noticed. Had we forgotten last year to take the boys to see the giant mechanical Santa's village in the front window of the Caerphilly Toy Town? No, we had a picture of the boys staring openmouthed as the red-and-green North Pole Express train chugged its way around and around. And yet Josh was as excited as if he'd never seen it before, and we spent a happy half hour watching it.

"Do you think Santa will bring Jamie and me toy trains?" he asked eventually.

"It was on your list, wasn't it?" I asked.

He nodded.

"Then trust Santa," I said. "I do."

Of course it was easier for me, knowing that two fabulous electric train sets were already wrapped and hidden in the attic. It would be interesting to see if the boys ran separate but equal railroad lines or if they joined forces to create one sprawling monster set of tracks. I made a mental note to bring them back here for inspiration. And then I dragged a reluctant Josh away so we could finish shopping for his dad. Eventually, at the hardware store, we decided on a new Craftsman hammer for Michael.

After a couple of hours Josh and I met Jamie and Michael at the ice cream store. In spite of the weather, both boys were begging for ice cream, so we indulged them, while Michael and I enjoyed a more seasonal cup of hot chocolate. Then we swapped twins, so Jamie and I could shop for Michael while Josh and Michael found a present for me.

Jamie also liked the train set, but his favorite place to linger was the Caerphilly Bakery, which had recently installed a viewing window so the tourists could watch as the staff pulled a seemingly neverending supply of cookies and gingerbread men out of the ovens. We finally chose two gingerbread men—one for him and one for Josh—and made our way to Caerphilly Sporting Goods, where he decided that a baseball and a pair of bright red baseball socks would be the perfect Christmas present for Michael.

We ended up for dinner at Luigi's, our favorite Italian restaurant, and Michael and I briefed each other while the boys went over to shake the wrapped boxes under Luigi's Christmas tree. My shopping had gone well, but apparently Michael wasn't having much luck helping the boys find something I'd like.

"I assume you're still opposed to hamsters, guinea pigs, and gerbils," he reported. "Persian cats and Siamese fighting fish were also discussed and vetoed. Josh and I spent quite a lot of time at the perfume counter, but in the end he decided that Rose Noire makes much better smells."

"He's probably right."

"Josh still thinks maybe you'd enjoy an electric train set once you started playing with it," he went on. "And he was disappointed that the diamond earrings he likes are a couple of thousand dollars over what he's saved up in his piggy bank."

"I do wish you could convince them just to make something," I said. "I'm sure I'd be delighted with anything they made."

"I know that," he said. "But for some reason this year they are determined to buy you a present. If you can think of anything you'd like, let me know and I'll try to talk them into it."

"Will do," I said, just as the boys scampered back to the table.

By the time we finished, the snow had started falling.

But we weren't about to let a little snow ruin our plans for the evening—going to see the world famous New Life Baptist Church's gospel choir. Every year they did a Christmas concert at the church for the unfortunate townspeople who, not being Baptist, wouldn't get to hear them sing at their Christmas services.

This year was especially exciting because it was New Life's first Christmas concert since my friend Minerva Burke had taken over as choir director. My friend Aida Butler was a nervous wreck, because her daughter Kayla was doing her first big solo, so I made her sit with us and distracted her by telling her all about the designers' antics.

Aida was still in her uniform as a sheriff's deputy. The boys were fascinated by the various objects hanging from her belt.

"Mommy, wouldn't you like one of those?" Jamie asked, pointing to Aida's police radio.

"No, that," Josh said, pointing to Aida's holster.

"They're both very nice," I said. "But I don't think anyone but police officers are allowed to have police guns and police radios."

The boys pondered this in silence for a few moments.

"Is it hard to become a police officer?" Jamie asked.

"You have to go to the police academy," Aida said. "For six months. And I'm sure your mom is smart enough to do very well there, but I don't think she wants to spend that much time away from her family."

Jamie seemed satisfied with this answer, but all through the concert Josh continued to study Aida's uniform and then look at me as if picturing me in one.

Nothing put me into a holiday mood more certainly than really good carol singing, and I was also looking forward to seeing how well the choir did with Minerva as its new leader.

We all knew the choir had become happier since its former much-hated director had departed under a cloud. But would they sing as well?

I should never have doubted Minerva. Or Kayla.

"They've outdone themselves," Mother exclaimed. "I don't think I've ever heard them this good, and that's saying something."

As we were filing out—slowly, because everyone kept stopping in clumps to chatter about how lovely the choir sounded and how beautifully the church was decorated—I ran into Randall.

"So is Clay in or out?" I asked him.

"Don't know yet," he said. "The only time I could get the whole committee together was just after the concert. I'm heading to the meeting now. I'll call you when I know."

After the concert, I took the boys home and put them to bed and then wrapped presents while Michael went to the college theater for a quick tech rehearsal. Tomorrow was the first of two nights that he'd be doing his annual dramatic reading of Dickens's *A Christmas Carol*.

It should have been a peaceful evening. I lit a fire in the fireplace, and the smell of juniper and cedar filled the room. Rose Noire and my brother, Rob, joined me, and we all wrapped presents and wrote cards while listening to Christmas music.

Rob was trying to be secretive, doing his wrapping behind one of the sofas. But since every single present he brought out to place under the tree was a flat rectangle about five and a half by seven and a half inches, I deduced that we were all getting our own personal copies of whatever new computer game Mutant Wizards, his company, had developed for the holiday season.

But his attempts at discretion and secrecy, however unsuccessful, made him so happy that Rose Noire and I both stifled our giggles and tried to look properly mystified at each stack of presents he deposited under the tree.

Rose Noire was humming happily as she wrapped another batch of her expensive gift baskets. The fact that Rob and Rose Noire, two of the least practical and businesslike people on the planet, had achieved financial success by doing what they loved usually cheered me and made me believe there was hope for humanity.

But tonight I was restless. I couldn't write a coherent note on a Christmas card. I mangled the paper whenever I tried to wrap a present. I kept thinking that I should have gone over to the house to make sure Randall's workers had cleaned up all the damage.

Rob, who was happily singing along with the Mormon Tabernacle Choir on the radio, didn't seem to notice my mood. Rose Noire did, though, and did her best to distract me from it.

"Are you sure you're okay with me giving ant farms to the boys?" she asked. "Because if you're not, there's still time to get the organic crayons."

"I think we'll be fine with the ant farms," I said. "As long as you can provide some kind of natural, environmentally safe ant repellant if they get out."

"They're vegan, wheat-free, sugar-free, preservative free—"

"The ants?" I asked.

"The *crayons*. And yes, I have a plan for when the ants get out."

When they get out? I'd have preferred *if.* But still, worrying about a hypothetical ant invasion distracted me, at least briefly, from my larger worries. When the Mormon

Tabernacle Choir began booming out "Joy to the World" we all three joined in.

A little after eleven, I finally got the long-awaited call from Randall.

"Show house committee just broke up." He sounded exhausted.

"This late? Well, is Clay in or out?"

"In, dammit. Not because we really want him, and he can kiss next year's house good-bye. But he's known to be litigious."

"And you think he'd sue if we really kicked him out." I sighed. "You're probably right. And I doubt if he'd win, but beating him would cost a lot of money."

"Probably more than the show house will clear. So we're counting on you. Just hold it together till the opening."

"Will do. Have we fixed everything he did today?"

"It was going well when I had to leave. I didn't have a chance to drop by after the concert—the committee's been meeting ever since it ended."

A two-hour meeting? To decide to do nothing at all? Not for the first time, I uttered a small, silent prayer of thanks that I had resisted Mother's attempts to talk me into joining the committee.

"I think I should go down and check, then," I said. "How are the roads?"

"Roads are fine, but why not wait until morning to check?"

"Because I won't be able to sleep till I do," I said. "I'll call you if I spot any problems, and then if anyone complains, we can say we already know and already have a plan to deal with it."

"E-mail me." He was obviously stifling a yawn. "Because I hope to be asleep in about ten minutes."

I decided that since Michael should arrive soon, I'd wait

and get his opinion on the roads. Randall drove a truck and prided himself on being able to drive on anything the weather threw at us. Michael had a more normal view on snow. I tried to concentrate on my Christmas cards.

By the time Michael arrived it was nearly midnight. Rose Noire had said goodnight and gone upstairs an hour before, and Rob was yawning. I was still wide awake.

"How was the rehearsal?" I asked. "And how are the roads?"

"Fine and fine," he said. "It's a nice, light snow. Easy for the plows to keep up with. But you're not going out again, are you?"

I had started putting on my coat.

"I want to check on the house," I said, as I stuffed my phone in my pocket and pulled on a thick wool cap. "I told you about all the stuff Clay ruined. Some of it happened last night, when I went home before he did. I like to be the last one out of the house, and while I wouldn't have given up this afternoon and evening with you and the boys for anything, now I'm anxious. And I want to see if Randall's workmen have finished fixing everything. Make sure there are no new problems. As long as you don't think the roads are unsafe."

Michael shook his head, but he knew better than to argue with me when I was in what he called my "taking-charge mode."

"Drive carefully," he said, giving me a quick kiss.

The snow, though steady, was light, and all fifteen or so miles of the road from our house to town had been well and recently plowed—fringe benefits, I suspected, of the county crew knowing Michael and I were among Mayor Randall Shiffley's closest friends. I found the drive curiously exhilarating. The Twinmobile, with its four-wheel drive, handled the road beautifully, and there wasn't another car in sight. At first I saw only snowy fields and snowflakes drifting down outside, and heard only the faint swish of my tires and the steady rhythm of the windshield wipers. As I drew closer to town, I began to see houses and fences strung with Christmas lights. The growing layer of snow on the outdoor reindeer and Santas made them more obviously fake, but I liked the effect of the snow on the manger scenes and snowmen.

I pulled up in front of the show house and parked. The house was dark and mine was the only car in front of it, though there were a few nearby. I could see faint car-shaped indentations that suggested some of the designers had stayed until the snow had started, but the places where they'd parked were covered with at least an inch of snow by now. Good. The house was a lot more peaceful when the designers had all gone home for the day. Even the ones like Sarah and Eustace who had become friends.

I found myself humming "Silent Night" as I got out and locked my car. I liked the way the snow muffled all the sounds around me, and the way my footsteps looked crisp and clear in the smooth snow on the walk. Should I e-mail Randall to remind him to send one of his workmen to shovel the walks tomorrow? Later.

I opened the door, stepped in, and began stomping on the doormat to shake the snow off my boots. I was reaching for the light switch when—

Something tinkled and broke in the distance. Upstairs.

I glanced up. The house was dark, but had I seen a faint flicker of light out of the corner of my eye—like a flashlight being switched off?

I stood in the darkened hallway and waited.

Silence. I was just reaching for the light switch, when the

hall light came on, half blinding me, and I heard two loud pops followed by the tinkling of something breaking nearby.

Gunshots?

I dashed into the study and dropped to the ground behind one of the armchairs. I pulled out my cell phone.

The hall light went out again, and I could hear racing footsteps upstairs. Racing away from me, thank goodness.

I dialed 9-1-1.

Chapter 5

"9-1-1; what's your emergency?"

"Debbie Ann!" I found the familiar voice of the local dispatcher comforting. "I'm at the show house—there's an intruder, and he fired a gun at me. I think he's upstairs, and running for the back stairs."

I rattled off the address.

"Are you in a safe place?"

Was I in a safe place? If there was only one intruder, yes. I heard the garage door opening, so evidently the intruder had gone down the back stairs and was leaving through the garage. He was fleeing.

But what if there was more than one?

"No idea," I said. "I think so. I think he's leaving."

"Stay put," she said. "And stay on the line."

Easier said than done, at least the staying put part. I felt like a sitting duck. I crawled toward the front windows. The garage doors faced to the side of the house, so it wasn't as if I could see someone leaving through them. But he had to make his way down the driveway. And when he got to the street—

A car motor started up outside. I couldn't see anything. I suspected one of those cars covered with soft mounds of snow would be gone when I went back out. And that whoever was driving it was waiting till he got away from the house before turning on his lights.

I described all this to Debbie Ann and crawled back behind the armchair. As usual, the adrenaline that had carried me through the crisis was deserting me now that the immediate danger seemed to have driven off. My knees felt weak. The hand holding my cell phone was visibly shaking. And I decided I had to do something, if only to distract myself. After all, if someone wanted to get me, they'd had plenty of time by now. In the dead silence of the house, my side of my conversation with Debbie Ann had been clearly audible.

"I'm going to check upstairs," I said.

"I said stay put!"

I didn't bother to explain that I'd go crazy if I stayed put a minute longer. I got up from my refuge behind the armchair. I walked back to the hall as softly as I could and paused at the foot of the stairs, listening.

Another faint noise. Was it just an old board squeaking? Or something else?

I crept upstairs and paused at the landing. The intruder seemed to have come from the master bedroom. The sound seemed to have come from there.

"Meg . . . Meg . . ." the faint voice on my phone kept saying.

I stepped into the master bedroom doorway and turned my phone so the light of its screen shone into the room.

There was something on the bed. My phone didn't give off enough light to see what it was.

I reached for the light switch and then stopped. The intruder had been in here, and might have left fingerprints.

I pulled my right glove out of my pocket and put it on before turning on the light switch.

Clay Spottiswood was lying in the middle of the enormous bed. His eyes were wide and staring, and blood had run down from a bullet hole in the middle of his fore-head.

"We're going to need an ambulance," I said. "Clay Spot-tiswood's been shot."

Chapter 6

"What in the world were you doing here at this hour?"

I opened my eyes to find Chief Burke standing in the study doorway. I'd retreated downstairs, to one of Sarah's comfy Art Deco armchairs, emerging only to let in Sammy Wendell, the deputy who arrived first. Several other deputies had followed, including my friend Aida Butler and Randall's cousin Vern. Then my cousin Horace, who was not only a deputy but also the county's crime scene technician. And Dad, who was now the local medical examiner. He'd insisted on checking me out briefly before trotting upstairs to examine Clay. I'd stayed in the study, out of their way, while they searched the house and did their forensic thing in the master bedroom.

The crime scene.

"Are you okay?" the chief asked.

"Just tired," I said. "And a little shaken. What was I doing here? Checking on the place. Usually I'm the last to leave, or nearly so. But today I left early to take the boys Christmas shopping. And that took longer than expected, and it bothered me that I never got back to the house. I like to make sure the place is locked up. Check on what the designers are up to. Especially if we've had problems, as we did today, I hate going to bed without knowing that everything's okay. And obviously it's not."

"What kind of problems did you have today?"

I brought him up to speed on what I knew about Clay's last day on earth. The chief listened in silence, scribbling occasionally in his notebook. He pondered for a while after I finished speaking.

"Not a particularly likable man," he said. "But—spattered paint, a misunderstanding about a vase, and some accidental water damage. Are you suggesting that any of these incidents could be related to his murder?"

"I have no idea," I said. "None of them seem important enough to kill over. I know Mother wouldn't kill him for stealing her vase—she'd just make sure anyone who might possibly want to hire him for a decorating job knew about it. I can't imagine Princess Violet killing anyone over anything. She's like Rose Noire—she escorts spiders out to the garage. Martha was positive we were going to kick him out and let her take over his room, and I'm pretty sure she'd want him alive to gloat over it. I can't imagine any of them doing it."

But what if one of them had?

"It's not just these incidents," I said. "They were just the latest in a series of things Clay did that upset everyone in the house. He was a poisonous influence. There was a cumulative effect."

The chief nodded, but didn't look convinced.

I remembered something else.

"Talk to Stanley," I suggested. "Clay and one of his former clients were in a big legal battle. Stanley knows more about it. He was trying to find Clay yesterday to serve some papers on him. No idea if he succeeded."

He nodded and scribbled.

"You look done in," he said. "Go home."

"Roger," I said. "Will you be keeping us out of the house in the morning?"

He looked tired.

"I don't know yet," he said. "I realize that you are supposed to open in a couple of days, and a lot of people have spent a ton of money on this, and the historical society will be pretty badly hurt if anything cancels or delays the show—"

"But it's a murder," I finished for him. "You have stuff you've got to do."

He nodded.

"I should let all the decorators know that they won't be able to get in," I said. "And tell Randall that the committee will need to decide what happens with Clay's room."

"Let me handle that," he said. "I've already called Randall—he's on his way. And let me tell the other decorators. It could be interesting to observe their reactions."

"Because they're all suspects," I said.

"Yes. Can you give me their contact information?" He held out his notebook, open to a blank page.

I pulled out my own notebook and copied out the names and telephone numbers of the designers for him.

"I've got e-mails and home addresses if you want them," I said.

"Tomorrow." He closed his notebook and stood up. "You'll be my first call when I'm ready to reopen the house. Sleep well."

Fat chance.

I drove home. It was nearly two o'clock. My mellow Christmas mood had vanished. When I looked at the snow, instead of appreciating its beauty and being grateful that it was coming down at a pace the county snowplows could handle, I started to feel claustrophobic. I was relieved when I finally let myself into the house and breathed in the evergreen scent. And someone had been cooking. Gingerbread?

Yes, and apple pie, too. Unless Rose Noire was experimenting with a new holiday potpourri. If so, it had my approval. She could call it Holiday Happy. Or Mistletoe Mellow. I could feel my spirits rising.

All the little LED fairy lights Mother had used to decorate the hall still twinkled merrily, so I didn't have to turn on the overhead light. The tree and the poinsettias and all the other holiday frills were merely shapes in the darkness, but shapes that gleamed here and there when the light from the LEDs hit some bit of tinsel or glitter.

The boys wanted leave the fairy lights up all year. I had pointed out that we'd take them for granted if we had them all the time. But tonight I decided maybe the boys might have the right idea. Hard to take for granted anything that cheered me so, I thought, as I tiptoed up to bed.

I didn't get much sleep that night. I know I got some sleep, because the boys woke me out of it at five.

"Mommy, there's a foot of snow!" Jamie shrieked as he bounced onto our bed.

"*Only* six inches," Josh said.

"I'm thinking eight or nine inches," Michael said. "But who cares how many inches—the important thing is that it's perfect for sledding!"

The boys cheered and began jumping up and down on our bed as if it were a trampoline. Michael observed my feeble attempts to share their enthusiasm.

"Anyone who wants to eat pancakes and then go sledding had better get dressed pronto," he exclaimed.

The boys cheered again, bounced off the bed, and disappeared.

"I didn't even wake up when you came in," he said. "I gather you had something to deal with at the house."

"Someone decided to get rid of Clay," I said.

"The committee finally got enough nerve to kick him out?" Michael was throwing on jeans and an old sweater.

"No, they voted to keep him, for fear he'd sue," I said. "And then he went back to the house, where someone shot him."

"He's dead?" Michael paused in the middle of pulling the sweater over his head.

"As the proverbial doornail," I said. "Someone shot him right between the eyes."

"Oh, my God! Are you all right?"

He hurried back over to the bed, sat down beside me, and put his arm around my shoulder.

"I'm fine," I said. "Just a little short of sleep."

"How late were you up last night?" he asked.

"Past two."

"Then go back to sleep," he said. "Rob and Rose Noire and I can keep the kids busy. And you'll need sleep to deal with whatever happens when you're able to go back to the house."

Thank goodness for family. Even family who, like Rob and Rose Noire, seemed to have settled in as permanent residents in several of our extra rooms. And thank goodness that Caerphilly College was on winter break, and that Michael, as always, was eager to spend his vacation time with his sons.

I turned over to go back to sleep. But I didn't drop off right away, or I wouldn't have heard Rose Noire's soft voice.

"Meg? You awake?"

"Yeah," I said. "What's up?"

I sat up and turned to look at her. She was standing in the doorway wringing her hands.

"Michael said that someone shot Clay Spottiswood."

"Yes," I said.

"That poor man." She shook her head. "He was such an unhappy, troubled soul. Such a waste."

She was right, of course, but I found myself wondering if anyone else would feel much sadness over his demise.

"And did it happen in the house?" she asked.

"In the middle of his room. I'm sure by now the house is filled with all kinds of bad karma and negative energy. Maybe you can do some kind of cleansing before we all get back to work there." Even though I only half believed in them, Rose Noire's cleansings and blessings always raised my spirits.

"Of course." She nodded absently. "But who did it? It wasn't Vermillion, was it?"

"I have no idea who did it." I sat up straighter, suddenly feeling a lot more awake. "Why would you think it would be Vermillion?"

"Your mother and Eustace and I were sort of keeping an eye out for her," Rose Noire said. "Clay made her anxious. She was bothered by the way he was flirting with her."

"Probably because Clay's idea of flirting corresponded with most sane women's idea of sexual harassment and sometimes actual assault," I said. "Do you mean he kept it up after the tongue lashing I gave him the first week we were all there?"

"Not that I saw," she said. "But of course I'm sure he'd have been very careful about doing it when you were around, or your mother or me."

"And you didn't trust him not to do it when she was all alone."

"No." She shook her head vigorously. "So we made sure she never was alone. She felt very safe when you were around, which was most of the time, and when you were gone, your mother and I kept an eye on her."

"So as far as you know, he didn't bother her again."

"As far as we knew."

I could see from her face that she was worried. Afraid that perhaps her watchdog mission hadn't been as successful as she had thought.

On the surface, the idea of Rose Noire protecting Goth Girl seemed funny. Rose Noire had never met a New Age theory without embracing it, was an ardent vegetarian, dressed in romantic flowing dresses trimmed with ethereal wisps of gauze and lace, and felt guilty thinking bad thoughts about anyone. Goth Girl wore a lot of black leather pocked with spikes and studs, sported jewelry featuring skulls and snakes, and liked to imply that she knew quite a lot about vampires, necromancy, and abstruse poisons.

But Rose Noire, at five eight, was only two inches shorter than I was, in excellent condition from working in her organic herb garden, and fierce as a mother hen about anything smaller or weaker than she was. Goth Girl was reed-thin, nearly a head shorter than me, and I'd always suspected her bark was much worse than her bite. Yeah, Rose Noire would protect her. And besides, they were both part of the sisterhood who, like Cher and Madonna, were on a first-name-only basis with the rest of the world.

"He was shot," I said. "That doesn't seem in character for Vermillion. Unless we find out it was done with silver bullets, or maybe a special antique revolver with an onyx handle."

Rose Noire smiled faintly at that.

"You really think she could have done it?" I asked.

"No." She sounded uncertain. "But I think we should make sure the chief knows about the harassment. Because it would look suspicious if he found out the wrong way."

"I'll make sure he knows about all the harassment," I said. "Vermillion wasn't the only one."

"Thanks." She looked relieved to have delegated her worries to me. "Get some sleep now."

I tried. But I lay awake a long time, thinking about Vermillion. Would it really be out of character for her to shoot Clay? The more I thought about it, the more I realized that she seemed like someone who'd been through a lot, but hadn't necessarily emerged unscathed.

Could I see her as fearful, and anxious, and deciding to protect herself by carrying a gun in her coffin-shaped black leather purse? Unfortunately, yes.

What I couldn't see nearly as easily was her showing up at the house at midnight. She always seemed very cheerful in the mornings, with the sunshine streaming through the faux stained glass she'd applied to all her room's windows. And always seemed in a hurry to leave before sunset.

A Goth who was afraid of the dark?

Or maybe just one who knew better than to be out "in those dark hours when the powers of evil are exalted."

Now where had that quotation come from? Thanks to Michael's annual one-man _Christmas Carol_ shows, I was now incapable of getting through a December day without quoting Dickens at least half a dozen times, but I was pretty sure that line had nothing to do with Scrooge. Or did it?

I began silently reciting the text of the show to myself to make sure and fell asleep long before even the first of the three ghosts arrived.

Chapter 7

December 21

"Sherlock Holmes," I exclaimed.

"What's that?" Randall said.

I appeared to be holding the phone. Evidently, Randall had called, and the phone's ring had awakened me from a dream in which I'd identified the source of the quote about "the powers of evil" that I'd gone to sleep muttering. Sherlock Holmes. I didn't remember which book, but I could always ask Dad, the mystery buff, who could quote countless pages of Conan Doyle from memory.

"Meg?" Randall again. "Something wrong?"

"Long story," I said aloud. "Please tell me you're calling to relay the news that the chief's letting us back in the house again." It was—good grief, nearly 10:00 A.M. Sunlight was pouring through the window, and I could hear giggles and shrieks of delight from the backyard.

"Not just yet," he said. "Although I think the chief's getting close. I've been hanging around here at the show house wearing my mayor's hat and kibitzing, and I think they're close to finishing up. No, I was calling to let you know that the committee decided not to give Clay's room to another designer."

"What are we going to do—exhibit the crime scene?" I asked. "Complete with bloodstains and an outline of the body and those little numbered cards they use to keep track of evidence in the crime-scene photos?"

"It's a thought," Randall said, with a chuckle. "Bet we'd sell tickets. No, we decided to complete his room as close as possible to the way he was doing it. Like a memorial. We thought we could get a couple of the other designers to supervise the workmen doing it. He left behind some sketches of his plan for the room—I found them in the dresser drawer. We can use those."

"Nobody's going to be thrilled with this solution," I said. "Every other designer in the house thinks his style is hideous."

"If they're right, all the more chances for their rooms to win," he said. "And won't it be a little bit of consolation that they'll never have to put up with him again?"

"Good point," I said. "I'll ask Mother, Eustace, and Martha. They've kind of got seniority. And I trust Mother and Eustace to be balanced about it. Martha will hate the whole thing, but she'd be furious if we didn't ask her."

"Sounds good to me and—hang on. . . . Yes, I'm talking to her now . . . Meg, the chief wants to know if you can come down to the house. He wants to go over a few things before he's ready to release it."

"On my way," I said.

I threw on my clothes, ran down to the kitchen, and stuck my head out the back door. Michael, Rob, and the boys were making snowmen, snow dogs, and snow llamas in the backyard.

"Going back to the house," I shouted.

Michael waved, and the boys followed his example.

I ran down the hallway to Michael's office and photocopied a page from my notebook—the page on which I had the names, e-mails, addresses, and phone numbers. I remembered the chief would be wanting it. Back in the kitchen,

I grabbed a yogurt and some granola bars to eat on the way, and then dashed out to my car. It was gloriously free of snow, and someone—probably the snow creature construction crew—had done a beautiful job of shoveling our driveway.

I'd heap praise on them later.

On my way to the house, I turned on the radio and hummed along with the carols. Carols—at least the old-fashioned kind—always helped me focus on the here and now instead of the long list of holiday tasks waiting in my notebook. The sun was shining, the snow made the Caerphilly countryside look like a Christmas card, and while I would rather be making snowmen with the boys, I knew they were happy and safe at home with Michael. And we had tonight's *Christmas Carol* performance to look forward to.

I tried to enjoy my Christmas mood while it lasted, since I suspected that between Clay's murder and having to deal with the stressed-out designers, the house would bring my spirits down soon enough.

There were a lot of cars parked in front of the show house. Several police cruisers. The chief's sedan. Cousin Horace's Prius—not surprising that he'd still be there, since his crime-scene investigation work could easily take hours. I was a little worried to see Dad's minivan—was he still there in his official capacity as medical examiner? If he'd stayed on to kibitz, the chief's patience might be wearing thin.

Most of the cars that had been parked up and down the street were still there, but someone had dusted off the back or front of each so they could check the license plates. Across the street from the house, one car had been completely cleared of snow, and I recognized Clay's silver Acura.

The front walk was nearly shoveled, and Tomás was finishing off the last bit.

"*Buenas dias, señora,*" he said as I passed.

"*Buenas dias,*" I echoed. I hadn't seen him quite so cheerful the whole time he'd been in the house. I wondered if the designers would be quite so honestly upbeat this morning, or if they'd all feel obliged to put on sober looks and struggle to find something nice to say about Clay.

I couldn't help thinking of the scene in *A Christmas Carol* in which the Ghost of Christmas Yet to Come shows Ebenezer Scrooge exactly how little his death would mean to any human soul. Instead of three spirits bent on his reformation, Clay had encountered a single vengeful one. No chance at reformation for him.

In this somewhat pensive mood, I entered the house. I found Dad, the chief, and Randall standing in the hallway.

"Meg—good!" the chief exclaimed. "I was hoping you'd get here soon. I want to hear again exactly what happened when you got here last night."

My stomach churned, making me regret the yogurt, just for a moment. I'd been staying pretty calm by shoving last night's events out of my mind—focusing narrowly on what we needed to get done in the show house. It had been working fine. But now the chief needed me to go back to last night.

He ushered me into Sarah's study. I took one of the armchairs, the chief took the other, and Randall and Dad perched on metal folding chairs that had been brought in from somewhere. Clearly the chief was using the study as his on-site headquarters. I hoped to clear him—and the battered metal chairs—out before Sarah returned.

"So tell us everything that happened," he said. "Start from when you were approaching the house."

I took a few of the deep, calming yoga breaths Rose Noire was always ordering me to take, and then I told him everything. The snow-covered cars. Stepping into the dark hallway. Hearing the faint noise upstairs. Dodging the bullets. Seeing—well, hearing—the intruder drive away.

He didn't interrupt me once, which was rare for him. When I finished, I felt curiously better, as if I'd gotten something nasty out of my system. He waited a few minutes before asking anything.

"Her 911 call came at twelve eighteen," he said finally.

"That fits," Dad said.

"Meg, how many shots did you hear again?"

"Two," I said. "Close together."

"You're sure," he said. "No chance it was more?"

"Positive."

"And you didn't hear any shots as you approached the house?"

I shook my head.

"That fits, too," Dad said.

"Fits what?" I asked.

"It appears that Mr. Spottiswood was shot shortly after eleven," the chief said.

"The wound would have been almost instantly fatal," Dad added.

"And then the killer stayed around to vandalize the house for approximately an hour," the chief said. "Not leaving until you interrupted him or her at around twelve fifteen."

"Vandalize the house?" I shot upright and looked around frantically. "How bad is it?"

"Calm down," Randall said. He was gesturing with both hands for me to sit down, so I sat. "Most of it's in the master bedroom, which is going to need some cleanup anyway. The boys and I can knock it all out in an hour or two. I already sent Mateo for supplies."

"So," the chief went on. "Let's assume Dr. Langslow's

estimates are correct—and I have no reason to think they're not," he added, nodding and smiling at Dad. "You did not interrupt the murder, but you did interrupt whatever the killer was doing after the murder. And it's possible that Mr. Spottiswood wasn't deliberately targeted—merely unfortunate enough to interrupt an armed intruder."

"That would be ironic," I said. "The guy everyone hates gets knocked off just after one of his worst rampages since we started working here, and it turns out to be a coincidence? Something that could have happened to any one of us if we'd been unlucky enough to come here at the wrong time?"

Something that could have happened to me if Michael's rehearsal had ended an hour earlier and I'd shown up to do my inspection at eleven instead of midnight. I shoved that away with all the other things I didn't really want to think about, until later, when the killer was behind bars.

"That's one theory," the chief said. "I'm not discounting the possibility that someone with a strong motive to kill Mr. Spottiswood lay in wait and staged the damage to make it look as if an intruder had been here."

"Makes sense to me, because the damage was so random and illogical," Randall said. "Drawers pulled out as if they were looking for something. Chunks of wall hacked out as if all they wanted to do was cause maximum chaos. Curtains and bed linens slashed. Stupid, mean stuff. But almost entirely in that one room."

"Maybe that was all they had time to do before I arrived," I said.

The others nodded.

"There's also the question of how the intruder gained entry," the chief said. "No sign of a break-in, and I understand it's only the designers who have keys."

"The designers, and a couple of the show house committee members, and anyone clever enough to pick up one of the dozen or so keys various designers have managed to lose over the last several weeks." I could tell my irritation was showing, so I took a couple of deep breaths before going on. "Violet alone has lost at least seven keys."

"That would be Miss Madsen, in the . . . frilly bedroom upstairs," the chief said.

"And one of the reasons I came back to check on the house is that half the time, even when they've got keys, they don't use them," I went on. "I seem to be the only one who ever bothers to go around and see that all the doors and windows are locked at the end of the day."

"This in spite of our attempts to make sure all the designers were aware that there was a history of vandalism here at the house," Randall said. "Not surprising, given how long it's been vacant."

"Only surprising it took several years for the vandals to find it," the chief said. "Getting back to the murder—do you know if any of the other decorators particularly disliked Mr. Spottiswood?"

I thought about it for about two seconds.

"Particularly disliked—no. Though I can't think of anyone who actually liked him. At least half of them resented him because they thought they should have been given the master bedroom. And he was harassing most of the women. Probably not Mother," I added to Dad, who was frowning thunderously. "Or he wouldn't have survived till last night. But pretty much everybody else."

"Did he harass you?" the chief asked, scowling.

"Until he figured out what a bad idea it was."

Randall made a snorting noise that I suspected was suppressed laughter.

"Define harassment," the chief said.

"Patting me on the rear," I said. "Finding it necessary to squeeze past me when I was standing in a narrow space. Stuff like that."

"And this was typical of his behavior toward the women in the house?"

"As far as I know, yes," I said. "He was a pig. And it's possible he was more offensive toward the women who weren't as comfortable confronting him. Rose Noire thinks Vermillion had some kind of run-in with him, so she and Mother made sure never to leave her alone. And I wonder about Violet, or even Sarah."

The chief nodded.

"You were going to give me the full contact information for all the designers," he asked.

I pulled out my notebook and handed him the photocopy I'd made.

"While I'm here—" I began.

"Meg!" It was Mother. "Are you really all right?"

She put her hand to my forehead, as if expecting the shock of encountering a murderer to have given me a dangerous fever.

"I'm fine," I said.

"James, you were supposed to call me once you'd seen her." Mother turned to Dad with a look of deep disappointment on her face.

"I was caught up in the case," Dad said. "Trying to find whoever took a shot at Meg."

Mother looked somewhat mollified.

"And do you have any idea how soon we can get back to work?" she asked, turning to the chief.

"I'm going to hold the master bedroom a few more hours," the chief said. "But there's no reason not to release the rest of the house. If you don't mind, I'd like to ask you a few questions, and when I'm done, I can let you get back to your work."

"That would be fine," Mother said.

"Here, take my chair." I stood up and stepped aside. "Chief, may I do a tour of inspection?"

"Just stay out of the master suite till I give the word," he said. "I'll be interviewing all the designers this morning. Try to avoid discussing the case with any of them until after I've had my chance. Sammy!"

The deputy raced into the study.

"Start calling the designers." The chief held out his copy of my contact list. "Start with Mr. Goodwin."

"Right, chief!" Sammy dashed out again.

Randall, Dad, and I followed, and the chief closed the French doors that separated the study from the foyer.

"Meg, if you're sure you're all right . . ." Dad began.

"Nothing wrong with me that a real night's sleep won't fix," I said.

"Then I'm going to head down to the hospital," he said. "I don't want to miss the autopsy."

He dashed out.

"I've already got a punch list of things we need to fix," Randall said. "Most of them in the master bedroom, so I'll have to wait till Horace finishes his forensic work. In here, nothing much. Couple broken crystals in the chandelier, and a bullet hole over there."

He point to one wall.

"That's a bullet hole?" I exclaimed. The hole was more fist- than bullet-sized.

"Okay, the hole where Horace dug out the bullet. Looked to me like a .22, which is also what I bet they'll be taking out of Clay. I saw the wound. Luckily the bullet that hit the chandelier just ricocheted and landed down the hall. Anyway, we can patch the hole pretty quick, though I'm afraid Miss Ivy will need to redo that part of her mural."

Poor Ivy. She had already been worrying about how to finish all the walls. And she was making it harder for herself by having pretty much nothing but wall. At the moment, the only pieces of furniture in any of her spaces were a small nondescript cabinet in the back of the foyer and a large bronze Art Nouveau umbrella stand beside the front door. I had a feeling she was only using the cabinet to store her paints in and would whisk it away before the house opened. The umbrella stand was probably staying, because she clearly enjoyed seeing her painting of "The Little Match Girl" peeping out from behind it. Maybe I should suggest altering her design to cover the unpainted stretches with a big piece of furniture or a tapestry.

No, better not. I'd figured out that the designers rarely appreciated what I thought were brilliant practical suggestions.

"We've pretty much cleaned up what the water leak did to the den," Randall said. We both glanced over at the French doors. Mother was gesticulating dramatically. I suspected she was giving the chief chapter and verse of Clay's sins.

I walked through all the rooms, starting with the upstairs, with Randall trailing me. We found a few small things to add to his list, but none of them appeared to be the result of the intruder. No sign that the intruder had damaged anything on his flight path through the Princess Room, the back bathroom, the quilt room, or the garage. No sign that he'd been in the Goth room, the kitchen, the dining room, or the great room.

"Tree looks nice in that new position," Randall said when we'd finished our detailed inspection. "I just hope your mother doesn't up and decide to move it again."

"If she does, I'll talk her out of it," I said. "It looks glorious there. You'd hardly know the dining room existed."

"Yeah, I gathered that was the whole point," Randall said with a snicker. "But your mother made me cut a couple feet off the bottom to make sure folks could still see Ivy's 'Nightingale' mural."

The mural that at the moment was still only a few pencil marks on the wall of the upper hall, marks so faint that from down here it still looked like a blank wall. I felt a twinge of increasingly familiar stomach-churning anxiety. Would Ivy still have time to finish all the paintings she'd planned? And if she didn't, would it be playing favorites to hint that maybe she should give priority to the one Mother had planned to showcase in her room?

Just then the front door opened.

"Meg, darlin'!" Eustace sailed in with a travel coffee cup in one hand and a large brown grocery bag in the other. He bent over to land an air kiss near my cheek. "I hear it was like the shootout at the O.K. Corral in here last night."

"I was only here for two of the gunshots," I said.

"I'm going to round up my workmen," Randall said, and strode off, pulling out his cell phone.

"*Only* two! Good Lord!" Eustace exclaimed. He was heading through Mother's room to his own domain, the breakfast room and kitchen. "But I heard someone knocked off Clay, and you found him. I want to hear every detail! Spill!"

"Not till after you've talked to the chief," I said.

"You sure he wants to talk to me?" Eustace asked.

"He wants to talk to everyone." I followed him into the breakfast room and sat down at the round glass-topped table while he continued into the kitchen.

"Well, I won't grill you till after the chief has grilled me." He had opened the refrigerator door and was putting things away: diet sodas, several brown paper-wrapped deli pack-ages, and bottles of water. "But after that, I expect all the dirt."

"Every bit," I said. I was staring at something that seemed out of place in the otherwise impeccable breakfast nook. A dirty glass. No, a half-full glass, and unless my sense of smell was playing tricks on me, it was half-full of cheap scotch.

I found myself remembering a night shortly after we'd started working on the house, when Randall had sent over beer, sodas, and pizza for everyone. I'd held out a can of soda and a bottle of beer for Eustace to choose from.

"I'll take the diet soda, darlin'," he'd said.

"I'm not a big beer drinker myself," I'd replied.

"Dear heart, I'm a dry drunk," he'd said. "Ten years so-ber come New Year's Day. If you ever see me popping the top of one of those beers, you tie me down and call my sponsor."

So why was there a half-full glass of scotch in his room?

He saw what I was looking at.

"Is that what I think it is?" he asked.

"If you think it's a stale glass of cheap, smelly scotch, then yes," I said.

"Another little offering from Clay," he said. "The last, I assume, unless he comes back to needle me from beyond the grave. Do me a favor—pour it out and rinse that glass out real good so I won't smell it."

"Offering from Clay?" I echoed, as I got up to follow his instructions. "You mean he left this here deliberately. Did he know—"

"That I'm a recovering alcoholic? Hell, yes. He did it all the time, bless his evil little heart. That's the kind of guy he is. Was."

I dumped the scotch in the sink, rinsed out the glass twice, and ran enough water to make sure the alcohol smell was long gone from the sink. Then I carried the glass back to the breakfast table so I could take it with me when I left. It was a cheap, heavy tumbler, and clearly didn't belong in Eustace's elegant kitchen.

"Chief's going to want to know my alibi." Eustace looked somber. "And that's going to be a problem."

"If only we'd known someone was going to knock Clay off," I said. "We could all have arranged to be with someone who could alibi us."

"I was with someone, but I'm not sure it's going to do me any good," Eustace said. "I'm sponsoring someone. He's almost made six months."

"That's great," I said.

"But holidays are a bad time for him. For most of us. I was with him, helping him through a bad night, from about nine thirty till well past two in the morning. But I can't give the chief his name unless he's okay with it. And if he's not . . ."

He shook his head.

"Maybe it won't be a problem," I said. "Even if he says no, you probably won't be the only person in the house without an alibi."

"No," he said, looking slightly more cheerful. "Not even the only person without an alibi who hated Clay's guts. I do hope your mother's alibied."

"Probably alibied ten times over," I said. "Michael's giving his one-man show of Dickens's *A Christmas Carol* tonight, so we have tons of family and friends coming into town to see it. If I know Mother, she was up till midnight visiting."

Deputy Sammy appeared in the doorway from the living room.

"Mr. Goodwin? The chief's ready for you now."

Eustace stood up and squared his shoulders.

"Wish me luck," he said, and sailed out.

I followed him and Sammy out into the living room. Mother was standing in the center of the room, gazing at the tree. Apparently she'd recruited Tomás and Mateo to work on the redecoration. They'd placed two stepladders next to the tree and were scampering down to grab ornaments and then back up to put them on the tree with Mother directing them in sign language and scraps of broken Spanish.

I glanced over at the French doors. Eustace was talking, gesticulating dramatically. I had a feeling he'd be there for quite a while.

Randall and my cousin Horace were standing at the top of the stairs. I ran up to join them.

Chapter 8

"Hey, Meg," Horace said. "The chief says it's okay for you guys to have the room back."

"Great," I said. "How bad is it?"

Randall stepped aside so I could see.

The master bed frame stood, stripped of its hangings, its bed linens, and even its mattress.

"We took all the bedding down to the lab," Horace said, following my look. "And there was almost no blood on the walls."

I didn't see any blood on them. But it looked as if someone had gone after the walls, the floors, and the furniture with an ax. And there was fingerprint powder all over everything—the furniture, the carpet, and the walls up to a height of six or seven feet.

"Soon as your mother's finished with Tomás and Mateo, I'm to turn them loose in here," Randall said. "First thing's to scrub off all that powder. Then we can patch and re-paint."

"And clean or replace the carpet," I suggested.

"Roger." He was scribbling on his list. "Couple of my guys are headed down here with some new drywall, and the hardware store's mixing up a big batch of that god-awful red paint. We'll get it back as fast as we can to where it was when Clay left yesterday, so start talking to whoever you think you can get to finish it off."

"We'll also need a new mattress," I said. "King-sized."

"And I assume we should be replacing the black sheets."

"Part of the design," I said.

"See you later," Horace said. "Got to get back to the lab."

"Oh, my!"

I looked over to see Violet standing in the doorway. She was holding something—a rolled-up rug, by the look of it—and staring at the room.

"What's left of the crime scene," Randall said.

"Horrible," Violet said. She turned and fled—presumably across the hall, to her room.

"I should go and see if she's all right," I said.

Randall nodded. He was holding a box of trash bags. As I was turning to leave, I saw him pull one out and stoop down to start picking up some of the debris on the floor.

I followed Violet. She was standing in her room, holding her head.

"You okay?" I asked.

"I've got a bit of a headache," she replied.

Probably a monster headache, by the look of her. She was pale and hollow-eyed, and I noticed she was shading her eyes against the light.

"Want me to help you with that?" I asked, pointing to the rolled-up rug.

"Please."

I tore the brown paper off the roll and set it down on the floor. I figured it would go where the damaged rug had gone, and Violet didn't correct me. Then I unrolled it, revealing a very familiar-looking petit-point rug.

"Is this a new rug or the one Clay damaged?" I asked.

"The damaged one."

"It looks great!" I exclaimed.

"It's Daphne's doing," she said. Daphne, the proprietor

of the Caerphilly Cleaners, was well known as a miracle worker when it came to removing stains. In a less enlightened era, her competitors would probably have tried to have her burned at the stake. "I can still sort of tell where the paint was," she added.

"But it might be your imagination," I hurried to say. "And no one else would ever guess. It looks great. The whole room looks great."

I must have been able to say it with a straight face, because she beamed happily. Actually, I suppose if you liked pastel colors, glitter, ruffles, lace, and stuffed animals, it probably was great. It was certainly the most extreme example I'd ever seen of the whole uber-feminine girly girl style. If Mother had done up my room like this when I was ten or twelve, I'd have run screaming into the night and slept in the tool shed.

Martha stuck her head in the door.

"You okay?" she asked. "You want more of that Alka-Seltzer?"

"I'm fine," Violet replied.

"You don't look fine," Martha said. "Here." She handed Violet a bottle of water. "Keep hydrating. Best thing for you."

Violet nodded, opened the bottle, and sipped.

Martha nodded and left. I was puzzled. I hadn't noticed that the two of them were particularly close before.

"She's a mother hen," Violet said. "We sort of bonded over the whole horrible experience of having Clay ruin our rooms."

"I can understand that," I said.

"We went out to dinner last night," she said. "To vent about the whole thing. Isn't that lucky?"

"Lucky? How so?"

"Well, I had a couple of glasses of wine, which I shouldn't have done, because even one glass puts me under the table." She giggled girlishly. "Martha put me up in her guest room, and we stayed up past midnight gossiping."

I suddenly realized where she was going with this.

"So you're alibied," I said. "Congratulations!"

It must have sounded as silly to her as it did to me, because we both burst out laughing. Or maybe it was the relief. She was happy to be in the clear. I was happy for her. She was one of the nice ones. Silly, but nice. And knowing that Martha had looked after her properly made me think better of her, too.

"What's so funny?" Martha had appeared in the doorway again.

"We were just—" Violet began. And then she paused and held her hand to her mouth. "Oh, dear. Mind if I use your bathroom for a sec?"

"Don't touch the walls," Martha said. "Wet paint."

Martha stepped into the room. Violet scurried into the bathroom and closed the door.

"Nice of you to look after her," I said.

"Some people shouldn't be allowed out on their own."

"And your good deed is rewarded."

"Rewarded?" Martha raised one eyebrow in a puzzled expression.

"At the very time when Clay was being murdered here in the house, the two of you were sharing girlish confidences over your wine."

"Actually, I was probably holding her head while she worshiped the porcelain goddess," Martha said. "No head for alcohol, that girl. And I feel a little guilty—we must have spent half the evening trading stories about nasty things Clay had done, and planning silly little pranks to play on

him. If I'd known he was about to get killed . . ." She shook
her head.

"But you didn't," I said. "And being dead doesn't make
him a saint."

"I guess we'll have to go to the funeral," she said. "And
look solemn. And make sure he's really gone."

Violet opened the door and scurried out into the room.

"Thanks, Martha," she chirped.

"Let's go see if Eustace has any coffee," Martha said.
"Might settle your stomach."

As they went down the stairs, I could hear Violet chatter-
ing with determined cheerfulness about ruching, whatever
that was. And Martha answering that proper thread ten-
sion was the key.

Not the most likely pair of new best friends, but perhaps
working in adjacent rooms under the pressure of our
deadline—and with the odious Clay nearby—had worked
some kind of magic. And it would be interesting if their
newfound alliance survived the end of the show house. But
it was nice, for the time being, to see Violet opening up and
Martha behaving kindly rather than waspishly.

I heard the toilet flush in Martha's bathroom. The door
to the first part of the bathroom, with the sink and tub in
it was open, but the door to the toilet compartment was
closed. I waited until after I heard water running in the
second sink, in its own compartment on the far side of the
toilet, to knock on the door.

"Out in a minute."

It was Alice, one of the two Quilt Ladies.

"I was just coming to see how you two were doing this
morning," I said.

"Pretty well, considering," she answered, as I followed her
into the bonus room beyond. "Last night was a tough night."

"You're telling me," I said.

"I don't just mean here," she said. "Mrs. Stavropoulos broke her hip. Dr. Stavropoulos's mother," she added, seeing my puzzled look. "She lives at Caerphilly Assisted Living."

"It didn't happen when we were over there caroling?" I asked. I was always deathly afraid that the boys would start running and knock over one of the frailer seniors.

"No, around midnight, while I was on duty. I'm the night shift receptionist, you know, five nights a week."

Actually, I hadn't known, but I nodded as if I did.

"It's really the perfect job for us," she said. "Until we can afford to do this full time. For me, actually—Vicky's retired, of course. But she comes over most nights when I'm on duty, and we sit together behind the desk and quilt all night. Or work on our room designs. Management doesn't mind—as long as I'm there to answer the phone and buzz people in, they don't care what I do. And sometimes, like last night, it's a real blessing to have the two of us there."

"What happened last night," I asked. "With Mrs. Stavropoulos?"

"Got up to go to the bathroom and fell," Alice said. "Luckily, she could still reach the emergency cord. I called 9-1-1 and Vicky went up to sit with her and keep her spirits up until the ambulance got there. And a few of the residents heard the ambulance, and we had to reassure them and walk them back to their rooms. And old Mr. Jackson took it into his head again that General Sherman's army was coming to burn the town, and Vicky calmed him down by filling the water buckets and keeping watch out his window till he fell asleep. I had to stay at the desk all this time—I was trying to reach Dr. Stavropoulos to let him know—so having her there was a lifesaver."

"When did all this happen?" I asked.

"Around eleven thirty," she said. "And I don't think we got everyone calmed down and back in their rooms until well after one a.m. Not much progress on our quilting last night! But Mrs. Stavropoulos is going to be all right, so all's well that ends well."

"Where is Vicky?" I asked. "Sleeping in after all that excitement?"

"I wish. That both of us could sleep in. No, she's downstairs, talking to the chief. My turn next. You poor thing! Here I'm rattling on about our night—and did I hear that you found poor Clay's body right here in the house?"

"I did," I said. "And I'll be happy to tell you all about it after you talk to the chief. I just came over to see how you two were doing. Find out if this morning's delay has you in a panic."

"Oh, we're fine," she said. "We'd be fine if the house opened tomorrow. Mind you, there's a few more things we want to do if we have the time. And we might do a little fine tuning of what's here. For example, do you think we should swap the tumbling blocks with the Irish chain? Or leave them were they are?"

From her gestures, I deduced that we were talking about quilts, not actual blocks and chains.

"I'm not sure I know which one is which," I said. "And if I had any design sense whatsoever, Mother would long ago have co-opted me to work in her room. But for my money, that quilt is the most awesome one you've got." I pointed to a quilt that looked like a bunch of three-dimensional squares done in black, purple, and turquoise. "So if you put it where it was the first thing visitors saw when they walked into the room, they would be seriously impressed."

"That's the tumbling blocks," she said. "And yes, we were thinking we should make it more prominent. Don't tell me you have no design sense. Can you help me with this?"

We'd done this before, so I knew the drill. We each grabbed one end of the long pole from which my favorite quilt was hanging and lifted it down from the pegs that held it up. We laid it down carefully on the worktable while we picked up the other quilt—presumably the Irish chain—and moved it into the place where the tumbling blocks had been.

"Definitely an improvement," Alice said, as we lifted the tumbling blocks quilt into place, right inside the door where the visitors would enter after touring Martha's bathroom. We stood back for a few moments and admired the effect.

There were a dozen large quilts hung around the room— some modern, some traditional, all different and all beautiful. Along one wall they'd put a shelf with dozens of bolts of fabric, arranged in order from blue on one end through green, yellow, orange, red, and purple at the far end, like a bright rainbow. And they hadn't forgotten to work in the Christmas theme. One of the quilts was a special Christmas quilt in reds and greens, using fabrics with patterns of holly and presents. Another was in blue and silver with stars and snowflakes—both beautiful, though neither outshone the tumbling blocks quilt I so admired. The small Christmas tree in the corner was decorated with a garland of metallic fabric and ornaments quilted from red and green satin.

"Even the late Mr. Spottiswood allowed as how that quilt wasn't too bad," Alice said as she carefully tucked a few sprigs of evergreen at either end of the pole, being careful not to let them touch the fabric. "I confess, I feel sorry for the poor man, but I won't miss him."

"Sorry for him?"

"You have to be pretty unhappy to be that mean, don't you?"

I nodded.

"Well, anyway," she said. "Things will be a bit more pleasant around here with him gone, won't they?"

"Yes, we might actually see a bit of Christmas cheer around here."

"True," she said. "I think Clay's idea of Christmas decorating was to put a bit of mistletoe in the doorway so he could bother all the pretty ladies. But actually by around here I meant here in Caerphilly. The design world's a small town, you know. Having Clay barge in has shaken things up a bit. And not in a good way."

"Who was the most hurt by his arrival?" I asked.

"Sarah and Martha," Alice said, with surprising promptness. "Your mother and Eustace have a much more traditional sensibility. So do Linda and Violet, though they're not in the same league. Violet's barely making a living, and poor Linda's lucky her late husband left her comfortably off."

Linda, I remembered, was Our Lady of Chintz's real name.

"And he didn't much hurt Vicky and me, either. If you want a quilting room, or a room designed with plenty of quilts, we're the best. But we don't do anything outside of our niche. And I suppose our vampire girl has her own niche. Not a big call for decorating with bats and coffins, is there? I understand she makes the better part of her income selling Goth crafts on Etsy."

I nodded as if I'd already known this.

"But Sarah and Martha are both working in similar areas," she said. "More modern styles. A clean, open minimalist look. Strong colors. I think when he arrived here a few years ago, he took quite a bite out of both their businesses," she went on. "They've been bouncing back—people are starting to see Clay for the one-trick pony he is. Oh, it's quite a handsome pony, but it's always the same, and frankly, a little too much Clay and too little client. He's not a bad designer if you like what he likes, but if you don't, too bad—that's what you get anyway."

"Mrs. Graham?" Sammy appeared at the head of the stairway that led down to the garage. "The chief would like to see you now."

Chapter 9

"I'm ready," Alice said. "Dying to get it over with so I can pump Meg for all the details she won't tell me!"

Bless her for that—it might reduce the chief's annoyance, if he heard I'd been talking to a witness he hadn't yet interviewed.

I decided it might be wiser for me to stick to talking to people who'd already been debriefed. So I followed them down the stairs and through the kitchen, intending to see what Mother and Eustace were up to.

They were standing together in the archway that separated Eustace's breakfast nook from Mother's great room. As I watched, they looked into the great room. Then the breakfast nook. Then the great room again.

"No," he said. "You're right."

"Too abrupt," Mother said.

"I could change the paint color?"

"No, it's not that," Mother said. "Maybe if we mass a few poinsettias on either side of the archway."

They studied the archway some more.

"No," they said simultaneously.

I'd seen this before. They could keep up these conferences for longer that I'd ever imagined possible. Sometimes the conference erupted into painting and furniture moving, and anyone foolish enough to be nearby would get drafted into the action and could kiss the rest of her day good-bye.

"Oh, hello, Meg," Eustace said, spotting me. "What do you think of—"

"Hang on," I said. "I've got to check on—on Linda."

I'd almost called her Our Lady of Chintz in front of someone other than Mother. I needed to be careful. Linda. Linda. Linda.

I went back through the kitchen and into the dining room.

Linda was standing in her room, looking frazzled. She was batting uselessly at the branches of spruce that protruded into her room as if she'd caught them trying to sneak farther in and dump needles on her fabric. One of them had snagged her shapeless brown woolen tunic.

"This tree is impossible," she said, turning to me. "The branches take up half the room."

Half was an exaggeration, but the branches did stick out rather far.

"We need to move the tree," she said.

I'd been afraid of that. Tomás and Mateo were nearly finished redecorating Mother's side of the tree. We couldn't ask them to move it again.

"Oh, no," I said. "I think the tree adds just the right touch. We only need a little less of it in the room. I'll have Randall get someone to prune it back."

I stepped into the hall and called. Randall didn't answer, so I left a voice mail—one that wouldn't offend Linda, in case she was eavesdropping.

Then I stepped back into the dining room. Linda had turned her back on the invading vegetation and was sitting on one of her chintz-covered dining room chairs, threading red and gold beads and green holly leaves onto a string to make a garland.

"So," I said. "Apart from the branches, how's it going?"

"Fine." She looked up and gave me a tight little smile. The kind of smile that's supposed to say "Don't worry, everything's fine," but makes you pretty sure everything isn't. "Just need to add those few Christmassy touches," she went on. "I'm essentially finished with the room itself."

For my taste, she should have declared it finished a week ago. It was a big dining room, but now it felt small and claustrophobic. There were too many things here. Too much going on. Too many small bits of furniture. Too many precisely arranged groups of small prints or decorative plates on the wall. Too many whatnots containing too many delicate tchotchkes. And above all, too many different chintz prints. One for the wallpaper. A similar but not-quite-matching one for the curtains. A third print for the dining room chair seats. Yet another for the occasional chair in the corner, not to mention another for the skirt covering the side table. Even the rug had a busy pattern all too reminiscent of chintz. I knew the effect she was aiming for—she'd told me the first time I met her.

"I like that cluttered, homey, English country look," she'd said. "Where it doesn't look as if everything was bought as a set, all matchy-matchy. Where the family just accumulates objects it loves, over the centuries, and doesn't care whether they're *supposed* to go together."

I had liked the sound of that. I'd expected something low-key and comfortable. Unfortunately, her room looked more as if she'd found a sale on chintz remnants and handed them over to a crew of blind seamstresses.

Of course, I made no pretense of understanding decorating trends, so for all I knew this could be the coming thing. Total sensory overload as a decorating strategy. Maybe I'd be seeing rooms like this in all of Mother's decorating magazines, if I ever bothered reading them.

Then again, there was hope. Mother hated Linda's room, I reminded myself, as I gazed at the offending spruce branches.

Linda herself didn't match the room at all. She was an attractive woman of forty-five or fifty, and I could tell her skirt and sweater were not cheap, but the overall effect was drab and lugubrious.

But she was pleasant and undemanding and went about her decorating business without any of the angst and drama that seemed part of the process for so many of the other designers, so on the whole, I liked her.

A stack of cardboard boxes sat in one corner, all with the words "Christmas ornaments" scrawled on them in one place or another.

"Oh, dear," I said. "Did you have to bring in your own personal Christmas decorations to cope with the tree?"

"Yes, but that's not a problem," she said. "I'm not going to do a tree this year anyway. There's just me, and I won't be home enough to really enjoy it. The tree here's a godsend. I was worried that the room wasn't turning out Christmassy enough."

Not Christmassy enough? She'd already looped red, green, and gold garlands, like the one she was making, along the crown molding all around the room near the ceiling. Tucked sheaves of holly and ivy behind every picture. Covered the table with a red-and-green holly print table runner. Scattered china elves and angels along the runner. And placed both wreaths and battery-operated candles in the two windows. To me, the as-yet undecorated branches of the Christmas tree poking through the archway were the one soothing, peaceful, truly beautiful element in the room.

"Don't work yourself into a frazzle," I said. "We women are all too prone to do that around Christmas. Take care of yourself."

"Oh, don't worry about me," she said. But I was startled to see that there were tears in her eyes. She bowed her head over her work, clearly not wanting me to see the tears.

Part of me wanted to stay and find out why a few kind words reduced her to tears. But another part of me— probably a better part—wanted to give her some privacy.

Maybe she was even crying over Clay's death. I didn't think they'd known each other that well. I couldn't recall any run-ins between them.

Maybe not knowing him that well made it easier to feel sad over his death. She could be the one person in the house who had no negative feelings about Clay, and could react to it simply as the death of another human being.

"Got to run," I said. "Call me if you need anything."

She nodded but didn't raise her head as I slipped out of the room.

I went back into the hall. It looked as if the chief was about to finish up with Alice. Sarah was sitting on the stairs with her chin in her hand, watching Ivy paint. Overnight the blue streak in Sarah's hair had morphed into a rich purple that matched her sweater. I decided it was an improvement.

"I'm sorry," I said. "The chief's got your room."

"He's only got a couple of people left to interview," she said. "And he did point out that this was faster for us than having to go down to the station. I'm good with it."

Ivy smiled over her shoulder at us, then got up and slipped

down the hallway. In her brown skirt and brown sweater, she seemed to disappear into the shadows after a few steps. But oddly enough, she didn't seem drab like Linda. More elfin.

"If we're bothering you, we can leave," I called out.

"Just going to the basement to mix some more pigments," she said.

I heard the basement door close.

"I don't think we're bothering her particularly," Sarah said. "She just needs a lot of time alone. It's not quite the same thing."

I nodded.

"Hell of a night last night," I said.

Sarah nodded but didn't say anything.

"What I wouldn't give to have been anywhere but here," I said.

Sarah giggled.

"Meg, if you're trying to find out whether or not I have an alibi for the time when Clay was killed, you could just ask me," she said.

"Okay," I said. "I gather you do have an alibi."

"Yes," she replied. "I was neutering tomcats."

I wasn't quite sure what to say to that.

"Actual feline tomcats," she went on. "Not Clay's kind. And spaying the females."

"I didn't know you moonlighted as a vet," I said.

"I was helping Clarence Rutledge. He's been doing a lot of pro bono work down at the animal shelter, spaying and neutering that whole feral cat colony that lives in the woods behind the New Life Baptist Church."

That made sense. Clarence was Caerphilly's most popular veterinarian. And although his appearance was intimidating—he was six feet, six inches tall and almost as wide, and usually wore leather and denim biker gear, even under his white lab coat at the clinic—he was a notorious softie when it came to any kind of animal.

"His clinic's so busy during the day that the only time he can do the surgeries is after hours," she said. "And we'd trapped a lot of feral cats. We were running out of cages. So every night this week I've been going over there at nine or ten o'clock, as soon as I can get away from here, and we work until he's too tired. Usually one or two in the morning."

"That's great," I said. "Best alibi I've heard all day, in fact."

"There is one thing I'm worried about," she said.

"What's that?"

"My fingerprints might be on the murder weapon."

Chapter 10

My jaw fell open, and I couldn't think of anything to say for several moments.

"How did that happen?" I asked finally.

"I don't know for sure," she said. "But there's a gun missing, and for all I know, it could be the murder weapon, and if it is, my fingerprints will be on it."

"Missing where?"

"From the house," she said. "From my room."

"You were keeping a gun in your room?"

"Not on purpose," she said. "It's not even mine—it's Kate's."

Kate—her business partner, the one Sarah had been having such an angry conversation with the day before—Kate saying "keep it" and Sarah saying "I don't even want it around me."

"Her husband got it for her when he started having to commute to Tappahannock for his job," Sarah said. "She never really wanted it around. But then when I began working here at the show house, she kept telling me I should take it with me, for protection. Because of Clay."

"She was afraid of Clay?"

"He's got a temper," Sarah said. "He had a booth near us at the Caerphilly Home and Garden Show last year, and he was just a pill the whole time. Flirting with us, and smirking at us, and then snaking people away from us the whole time,

and then at the end of the show, during the teardown, someone ticked him off and he just went berserk. Wrecked part
of his booth and the booth next door. He was like a crazy
man. And Kate freaked. Ever since then, she's wanted nothing to do with him. He works out of his house, which isn't
that far from our office, and for a while he kept trying to
drop in and schmooze. Until Bailey tried to bite him."

"Bailey?" I echoed. "The third partner in Byrne, Banks,
and Bailey?"

"Bailey's an Irish setter," she said, with a giggle. "And he
pretty much hates Clay, too."

"Dogs can be good judges of character," I said.

"Tell me about it," Sarah agreed. "Anyway, when Kate
heard Clay was part of the show house, she wanted us to
pull out. And I didn't think that would be good for our rep.
I said she could pull out, but I'd do it myself. We had a
pretty big fight over it."

"And then she brought her gun over here."

"Yesterday morning," she said. "I was off running an errand, and evidently, while I was out, she came in and put it
in the drawer in one of my end tables. I found it there a
little later, and told her to come and get it. And then the
whole flood thing happened, and when I remembered the
gun and looked in the end table drawers, it was gone. I was
hoping she'd taken it after all, but I asked her this morning and she didn't. It's gone."

"And you think someone took it while we were moving
everything out from under the flood?"

Sarah nodded.

"Damn," I said.

"Yeah."

"What kind of gun was it?"

"I have no idea."

"How big was it?"

She held her hands out about eight inches apart. Then moved them out to ten inches. And down to six. And then threw them up in frustration.

"I don't know," she said. "Gun-sized. Kind of small, I guess."

Her inability to identify the gun very accurately might have been more frustrating if I knew more about guns myself. Or if we knew what kind of gun had killed Clay.

"Anyway—I figure I should probably tell the chief."

"Absolutely."

"Even though it will make Kate a suspect, and she'll be mad at me, and maybe her husband will be mad at her for losing the gun?"

"Even though."

"Damn," she said.

We waited in silence for a while, and then the door opened. Alice came out, looking relieved to have gotten her interview over with.

"Ms. Byrne?" the chief said.

Sarah stood up and slowly walked toward the study.

My phone rang. I answered it, my eyes still on Sarah and the chief.

"Goose or turkey?"

"What's that?"

"I said, goose or turkey?"

I looked at my phone. The number showing was Michael's and my home phone. But the voice—

Wait—it was Michael's mother. Who evidently had arrived, and was starting the preparations for Christmas dinner.

Last year, my mother and Michael's had each decided to cook a Christmas dinner for the family. No amount of diplomacy could convince them to combine their events, and

I heard that several people unlucky enough to attend both dinners developed a temporary aversion to eating and fasted for one or more days afterward.

One of the saving graces of Mother's involvement in the show house was that it would prevent a recurrence. Even the mothers realized that last year's excess had been over the top, and while we'd made progress on getting them to join forces, I'd been more than a little worried about the possibility of conflict in the kitchen. Not that Mother cooked, of course. She usually drafted one or two relatives whose culinary skills she admired and got them to cook for her. But while most of her family were quite willing to let Mother order them around in the kitchen, I didn't think Dahlia Waterston would be as patient.

So I'd been very relieved when Mother announced that, alas, due to the show house, she would have to withdraw from Christmas dinner preparation. Would Dahlia ever forgive her?

Michael's mother not only forgave her, she rejoiced in the opportunity to plan the dinner solo. And I'd been grateful to have at least one holiday chore completely off my plate.

Evidently I wasn't going to be completely uninvolved.

"I tend to prefer turkey," I said. "But goose is also nice."

"And goose is traditional," she said.

I decided not to say "So's turkey."

"But many people find goose a little too greasy."

"That's true," I said. "A lot of people have trouble digesting it."

"But turkey's so bland."

I wanted to say "that's why we put gravy on it," but I held my tongue.

"Maybe I should have both."

"That's an excellent idea," I said. "That should keep both parties happy."

"Not the vegetarians," she said. "But I'll worry about them later. Oh, by the way—do you really want an Xbox for Christmas?"

"No," I said. "I can't say that I do, and Michael and I agreed that we don't want the boys exposed to video games this young."

"I thought as much," she said. "So I told Jamie that I couldn't help him buy you one for Christmas."

With that she hung up.

Should I warn Michael that Jamie was trying to do an end run around him on the present-buying front?

No time. Mother and Eustace were waiting to ask me something. And one of Randall Shiffley's cousins was standing behind them. And Vermillion was peeking through the railings from the upstairs landing as if waiting for a time to get my attention.

I took care of Randall's cousin first, because he appeared to be in the middle of doing actual physical labor. Not that I didn't think what the designers did was work, but as a blacksmith I suppose I was ever-so-slightly more sympathetic to work that produced sweat. Then I had to listen to Mother and Eustace explain something that they felt was essential to do to smooth the flow between their two areas. After twenty minutes I finally interrupted them.

"Let's cut to the chase—does this involve knocking down any load-bearing walls or otherwise threatening the structural integrity of the house."

"Of course not, dear."

"Will what you're doing intrude on or inconvenience any of the other decorators?"

"Of course not, dear. You see, all we really want to do is put a little bit of crown molding right here—"

"Do you need any supplies or workman other than what Randall has already provided?"

"No, dear." Mother was starting to look a little provoked.

"Then make it so," I said. "I approve with all my heart."

As I strode back toward the hall, I heard Mother murmur softly to Eustace. "Clearly not quite herself again."

I climbed upstairs—noting, to my satisfaction, that the chief had finished with Sarah and was interviewing Ivy. Her tiny, brown-clad body looked oddly out of place against the rich red velvet of Sarah's armchair.

Upstairs, I found Vermillion wanted me to solve a dispute over what color to paint the door between her room and Martha's bathroom. Vermillion had painted her side glossy black, to match everything else in her room. But when the door opened, it looked like a blob of ink against the white tile, white walls, white shower curtain, and white towels of Martha's spa décor. Martha, of course, wanted to paint it white.

"The door will be open most of the time, which means it will be in my room," Martha said, tapping her paintbrush against the lid of the can of Benjamin Moore "White Dove" that she was holding.

"But when it's closed, it will look as if a polar bear has landed in my room," Vermillion wailed.

We went back and forth about that for half an hour or so. Neither of them would budge an inch.

Suddenly inspiration came.

I pulled out my phone.

"Randall," I said. "Can you come up to the back bathroom?"

"On my way."

When Randall arrived, I let him watch Martha and Vermillion going at it for a couple of minutes, just so he could see what we were dealing with. He glanced at me uneasily. Settling catfights between the designers was supposed to be my job.

"Ladies!" I shouted.

They both subsided reluctantly and glowered at me.

"Randall, you see the problem."

He nodded, and looked a little wild-eyed, as if trying to beg me to leave him out of it.

"Can you build us a door that will solve this problem?"

"A door that looks white when it's in one room and black in the other?"

"One of those doors that disappears into the wall when it's open instead of swinging one way or the other."

"A pocket door." Randall and Martha said it in unison.

"Yes," Vermillion said. "That would work."

"I'll get right on it," Randall said. "You ladies hold on to your paint cans for a little while. Help is on the way."

I fled the room, and he followed.

"Ingenious," he said. "Of course, it'll cost money."

"I will gladly pay for it myself if it shuts them up," I said.

"On the contrary, it will be my treat, on account of you took this job and kept me from having to deal with all of them."

"Of course, even once the pocket door is in, they won't get along," I said. "They'll each complain that every time the door opens, the other one's room will spoil the look of their own."

"Then I'll nail the damned door shut if that's what it takes," Randall said. We had reached the top of the stairway, right outside the door to Clay's room. Both of us couldn't help staring at the door for a few minutes.

"Puts it all in perspective, doesn't it?" Randall said.

I nodded.

He went downstairs, and I pulled out my notebook to see what other tasks awaited me.

Sammy came up to fetch Vermillion for her interview. As they went downstairs together, Martha came out into the hallway and started after Vermillion.

I decided that if she made another complaint about Vermillion, I'd tell Randall to forget the pocket door and paint the whole damned door black.

But she stopped beside me.

"Why's he spending so much time interviewing us?" Martha said.

I suspected this was a rhetorical question rather than a real one.

"Because all of us had access to the crime scene," I said. "And some of us could have a motive to kill Clay, and any of us could have seen something that would give him a clue to who did it."

"And they took all our fingerprints," she said. "Took me forever to wash that nasty stuff off. Even those of us with alibis."

"For exclusionary purposes," I said. "I expect all of us have been in Clay's room at one time or another, touching stuff. They need to identify our fingerprints so they'll know if there are any outsiders' fingerprints in there."

"Well, that makes sense," she said. Her tone implied that few other things the police were doing did. "And I suppose the police will have a better idea who might have done it once they trace the gun."

"First they'll have to find the gun," I said.

"What do you mean, find the gun?" she asked. "Haven't they searched Clay's room?"

"Yes, but apparently the killer took the gun with him."

"Took it with him? Are you sure?"

"Reasonably sure," I said. "I was there, remember?"

"Sorry," she said. "Yes, you should know. Well, that stinks."

"Why?"

"Means the gun is still out there somewhere," she said. "On the loose."

"Yes," I said. "Just like the killer." Was it just me or was it weird for her to be more focused on the missing gun than the missing killer?

"I felt a lot better thinking the police had the damned gun."

Did she think it was the only gun in the state of Virginia?

"Great," she went on. "We're stuck here in this house, sitting ducks, with an armed killer on the loose—maybe even among us."

"Well, that's why the chief is checking out everyone in the house pretty carefully," I said. "And what makes you think the killer was after anyone other than Clay?"

"Till we know why he killed Clay, we don't know that he isn't. Maybe we should ask for police protection."

I reminded myself, not for the first time, that Martha was a bit of a drama queen.

"I'll let you take that up with the chief," I said. "I just plan to be careful until the police catch the killer."

"With any luck, that will be soon," she said. "He must be a pretty stupid killer, taking the gun with him like that. If the police catch him with it, that will pretty much prove he's the one, won't it?"

"If he—or she—is stupid enough to hang on to it," I said. "If I were planning to shoot someone, I'd make sure to do it with a gun that couldn't possibly be traced to me, and then I'd dispose of it afterward someplace where there was almost no chance anyone would ever find it. Like dumping it in the middle of a river. Or down a mineshaft."

"How do you come up with stuff like that?" She looked at me as if she thought I might be speaking from vast criminal experience.

"My cousin's a crime scene specialist," I said. "And my father's the medical examiner. Sometimes they talk shop."

"Goodness." She shuddered slightly. "Well, I'm going to get back to working on my rooms. Got to take my shot at winning the prize for the garden club."

As she strolled downstairs, I reminded myself that at least, if Martha won, the garden club would benefit. Although come to think of it, so would Martha, since she'd recently staged a coup and taken over the presidency of the club, and was reputed to be running it like a personal fiefdom.

But that reminded me of something. I flipped to the page of my notebook where I'd listed which charities each designer had designated to benefit if they won the judging. And then I pulled out my phone and called Stanley Denton, Caerphilly's resident private investigator.

"Can you check out a charity?" I said. "I mean, is that something you've got contacts or access to do?"

"I can try," he said. "What's the charity?"

"Designers of the Future," I said. "Supposedly it gives out scholarships to needy but deserving art students."

"Supposedly?" he asked. "You think it might not be on the up-and-up?"

"It's the charity Clay Spottiswood designated to get the money if he won best room contest," I said. "And I suppose it could still get the money if his room wins—always possible he could get the sympathy vote."

"I hope not," Stanley said. "You got an address on that?"

"Seems to be local," I said. "The address is 1224 Pruitt Avenue in Caerphilly."

"That's familiar address," Stanley said. "Hang on a minute. Yeah, very familiar. That's Clay Spottiswood's home address. Home and business. I remember it from serving papers on him a couple of times."

"That jerk," I muttered.

"Don't jump to conclusions," he said. "It could be a small but legitimate charity that he's running in his spare time."

"Or it could be he was trying to pull a fast one. Randall has the paperwork Clay provided. That might give you a starting point."

"I'm on it."

I made a note in my notebook to bug Stanley if I didn't hear from him for a few days. And then I glanced over the other items on my list. Calling the graphic designer to see when we'd get the program proofs. Writing another press release to go to the Richmond, D.C., Northern Virginia, Hampton Roads, and other regional papers. Finding out if we had enough shuttle buses to take people to and from the satellite parking. And a dozen other tasks. All the practical minutiae necessary to make the show house actually happen.

Just then, my phone rang. It was Michael.

"Meg? Are you ready?"

"For anything you have in mind, always," I said. "But was there anything in particular I'm supposed to be ready for right now?"

"Santa Claus," he said. "Remember, Mom asked if we would wait to see Santa until she could be there?"

"Oh, my God," I said. "I forgot that was today. Are you still sure you want to do it? This late? They've already written their letters to Santa, remember? What if they come up with some enormous, important last-minute must-have thing that Santa can't get by Christmas?"

"Then we'll ask Santa to write them a letter explaining why their big present will be a little late," he said. "We'll manage. I'm more worried about a repeat of last year's disaster. Was it Josh or Jamie who bit Santa?"

"Josh," I said. "Jamie just ran away screaming and hid in the fake igloo."

"I warned Mom about that," Michael said. "But they are a year older. And Mom will be so disappointed if we cancel, so let's do it. Your dad and I are about to load the boys in the car. We'll be by for you and your mother in ten minutes."

"I'll tell Mother."

I found her staring at a white board on which someone had painted a dozen stripes in various shades of red.

"What do you think, dear?" she asked. "I'm leaning toward the 'Red Obsession.' But 'Ablaze' is also nice. And 'Positive Red' is rather more Christmassy—but maybe too Christmassy? Or should we consider 'Rave Red,' or possibly 'Habanero Chile'?"

"Time for Santa," I said.

"I don't think we have that one, dear," Mother said. She frowned slightly at Mateo, who was holding the board, and presumably had been under orders to bring back samples of every possible red.

"It's not a color, it's a family event," I said. "Michael and his mother and Dad are taking the boys to see Santa Claus. If you want to come and take cute pictures of your grandsons on Santa's lap, be on the steps in five minutes."

"Well, why didn't you say so, dear? *Mas tarde,*" she added to Mateo. He smiled and whisked the board away. "I do hope we can avoid bloodshed this year," she added as she followed me to the front door.

Chapter 11

The Twinmobile pulled up a few minutes later. Michael's mother, who was quite spry for a grandmother, had crawled into the third row and was sitting between Josh and Jamie. From the exuberance of their greetings to me and Mother, I suspected Granny Waterston had been bribing them with candy and they were riding the resulting sugar high.

I took a seat in the middle row, and once we got underway, I turned around to start preparing the boys for what lay ahead.

"Did Daddy tell you where we're going?" I asked.

"Santa!" they both exclaimed. There was a telltale whiff of chocolate and peppermint on their breaths.

"And we love Santa, don't we?" Michael added from the front seat.

"Santa! Love Santa! Santa!"

"I seem to remember that last year someone was a little nervous when we met Santa." Calling either boy's reaction "a little nervous" was like calling a blizzard "a few scattered flakes."

"Not me," Josh said.

"Him," Jamie countered, pointing.

"It's okay to be nervous," Michael said. "Santa's a very important person. But if you feel nervous, just tell Mommy or Daddy or Grandma or Grandpa or Grammy."

"We'll be fine, won't we?" Michael's mother said.

I pretended not to notice as she slipped them each another bit of candy cane.

"So, Meg," Dad said. "How's the mood at the house? Is everyone upset by the—"

"James!" Mother exclaimed. "Little ears!"

"By the M-U-R-D-E-R," Dad continued.

"Hard to say," I said. "No one much misses Clay, but I think everyone will be on edge till they catch who did it. What's that, Jamie?"

"M-U-R-D-E-R," Jamie repeated.

We all looked back at him, startled.

Josh had printed the word in the condensation on his window.

"Muh . . . Muhr . . . Murd . . ." Josh muttered.

"Murder!" Jamie exclaimed.

"Grandpa, what's murder?" Josh asked.

There was a brief silence.

"Adult communication suddenly becomes a lot more difficult," Michael said.

"Grandpa," Jamie began.

"Murder," Michael's mother spoke up. "Is when someone hurts someone else. It's a very bad thing to do."

She reached over and rubbed out the writing on the car window.

"Grammy, is murder an inappropriate word?" Josh asked.

"It's a little inappropriate," Michael's mother said. "You don't really need to use it."

"So, it's kind of like poopie or booger?" Jamie suggested. "And not a really bad word like—"

"Look! Is that a reindeer!" Michael exclaimed. I couldn't see anything that even vaguely resembled a reindeer, but his remark served the double purpose of distracting the boys and almost drowning out the highly inappropriate word Jamie had brought forth to appall his grandparents.

I was relieved that the rest of the ride downtown passed without further incident. And after the ride over, the actual visit to Santa was delightfully uneventful. These days, the Caerphilly Volunteer Fire Department hosted Santa's local stay. They had built a large Styrofoam igloo at the back of the vacant engine bay and hauled in a brightly painted red sleigh to serve as Santa's throne. If we ever raised enough money for a much needed fourth fire engine, they might need to find Santa a new home, but in the meantime, the kids—and grown-ups—enjoyed getting tours of the fire engines while waiting their turn on Santa's lap. And everyone seemed to enjoy the occasional days when the firemen got a call and Santa clapped on his fire hat and took off driving the ladder truck.

Michael's fellow firemen greeted him with enthusiasm. Perhaps all the times the boys had visited their daddy during his volunteer shifts at the fire station helped keep them from being scared of Santa this time. After staring at the burly, bearded man in red for a few moments, Jamie turned to me.

"Is that a real beard?" he stage-whispered.

"Of course it is," Santa said. "Want to give it a tug?"

Both boys were charmed by the idea, and after each had given Santa's beard a few relatively gentle tugs, they settled down to the business of reiterating their Christmas requests—no new major demands, to my relief—and having their pictures taken. Michael and all three grandparents drained their camera and cell phone batteries taking endless pictures—Jamie with Santa. Josh with Santa. Both boys with Santa. Both boys with Santa and various configurations of parents and grandparents. The boys climbing on the fire trucks. The boys wearing firefighter hats, with and without Fireman Santa.

At one point I noticed Josh in deep conversation with Santa, so I inched a little closer to eavesdrop.

"No, Josh," Santa was saying. "I don't understand it myself, but for some reason mommies don't usually like getting boa constrictors for Christmas."

"So you think a basketball hoop is a better idea?"

"To tell you the truth, Josh," Santa began.

I slipped away, reassured that St. Nick would save me from hoops and snakes. And reminded myself again to drop some hints for things the boys might enjoy giving me. As soon as I thought of some ideas.

Meanwhile, Mother was quite taken with the deep, glossy red of the sleigh, and I looked around several times to see her taking pictures of it with her camera and digging into her purse for fabric samples to hold against it.

"I hate to be a party pooper," I said finally. "But I'm getting hungry, and Grandma and I have to get back to the show house."

We had a quick lunch at Muriel's Diner, home of what had now been certified, by last year's fair, as the best apple and cherry pies in the state. And then Michael dropped Mother and me back at the show house, and took the boys off for naps so they could stay up late for tonight's show. I suspected he and his mother and Dad were also planning on a nap.

Mother and I were made of sterner stuff.

She returned to inspecting red paint. I was half expecting her to ask me to drive her back to the fire station to match her samples against Santa's sleigh. Or worse, send Mateo on the thankless errand of getting the local hardware store to match the sleigh's paint. But after another quarter hour of dithering, she made a decision. The walls would be resplendent in "Red Obession."

After dealing with a few crises that had popped up while I was gone, I decided the only way I'd get any work done was to retire to the garage. It was a little chilly, but at least it was out of the way. I'd begun to realize that if I was underfoot, the designers would come to me with every little hangnail-sized problem, but if I was in the garage, it took a much larger problem to make them take the trouble of hunting me down.

Though I did walk through the house every hour or so. Pocket door construction was going nicely. Mother and Eustace were positively cooing at each other as they watched Tomás doing whatever they had agreed to have him do to the archway. Mateo and Randall's workmen had almost finished returning the master suite to the condition it had been in before the murder—and for that matter, before the flood. Sarah's room looked back to normal, though she had a disconcerting tendency to jerk open drawers, look under chair cushions, and search every other nook and cranny of the room, all of which she'd already searched at least a dozen times. And to my relief, Ivy had begun working on her "Nightingale" mural in the part of the upstairs hallway that was visible from the great room below. Mother had been counting on that as a key part of her decoration.

I walked into the dining room to make sure the workmen had pruned Linda's portion of the Christmas tree, and that she was happy with the results.

Linda was sitting on one of her flowered chairs, crying, quietly but steadily. A small heap of tissues lay on the floor on the right side of her chair. As I watched, she dropped the tissue she was using with the others and took a fresh one from the box.

"Are you okay?" I asked.

I took a few steps toward her but paused when she held up her hand like a traffic cop ordering cars to stop.

"I'll be fine," she said. "This is just an upsetting time for all of us."

I nodded and watched as she added another tissue to the pile.

"It's a very small world, you know," Linda said. "The design community."

I'd figured that out weeks ago. Coming in to take charge of organizing I'd felt like the new kid starting school in the middle of a semester.

"We all fight over the same clients. The same vendors. Read the same publications. Follow—or try to break free from—the same trends."

"The designers in the show house all seem pretty individual to me," I said.

"That's because it's a small town show house," she said. "Half of these people wouldn't get into a sophisticated big city event. Sarah maybe, and your mother, and Eustace. But not Violet and Vermillion or those nice ladies with the quilts. And not me."

Maybe that was supposed to be my cue to reassure her. But I didn't think I could do it and fool her.

"And Clay?" I asked. "Would he have made the cut?"

"God, I hope not!" She plucked another tissue from the box with such a violent tug that it fell to the floor. "He was a horrible person."

"Tell me about it," I said.

"I'm sure somebody already has," she replied. "Did anyone tell you about the hilarious prank Clay played on me?"

"No one's told me about Clay doing anything hilarious," I said. "Or even mildly amusing. Remember, I'm a stranger in this strange land of Decoratorville. What nasty prank did he play?"

She looked up, assessed me for a few minutes, then closed her eyes and leaned back in her chair, as if surrendering.

"I've been widowed for ten years," she said. "No family. And a couple of years ago, I decided to try one of those on-line dating sites. And I didn't like it at first. I was almost going to close my account. Then I met this man who seemed really nice and normal. He was a doctor. A widower. Fifty-ish. We spent hours online talking. We bonded. I told him things . . ."

Her voice trailed off and she shook her head.

"We finally agreed to meet in person," she continued. "At a restaurant in Richmond. I was so nervous. I must have tried on a dozen outfits before deciding on one. I'm not young or skinny." She lifted her chin defiantly. "But I look pretty good for my age. I take care of myself."

"Absolutely," I said. And I meant it. I might not like her taste in décor and clothes, but I had a hard time imagining that the fiftyish widowed doctor wouldn't be pleased to see her across the table.

"I waited in that restaurant for an hour and a half," she said. "Drinking the water and nibbling the bread and eventually ordering a glass of wine so the waiters wouldn't think I was just some crazy person taking up space. And when I finished my wine, the waiter brought me another glass, saying it was from one of the other customers."

I had a bad feeling about this.

"It was Clay," she said. "I found out he'd overheard me telling a friend about joining the online dating site. He figured out what my user name was and he pretended to be that nice, widowed doctor. I told him things I'd never told anyone—not even my late husband. And then he sat there in that restaurant, for an hour and a half, watching me wait."

"What a horrible thing to do!"

"So, ever since then—as I said, a very small community. No way I could keep from running into him. And he was always digging at me. Dropping little hints about things I'd told him online. Calling me 'Linda May.' That's what my mama used to call me, but when I got out of high school I dropped the 'May,' 'cause it sounded too Southern and country."

She shook her head and blew her nose vigorously.

"And I'm sure everyone else knows all about it, and someone must have told the chief," she said, more briskly. "And he's right to suspect me of knocking off Clay. I didn't do it, but I half want to thank whoever did. I just wish I had some kind of an alibi."

"What were you doing instead of being alibied?" I asked.

"At home, watching TV and using the computer," she said. "All by my lonesome, so I can't prove a thing. So maybe the chief should just come and put the cuffs on now."

"Because you hated Clay?" I said. "Take a number."

She laughed a little at that.

"And besides," I went on. "Maybe you can prove you were home. Were you doing anything online with your computer?

"Why?" She suddenly looked wary again.

"Because creepy and Big Brotherish as it sounds, these days they might be able to trace what you were doing online, and where you were doing it from."

"Really?" She didn't look upset at the idea. More hopeful.

"Really. Mutant Wizards, the computer game company my brother owns, had a problem last year with confidential information getting leaked, and they were able to figure out that someone was logging into the company's computers from the house of an employee of his biggest competitor. They shut down the leak and I think the DA filed criminal charges against the data thief. So if you were doing something online . . ."

"I was." She looked embarrassed. And just when I thought she wasn't going to say anything else, she blurted out, "I reactivated my online dating profile. I've been talking to *two* guys, for a month or two now. Neither one of them seems quite as perfect for me as that nice, widowed doctor Clay pretended to be. But that could be because they're real people. At least so far I think they are. Could be a while before I get up enough nerve to meet either of them in the real world to be sure. You think there's any chance one of them might alibi me?"

"They would have no idea where you were chatting from," I said. "But whatever company you get Internet from might be able to tell that you were online, and where, and for how long. I don't know for sure, but it's worth a try," I said.

"How do I go about finding out?"

"Tell the chief. He's got excellent consultants he can use. And I know that for sure, because they work for my brother. After that data theft problem, he realized there was a big market for cutting-edge forensic data analysis, so he started a division to do it. If anyone can prove your alibi, Mutant Wizards can. Just tell the chief."

"Thanks." She stood up and squared her shoulders. "I will."

"If you like, I can tell him what you just told me," I said. "So you don't have to explain it all over again. I don't even have to tell him about what Clay did. Just that you were chatting online with friends, and had no idea that could be traced."

"Oh, would you?"

"Sure," I said.

"Thank you." She sat down again, and began stringing her garland again, but she wasn't quite so slumped, and she seemed to have more energy.

I decided not to call to tell the chief. Linda had already suffered enough from people overhearing her business. I typed out a detailed e-mail on my phone.

By around five, most of the workmen and decorators had left. Mother was still rearranging ornaments on her Christmas tree, and Ivy was painting away above her head, but the rest of the house was peaceful. And it was getting cold outside, so I moved my base of operations back into the foyer.

"Meg! It's lovely!"

My old friend Caroline Willner popped through the front door and begin shedding her scarf, gloves, hat, and coat. "Your mother invited me to come and get a sneak preview."

"Is this going to take long?" Grandfather came stumping in behind her. From his expression I suspected he'd have considered wrestling alligators preferable to inspecting interior design. But he and Caroline were good friends—she often accompanied him on his trips to rescue abused animals and endangered species—so I assumed he was returning the favor by coming along to keep her company.

"We won't be long," Mother said, giving Grandfather a kiss on the cheek. "Why don't you talk to Meg while we do our tour."

She and Caroline sailed off, and from the amount of time they were taking in the first room—Sarah's study—I could tell that her definition of "not long" would probably differ significantly from Grandfather's.

"So, is this where you had one of them bumped off?" he asked.

"Not here," I said. "Upstairs. And all I did was find him."

"Show me."

Chapter 12

I led Grandfather upstairs to the master suite, but since the workmen had done a good job of cleaning up and repairing it, there wasn't that much to see. But while he was poking around—hoping, perhaps, to find a stray blood spatter the workmen had overlooked—I went out into the hall to see how Ivy was coming along.

Her "Nightingale" mural was splendid. The Emperor of China, clad in cloth of gold, sat in the center, surrounded by courtiers, all staring at a tiny bejeweled clockwork bird. Up in the top left corner of the wall lurked a small bird whose muted gray-brown color echoed Ivy's soft, drab garments.

Grandfather ambled along the hall and studied the glittering court with little interest. Then he spotted the bird.

"So what's this?" Grandfather said. "Ah! *Luscinia megarhynchos!*"

"The common nightingale," I translated. Grandfather rarely stopped to consider the feelings of people who, not being professional zoologists, hadn't memorized the Latin names of every species in creation.

"Not bad." Grandfather was on his tiptoes, inspecting the nightingale at close quarters. "Not bad at all. What's all the rest of this?"

"You know Hans Christian Andersen's story of the nightingale, don't you?" Ivy asked.

"Not much for fairy tales," Grandfather said.

"The Emperor of China had a wonderful palace," Ivy began, not looking up from her work. "It was built entirely of porcelain, and in the garden all the flowers had tiny bells tied to them that tinkled gently with the slightest breeze."

"Hmph." Grandfather's snort seemed to suggest that he found this a silly kind of place, but he didn't actually interrupt Ivy.

"But the emperor heard that the nightingale's song was more beautiful than anything in his palace," Ivy went on.

Grandfather nodded approvingly at this note of natural history.

"So he sent for the bird to sing at his court. And everyone loved the bird's song so much that the emperor decreed that she should live at his court in a golden cage and sing for them every night. And she was only allowed to fly outside the cage with twelve courtiers holding on to her with silken ribbons."

I was relieved to see that Grandfather refrained from denouncing this shocking example of animal abuse, contenting himself with frowning thunderously.

"And then the Emperor of Japan, the Chinese emperor's arch rival, sent him another nightingale—a clockwork one, encrusted with gold and jewels. And even though it always sang the same song, the golden nightingale was so ingenious, and so beautiful compared to the plain brown nightingale—"

"Sounds perfectly ghastly to me, actually," Grandfather said. "Give me the real thing any time."

"—that they lost interest in the real nightingale, and forgot to close the door to her cage, and she flew away back to the forest."

"Excellent." Grandfather nodded with approval, clearly assuming this was the fairy tale's obligatory happy ending.

"But the emperor played the golden nightingale so much that it began to wear out," Ivy went on. "And the watchmaker called in to fix it couldn't. He warned the emperor that every time it sang could be its last. So they put the golden nightingale on a pedestal and only played it once a year. And the emperor began to pine away and grew sick, and all his courtiers and servants deserted him to flatter the one who would be the next emperor."

I had been watching Ivy's careful brushstrokes, but I suddenly realized that Grandfather had stopped interrupting. I glanced up and saw that he was intent on Ivy's words. Probably more worried about the real nightingale than the emperor, but still.

"The real nightingale heard of the emperor's illness and came to perch on a branch outside his window to sing to him," Ivy went on. "She found Death sitting on the emperor's chest, and she sang so beautifully that she charmed Death into leaving. And the emperor promised her anything she wanted as a reward. And she asked only that she be allowed to stay free and to perch on the branch and sing to him every night of what was happening in his kingdom."

"No more cages?" Grandfather asked.

"He'd learned his lesson," Ivy said.

"So they lived happily ever after," Grandfather said. "They always do in fairy tales."

"Not always in Andersen," Ivy said. "Some of his are downright depressing. But I imagine the emperor and the nightingale lived happily for a good long while. The story actually ends with the emperor saying good morning to all the servants who had run out on him the night before. Leaves it to your imagination what happens next."

She'd been working all this time on the emperor, and I had to smother a giggle when I realized that she'd given

him Grandfather's face. There he sat, incongruously dressed
in elaborate court robes and sitting on a bejeweled golden
throne, his face rapt with wonder as he listened to the nightingale that was perched near the ceiling.

"Very nice," Grandfather said. "You've got the nightingale pretty accurately. But I'm not sure about the foliage.
Doesn't look like anything that would grow in China. I can
recommend a nice botanist if you'd like some accurate information."

"Ah, but I'm not trying to portray real Chinese foliage,"
Ivy said. "Andersen was a Victorian, a child of poverty, and
a native of the frozen north. I'm painting the China of his
imagination."

Grandfather didn't try to argue with her, and we both
stood there for quite a while watching Ivy paint, until we
heard Caroline calling downstairs.

"Monty? We're leaving. Where's that old fool got to now?"

"On my way," Grandfather said. And then nodding to
Ivy, he said, "Nice bird."

Then he ambled back downstairs and left.

Vermillion appeared out of her room. She paused as if
she'd like to watch Ivy, then nodded to us and left. I noticed, as I always did, her elegant, expensive-looking coffin-
shaped black leather purse. But I waited until the door had
closed behind her downstairs before saying what came into
my mind whenever I saw the purse.

"She's got to be putting us on," I said.

"Vermillion?" Ivy looked puzzled. "What do you mean?"

"Everything she does is over the top," I said. "The coffin
sofa, the Spanish moss, the bats, and most of all that coffin
purse. Would a real Goth actually carry a coffin-shaped
purse?"

"I'm not sure a real Goth would carry anything else," Ivy

said. "And it's very nicely made. Your mother says she has a good eye. 'If she ever gives up this macabre obsession with death and spiderwebs she could be quite a good designer.'"

Her imitation of Mother's gently regretful tone was spot-on. I burst out laughing.

"And if she doesn't give up her obsession?" I asked.

"Then she will continue to be her very interesting self."

I watched Ivy paint for a few moments. It was curiously restful, watching the mural slowly come to life under her brush.

She glanced over her shoulder at me, and I suddenly remembered that she didn't always like onlookers.

"I can leave if I'm bothering you," I said.

"You don't bother me." She turned back to her painting. "Not like that reporter."

"Jessica? The one from the student newspaper?"

"That's the one." She nodded, and took a step back to study what she'd been working on. "She was driving me crazy last night."

"Last night?"

"Between eight and ten o'clock," she said. "She got on everyone's nerves after a couple of hours, so Rose Noire kicked her out—ever so politely. But someone must have let her back in and then gone off without making sure she was gone. She was driving me crazy—asking questions, darting around the house, tapping on things, coming up behind and startling me. But maybe it's lucky for me she came. I'd been planning to work as long as it took to finish 'The Nightingale,' but after just an hour with her underfoot I had such a headache that I went home early. Maybe Jessica saved me from encountering the killer."

Or maybe she'd cleared the field for the killer to work.

"Was she still here when you left?" I asked.

"Of course not," she said. "I kicked her out, and checked all the doors and windows before I locked up."

I tried to imagine Ivy kicking out so much as a stray kitten and failed. Clearly she had hidden depths.

"She shouldn't have been hanging around here at all after Rose Noire made her leave." I pulled out my notebook and began making a note. "I'm going to complain to her editor."

"Good idea," Ivy said.

"Meanwhile, we seem to be the last ones here," I said to Ivy. "And I'm about to leave. Should you be staying here alone?"

"Oh, nobody will notice I'm here," she said.

"I'll make sure all the doors and windows are locked," I said.

I made the rounds, checking every room, every door, and every window. Everyone had gone, and everything was locked up tight. I had the nagging feeling I was supposed to be somewhere else, doing something in particular, but then I'd felt that way at the end of most days lately. Time to head home for some rest.

As I headed for my car, I realized I wasn't sure if I should be pleased with my day or frustrated. On the positive side, I felt a lot more certain that none of the designers I was working with day-in and day-out had killed Clay. The only ones for whom I hadn't heard a plausible alibi were Vermillion and Ivy, and neither of them had ever been at the top of my list of suspects anyway. As the day wore on and as I talked to each of the designers, I'd started feeling less tense. Less apt to start if someone walked up behind me.

On the other hand, if none of the designers had killed him, who had?

"The chief's problem," I muttered to myself as I got into

my car. He'd be spending the coming days—or weeks—digging into Clay's life. Interviewing disgruntled clients, angry exes, and rival decorators. Poking and prodding the decorators' alibis to see if they held.

I had other things to worry about, I told myself as I set off for home.

Though I should probably tell him that Jessica had been hanging around only an hour or so from the time of the murder.

I was only a block from the show house when my phone rang. I glanced down—it was Michael. And I suddenly remembered what I was supposed to be doing—tonight was the first night of his one-man performance of Dickens's *A Christmas Carol*.

I felt guilty. Last year, on the day of show, I'd spent the whole day pampering him and distracting him. And this year I'd left him to take care of the boys all day. Well, at least he'd had the distraction part.

I pulled over to the curb and answered the phone.

"I'm so sorry!" I said. "I'm on my way to take the boys off your hands and feed them and—

"Don't hurry!" he said. "I figured after last night you needed a break, so I arranged for Mom and Rob to take the boys to the zoo. They'll bring them along to the theater full of pizza. And probably smelling like camels, but who cares."

As he was talking, I saw Vermillion drive by. Her black Subaru station wagon was festooned with moons and spiderwebs in silver paint, so it was pretty distinctive. I waved, but she didn't see me.

"That's great about the boys," I said. "I'll go home, clean up, and meet you all at the theater."

"Fine," he said. "Has the chief figured out who killed Clay yet?"

"Not that I've heard," I said. "But I've figured out that most of my friends didn't do it, in spite of pretty extreme provocation, so I'm feeling a lot more cheerful. I'll fill you in later."

I was about to pull away from the curb when I spotted Vermillion's car again, pulling up to the stop sign on the side street ahead of me. Weird. To get there, she'd have had to turn off the main road and circle back. Had she left something back at the house?

No. Instead of turning to go back to the house, she continued through the intersection along the side street. I waited a few moments, then pulled back onto the road and made a left to follow her.

I wasn't sure why I was doing it, but I followed Vermillion for the next ten minutes. She was making apparently random turns, zigzagging through subdivisions and circling some blocks two or three times. Was she looking for something? Or was she trying to make sure no one was following her? If that was what she was up to, she wasn't very good at it. I'd have had no trouble following her, even if she'd been smart enough to ditch her highly distinctive car for something more nondescript. And she didn't seem to have spotted me.

Eventually she reached the center of town and pulled into an alley that I knew was a dead end. I continued on past the alley and parked a little way down the street.

After a minute or two, her car backed out of the alley. I could see another person in the passenger seat. Then the passenger ducked down and Vermillion turned onto the street and continued on past me. I waited till she'd pulled a safe distance ahead and then took off after her again.

More perambulations through the byways of Caerphilly. I began wondering if I should give up following her. I was already running short on time if I wanted to get home and change for Michael's show.

But just as I was about to call off the chase, she stopped in front of a house with a high fence around it. I stopped, too, and watched from a distance as a gate swung open. Vermillion drove inside, and the gate closed after her.

Okay, now what? I parked my car and watched for a few minutes. I should be heading home.

What the heck. I could go straight to the show in what I was wearing. Who dresses up with a foot of snow on the ground?

I got out of the car and strolled down the street, as slowly and nonchalantly as I could. The house was surrounded by an eight-foot-tall wooden fence. There were lights in some of the windows, but all of them were protected by curtains, shades, or blinds.

I continued on to the corner and then paused. I was on a quiet residential street lined with small but tidy bunga-lows. Even if I had all night to carry out surveillance, there wasn't really anyplace to hide and keep an eye on the house into which Vermillion had gone.

I turned and headed back for my car, again walking slowly.

This is ridiculous, I told myself. I should come back to-morrow, in daylight, and figure out the address of the house behind the fence. If there were numbers, I couldn't see them in this light. And then I could look it up in the county records. Get Stanley to check it out. Maybe even tell Chief Burke about Vermillion's furtive behavior. And then—

"Psst! Meg!"

I was past the gate now. I turned and looked back.

The gate was open about a foot, and Reverend Robyn Smith from Grace Episcopal was peering out.

"What are you doing here?" she asked.

"I followed Vermillion," I said.

Robyn closed her eyes, sighed, and then opened them again.

"Come in for a minute," she said.

She swung the gate open. I stepped into the yard and waited while she closed and latched it. Then she led me into the house.

"It's okay," she called as she stepped inside. "I know her."

She moved aside so I could see. The room was filled with women and children and sparsely furnished with what looked like castoffs. Three children were playing Parcheesi on the floor. Another knot of children were playing with toy cars. A girl of perhaps eleven or twelve sat on one of the faded sofas, playing with a baby. At the far end of the room, three women were setting out plates and silverware on two card tables, and another woman peered out from the kitchen.

"Welcome to the Caerphilly Battered Women's Shelter," Robyn said.

Chapter 13

"I didn't know Caerphilly even had a women's shelter," I said.

"We like it that way," Robyn said. "If you tell anyone where it is, you could be putting these women's and children's lives in jeopardy. They're all taking refuge from dangerously abusive men."

"It's okay," I said. "I haven't the faintest idea where I am anyway."

Robyn smiled at that, and a couple of the women giggled.

Vermillion, carrying a toddler, came over.

"Why were you following me?" she asked.

"I'm sorry—" I began.

"The safe house is supposed to be a secret," she said. "I was supposed to pick up Eil—one of the residents—at her job and bring her back here without anyone following us, especially her horrible ex. And—"

"Then maybe you should take some lessons on how to lose a tail," I said. "Starting with driving a less distinctive car."

She blinked and took a step back as if I'd hit her.

"Now, now," Robyn said.

"Vermillion, I'm sorry," I said. "If I'd known where you were going, I wouldn't have followed you. But remember, we've had a murder at the show house, and you're one of the few people in the house whose whereabouts last night

I know nothing about, and you were acting incredibly furtive."

"Meg does have a point, Vermillion," Robyn said.

Vermillion's shoulders slumped.

"Yeah, okay," she said. "I just get really nervous when I'm bringing someone to the house. And if it makes you feel any better, last night I was here at the shelter. All night."

"Vermillion's been staying here on night duty," Robyn said. "And we had a new family move in last night. I arrived with them around ten thirty, and I didn't leave until past one. She was helping, too. So I think she's in the clear on the murder."

"Excellent," I said.

"If I knew anything, I'd tell you," Vermillion said. "I loathed Clay and I wanted him out of the house, but still, it's not right for someone to murder him."

"Why don't you go ahead and get dinner started?" Robyn said to the women at the table. "I just want to have a quiet word with Meg. Vermillion, can you help them?"

Vermillion lugged the child she was carrying into the kitchen. Robyn led me back out onto the porch.

"So how long has Caerphilly had a battered women's shelter?" I asked.

"Only been operating six months," she said.

"Keeping it secret for six months is a miracle in a small town like this."

"And Vermillion is one of our best volunteers," she said. "Although I've been worried about her lately."

"Worried? Why?" I asked. Would it have something to do with Clay?

"She's really good with the residents because she's been through what they're going through," Robyn said. "Not here, but back home, wherever home was. She hasn't told me much more than that. She was doing pretty well until the last few weeks. Lately she's taken to sleeping here overnight most nights."

"Did something happen to her here in Caerphilly?"

"No," Robyn said. "I asked her. She said no—and I believe her—but she also said there was someone in the house she didn't trust."

"Clay Spottiswood," I said.

"Yes." Robyn nodded. "Not that she said as much, but it stands to reason."

"Do you think he . . . threatened her in some way?"

"I think she'd have told me if he did," Robyn said. "But I trust her judgment. Not her fashion sense, mind you. But her ability to spot someone capable of violence, absolutely."

"Yesterday, when she arrived at the house, Rose Noire said she could feel the negative energy trying to keep her out," I said. "And that there was something evil in the house."

"Rose Noire is a good person," Robyn said. "I trust her judgment, too. Do you think this man Clay was evil?"

The question surprised me.

"No," I said, after thinking for a few moments. "Unpleasant, yes. Responsible for that negative energy, definitely. He was not a nice person. Maybe even a violent one. But evil? No. If there really was evil in the house, maybe it was that someone was already planning to kill him."

"Yes." Robyn nodded emphatically. "So be careful out there. There's an evildoer still at large."

Then her mood lightened.

"We're having chili for dinner," she said. "One of our current residents is a fabulous cook. Would you like to stay and share it?"

"I would love to," I said. "But I'm going to miss the start

of Michael's show if I don't rush over to the theater right now. Rain check?"

"Absolutely," she said. "And you do realize now that you've found your way here to the safe house, we'll figure out a way to make use of you."

"I'll count on it."

I tried to follow my own advice as I walked back to the car, matter-of-factly, no tiptoeing or looking furtively over my shoulder. But I still found myself breathing a sigh of relief that I saw only a few perfectly innocent-looking vehicles and pedestrians as I wound my way out of the quiet neighborhood.

And I realized, with a start, that the safe house was only about ten blocks from the show house. Vermillion could have walked here in ten minutes. We must have spent at least two or three times that driving around town. Of course, she hadn't just been coming here, she'd been picking up the resident who needed a safe way of getting home. Still—if Vermillion had been alone for as little as half an hour . . .

I'd have to trust Robyn on that. Robyn, and the chief's good instincts.

Of course, if Vermillion really had been afraid of Clay, knowing that he had been so close by could partly explain her growing uneasiness at the house.

I was getting close to the theater, and needed to focus all my attention on finding a parking space nearby. Or at least in the same time zone.

I raced in just in time to claim the seat my family had been saving for me on the far end of the front row. Not the best seat in the house, as Dad kept telling me apologetically, but I didn't mind. I'd heard Michael do his one-man show more than a couple of times now—part of the entertainment, for me, was to watch how the audience reacted to him. And I could do that more easily from the side of the theater.

And, of course, I also wanted to watch Josh and Jamie's reactions—they'd seen the show last year, of course, but now they were a year older, and considered themselves veteran theatergoers, thanks to our season tickets to the Caerphilly Children's Theater.

At last the house lights dimmed. A single spotlight lit the podium, and the sound crew played a few bars of a group of carolers singing "Good King Wenceslas." Then the music faded as if the carolers were strolling away, and Michael stepped onstage, to be greeted with thunderous applause.

He bowed, and waited till the applause had died down—and both twins had been induced to sit down instead of standing on their seats—before opening.

"*A Christmas Carol,* by Charles Dickens," he read out. "Stave one: Marley's Ghost."

I sat back to enjoy the show. But after a few paragraphs, Dickens's words suddenly drew me out of the story and back into thinking about the events of the last two days.

"Nobody ever stopped him in the street to say, with gladsome looks, 'My dear Scrooge, how are you? When will you come to see me?'" Michael proclaimed. "No beggars implored him to bestow a trifle, no children asked him what it was o'clock, no man or woman ever once in all his life inquired the way to such and such a place, of Scrooge."

He could be talking of Clay. Clay wasn't evil, any more than Scrooge was. Unpleasant, both of them, to be sure. Uncivil, rude, selfish, misguided—I could think of any number of uncomplimentary words that would apply to both.

But not evil. And Scrooge hadn't started off bad. At some point, for some reason, he'd taken the wrong path. But he'd reformed. Been redeemed.

Clay never would be.

As Michael recounted Scrooge's journey with the Ghost of Christmas Past, I tried to imagine what would happen if the same ghost had visited Clay.

And I drew a complete blank.

What if Clay's murderer wasn't anyone in the show house, but someone from his past?

The past I knew nothing about.

"None of my business," I murmured, causing Mother, who was next to me, to turn and raise one eyebrow inquiringly.

I smiled and shook my head.

I needed to focus on Michael's performance. But my mind continued to wander until my eyes, also wandering, lit on Rob, near the other end of our row of family members.

Of course. Rob. There had to be information online about Clay, and Rob was the one to help me with it. He might know next to nothing about computers himself, but as the CEO of Mutant Wizards, his highly successful computer game development company, he had access to all sorts of highly skilled techies. As soon as the show was over, I'd ask him to lend me one. Someone really good at online research, who could find me every detail of Clay Spottiswood's past.

With that decided, I was able to turn my attention to the show.

And not a minute too soon. I realized that while Jamie was sitting completely still, attention riveted to his father's every word and every gesture, Josh was displaying his devotion in a rather different way.

He was imitating Michael. When Michael rubbed his chin thoughtfully to indicate Scrooge's puzzlement, Josh rubbed his chin. When Michael threw out his hands to express Scrooge's delight at seeing his old master Fezziwig, Josh threw out his hands. And when Michael, describing the dancing at Fezziwig's Christmas party, leaped into the air and clicked his heels together, Josh bobbed out of his seat.

People were starting to notice. In fact, they weren't just starting to notice, they were staring and giggling. And Dad, on one side of him, and Michael's mother, on the other, weren't doing a thing.

"Josh!" I hissed. He was several seats down and didn't hear me at first. "Josh!"

He turned in the middle of pretending to play the fiddle and looked at me.

"Not now," I said.

He frowned.

"It's Daddy's turn to do the play," I said. "You can do it when we get home."

He slumped back into his seat.

"Okay," he said, in a small voice.

A voice I shouldn't have been able to hear.

I looked around. Everyone was staring. Even Michael, up on stage, was watching, and suppressing laughter. Then he bowed very deeply to Josh, who sat up a little straighter and smiled again.

Michael went on with the show. Josh, to my relief, remained silent, and mostly still. Though I could tell, from the way his mouth often moved, and the fact that his hands occasionally twitched in an almost imperceptible echo of Michael's hands, that he was planning to hold me to the notion of doing a performance of his own at home.

And the rest of the show went just fine. Even though I could repeat large chunks of it by heart, I never tired of hearing Dickens's words in Michael's voice. And all of the English holiday traditions Dickens described—and I suspect helped create—were exactly what I had grown up with. When the Ghost of Christmas Past took Scrooge to Fezziwig's party, with its mince pies and dancing, I felt nostalgic for the family parties of my childhood and eager to see the boys enjoy this year's celebrations.

When the Ghost of Christmas Present arrived laden with "turkeys, geese, game, brawn, great joints of meat, sucking pigs, long wreaths of sausages, mince-pies, plum-puddings, barrels of oysters, red-hot chestnuts, cherry-cheeked apples, juicy oranges, luscious pears, immense twelfth-cakes, and great bowls of punch" I began looking forward to the upcoming holiday meals and thanking my lucky stars that Michael's mother was in charge of providing them. And when Ghost of Christmas Yet to Come showed Scrooge the sorrow the Cratchits were suffering from losing Tiny Tim, audible sniffles could be heard throughout the theater, and I looked down the aisle to make sure the boys remembered that thanks to Scrooge's reformation Tiny Tim would not die. Jamie looked anxious and was holding tightly to Mother's hand, but Josh was fine—he was practicing the look of grave sorrow with which Michael read Bob Cratchit's words: "I promised him that I would walk there on a Sunday. My little, little child! My little child!"

The idea of being without one of the boys was bad enough—but at Christmas! I sniffled a little myself, and wanted to cheer when Scrooge woke from his ordeal and exclaimed "It's Christmas day! I haven't missed it."

As everyone in the audience slowly filed out of the theater, exclaiming about the show and exchanging Christmas greetings as they went, I caught Rob's sleeve.

"Rob," I said. "I need to borrow one of your employees. Have you got an online Sherlock who can find out anything about anyone?"

"Sure thing." He pulled out his phone and turned it on, scrolled through his contacts for a few moments, then nodded.

"Boomer's your guy," he said. "I'll e-mail you his info."

"Great," I said. "How early can I call him tomorrow?"

"Tomorrow?" Rob sounded amused. "Call him now."

"It's past eleven," I said. "It could be midnight before I find a quiet place to call him."

"He's up," Rob said. "He keeps vampire hours. If you wait till tomorrow, I wouldn't call him before three or four in the afternoon."

"And he works for you?"

"Flextime," Rob said with a shrug.

So while everyone else went backstage to congratulate Michael, I lagged behind, found a quiet corner, and called the number.

"Yeah?" said a voice on the other end.

"Hi, is this Boomer?"

Silence.

"This is Meg Langslow," I went on.

"Rob's sister," Boomer said.

I waited for a few moments, but clearly he thought that was enough of a response.

"Rob told me you could help me find out about someone," I said. "A guy named Claiborne Spottiswood."

"Spelled?"

Well, at least Boomer's terse style was efficient. I spelled the name and reminded him also to look under "Clay" and every possible misspelling of "Spottiswood" he could think of.

"Standard operating procedure," he said. "I'll call you when I find something."

When, not if. I liked the way Boomer thought.

"Thanks," I said, but he'd already hung up.

I pocketed my phone and headed for the dressing rooms. But along the way I stopped, almost by force of habit, by the rack that usually held copies of the student newspaper. It was empty. Not surprising this late in the evening. Well, I could check their Web site tomorrow to see if they'd run an article on the show house, or for that matter, on the murder.

Wait—the rack wasn't empty because of the late hour. We were on winter break. The newspaper wouldn't be putting out another issue until the students came back, in two weeks. There might be a few students still hanging around for the holidays—students from the area, grad students, students on tight budgets who couldn't afford the fare to go home for the holiday, and students who had something to do in town, like the ones working backstage at Michael's show. Presumably Jessica was one of the few still here. Maybe she was whiling away the long dark days on the near-deserted campus by pursuing stories from the wider community. But by the time the paper's next issue went out, the show house would be over, so an article wouldn't do us any good.

"Blast!" I muttered. I remembered all the time I'd spent talking to Jessica—time I could so easily have spent doing something more immediately useful. And who knew how much of the designers' time she'd wasted?

Ah, well. At least if she did the article it might get the decorators some publicity. And there was always the chance that once the chief caught up with her he might find some-thing useful in the photos she took.

I ran into Randall in the throng of family and friends crowding Michael's dressing room.

"Everything go okay at the house after I left?" he asked.

"Yes," I said. "Ivy was the only one still there when I left to come here. I'm going to drop by on the way home and make sure everything's locked up."

"I'll do it," he said. "You go home and rest."

"I'll think about it," I said.

Jamie was asleep on Michael's shoulder by the time we got to the Twinmobile. Josh was busily discussing the cos-tume he needed to have for his Dickens show, and was so wide awake that I was afraid I'd have to start assembling his miniature Victorian dress suit as soon as we got home. But a few seconds after I strapped him into his booster seat, he fell silent and his head lolled to one side in the sort of awkward position that never seems to bother children, though any adult who tried it would probably end up with a semipermanent sore neck.

Michael took off with the boys, and I headed up the street to where I'd parked my car. The streets that had been lined with cars belonging to shoppers and people going to the theater were nearly empty now that the stores were closed and the show over.

I was enjoying the peace and quiet and the crisp night air until I suddenly noticed the sound of footsteps behind me.

Chapter 14

Was I imagining the footsteps? I stopped and bent down as if to adjust my boot fastening. I stole a look behind me. There was no one in the street. And I heard no footsteps nearby.

Yet when I walked on, I heard it again. My footsteps made just a little more noise than they should. And the noise varied ever so slightly, as if someone was walking behind me, taking a step every time I did, and almost—but not quite—disguising the sound of his footsteps.

I walked along at a slow saunter until I came to a corner. Then, instead of crossing the street as I'd originally planned, I ducked around the corner. Once I had a building to keep me out of sight of anyone following me, I sprinted till I came to an alley in the middle of the block. I ducked down the alley and hid behind some trash cans.

I waited there, peering out from behind the trash cans to the mouth of the alley.

It wasn't my imagination. I could hear footsteps in the street I'd left. Soft footsteps approaching the mouth of the alley.

"Meg? Are you all right?"

I started, and whirled to find Muriel, owner of the diner, standing there with a full black plastic garbage bag in one hand. Not surprising, since this was the alley that ran behind the diner.

"You startled me," I said, a lot more softly than Muriel had spoken. "I thought someone was following me."

We both fell silent and listened while peering toward the end of the alley, but we didn't hear anything. At least I didn't, and after a few moments Muriel shook her head.

"You sure you're not just feeling spooked?" she asked. "What with finding a body last night and all?"

"Could be." I stood up and dusted my pants off. "Sorry if I startled you."

"No problem," she said. "Hey, just in case someone really was following you, how about if you walk me to my car and then I'll drive you to yours?"

"It's a deal," I said.

She deposited her garbage bag in the Dumpster and locked the back door of the diner behind her.

When we got to the mouth of the alley, I paused to look up and down the street. No one visible. Plenty of places to hide.

But was there a reason someone had left a brick lying on the snow just outside the mouth of the alley?

"From the construction site three blocks over," Muriel said, seeing me studying the brick.

"But what's it doing here?" I asked.

She looked at the brick for a few long moments.

"My car's this way," she said.

I was glad when we reached her car, and even gladder that she waited until she'd seen me start my car and drive off.

But I hadn't gone more than a few blocks before I began to suspect that a car was following me. A car with oddly distinctive headlights. Two sets of headlights, one on top of the other, with the bottom set slightly farther apart. And there was something on the inside of each top headlight that made it seem as if the car was looking at me cross-eyed. And frowning.

Maybe I'd been listening to the boys too much. Lately they'd developed very strong automotive likes and dislikes, based mainly on their impressions of the cars' faces, as they called the headlights and front-end decorations. Some cars looked as if they were smiling, others frowning. Some were sad, some happy. Josh was particularly fond of Corvettes, and Jamie thought most Audis looked mean. Once he'd burst into tears because a "mean car" was following us.

Was a mean car following me now? All I could see was those odd double headlights. Could be just a coincidence—there weren't that many streets in Caerphilly.

I took a leisurely detour through a residential neighborhood. The distinctive headlights never turned off, and never got any closer, even when I idled for a couple of minutes in front of a house well known for having some of the most over-the-top holiday lights in town.

Before moving on, I pulled out my phone. And then hesitated. Should I call the police?

I called Randall instead.

"What's up?" he said.

"Are you still at the show house?" I asked.

"For another minute or two. What do you need?"

"Could you stay there a few minutes longer? I think someone's following me. I'd call the police, but maybe everything that's happened lately has just got me jumpy. I don't want to look like a nervous idiot."

"What can I do?"

"Get in your truck, but don't leave yet. I'll drive by the house in a few minutes. If there's someone following me—"

"I'll get the license, call 9-1-1, and follow both of you till the police get there."

I felt better already. I took off again, and the headlights that had been stationary the whole time I'd pretended to enjoy the light show continued to follow me.

I cruised slowly past the show house. It was completely dark, but I spotted Randall sitting in his truck.

I went up a couple of blocks, then went around a block. Just as I was about to make a left turn to go past the show house again, the car behind me suddenly speeded up. It passed me, then turned sharply so it blocked the whole street. The driver's door popped open and a man jumped out and ran back toward my car.

I clicked the button to make sure all four doors were locked and then put the car in reverse and began slowly backing up as I picked up my cell phone to dial 9-1-1.

The man ran up to my window and banged on it, hard. Startled, I slammed on the brakes.

"Where is she?" he yelled. "I know you know."

"Meg, help's on the way," Debbie Ann, the dispatcher, said. "Randall just called to tell us about the guy who's following you."

"He's not following me anymore," I said. "He's banging on my car."

"I'll kill that bitch when I find her!" the man was shouting.

I turned my cell phone toward my window and took a picture of the angry red face pressed against it. But while I was still figuring out how to e-mail it to the police, the man suddenly flew backwards away from my window and landed in a snowdrift. Randall now stood just outside my window. I could hear sirens in the distance.

"Don't move," Randall shouted to the man. "And keep your hands where I can see them."

"Randall Shiffley's here," I said to Debbie Ann. "He's . . . confronting the guy."

The angry man was trying to struggle up.

Just then a police cruiser pulled up. Vern Shiffley, Randall's cousin, jumped out just in time to see the man lurch to his feet and aim a punch at Randall. Randall dodged neatly. Vern wasn't as lucky, but maybe it wasn't entirely a bad thing that my stalker had just opened himself up to a charge of assaulting a police officer.

Another cruiser pulled up and Aida Butler hopped out. By the time Chief Burke pulled up, she and Vern had the stalker handcuffed in the back of Aida's patrol car and Vern was holding a handful of snow on his injured eye.

"Are you all right?" the chief asked me.

"I'm fine," I said.

The chief strode over to Aida's patrol car and stood looking down at my stalker.

"Mr. Granger," he said. "What's the meaning of this?"

Someone known to the chief. I decided that was a good thing.

"She knows where my wife is," Granger said.

I controlled my impulse to protest that I didn't even know who his wife was, much less where she was.

"And what if she does?" the chief asked. "You do realize that you'd be violating the protective order if you followed her to find your wife, don't you?"

Granger shut his mouth as if determined not to say anything else.

"Take him down to the station," the chief said.

"I didn't go near the bitch," Granger protested. "I don't even know where she is."

"No, but you just assaulted a law enforcement officer while he was engaged in performing his duties," the chief said.

He waved to Aida, who got in and started up her patrol car. As she drove off, the chief walked back over to me.

"You willing to press charges against this clown?" he asked.

"Gladly," I said. "Though I'd really rather wait till tomorrow to do it, if it's all the same."

"Tomorrow will be soon enough," he said. "You want an escort home?"

I shook my head. I had the feeling Mr. Granger, whoever he might be, was the only person after me tonight.

Not that I wasn't glad when I got home and saw the house still brightly lit. And when Michael came out onto the porch to meet me.

"What took you so long?" he asked. "I was just about to call the police to have them check the ditches."

"We had a little excitement." I followed him and told him about Mr. Granger, while he went through the downstairs, performing his nightly ritual of shutting off lights and checking doors and windows.

"Quick thinking," he said, when I'd finished my tale. "But who is this Granger character, and why would he think you know anything about his wife?"

"No idea," I said. "I'll ask the chief tomorrow."

Though I had a feeling it would have something to do with the Caerphilly Women's Shelter. A good thing Granger hadn't been following me earlier in the day.

"Has the excitement given you an appetite?" Michael asked. "Want to join me in the kitchen?"

He never ate much before a show. He claimed it wasn't due to nerves but part of a deliberate plan to keep himself sharp for the performance. Whatever the reason, he was always starving afterward and ready to pig out.

"I won't eat much, but I'll keep you company," I said.

"Busy day tomorrow?"

"Two more days till we open," I said. "So yes. Remind me again why I ever agreed to do this."

"To protect this," he said, waving a hand around in a gesture that took in not just the foyer where we were standing but the surrounding rooms. "It was the price we had to pay to keep your mother from insisting on having the show house here. Having all those crazy designers invading our space, redoing rooms we've finally got looking the way we like them, letting hordes of strangers tramp through our home—madness!"

"Not to mention the possibility that we might have had a murder in our own master bedroom instead of someone else's," I said.

"Exactly."

Michael continued down the hall to the kitchen. I followed more slowly, looking around as I went, taking in the Christmas decorations in the foyer. I'd expected us to have to survive with minimal holiday decorations this year, since Mother, who normally insisted on decorating for us, would be totally immersed in the show house. But the day before she started work on her room, Mother showed up at seven in the morning with a dozen or so friends and relatives, and they'd transformed the whole house. The usual tall, narrow tree graced the foyer, this year completely decorated in red and gold with a musical theme—gold ornaments shaped like harps, trumpets, fiddles, drums, pianos, and French horns shared branches with chanting angels and singing choirboys. We had about the usual number of poinsettias, though this year most of them were plain red, which I preferred to the white or pink ones. Plain red dusted with a hint of gold glitter, anyway. This year Mother had put up red velvet ribbons crisscrossed on all the foyer walls, with little clips on them to hold Christmas cards. Every afternoon, providing they'd behaved themselves, the boys were allowed to take all the newly arrived Christmas cards and add them to the display. Mother had also festooned every corner of the room with so many tiny battery-powered LED candles in red-and-gold votive holders that the room sparkled like a convention of fireflies.

Just looking at it made me happier. When Michael and I had first moved into our house, I'd made an effort to trim it for the holidays with a wreath here and a garland there, but the sheer size of the space to be decorated overwhelmed me. Mother had taken over the chore of decorating the year I'd been pregnant with the boys—"You have so much else on your plate, dear"—and to my secret relief had never relinquished it. I might poke fun at some of her excesses, but I realized that I was okay with Mother doing the decorating. It brought back memories of Christmases when I was little. Not so much the way the house looked, but the fact that long before I'd have even begun seriously thinking about holiday plans, Mother and her helper bees would show up and transform the house from top to bottom in a single day. In fact, this was even better, because when I was living at home she'd enlist me as one of her minions, and now she preferred to finish the project when I wasn't even around. Maybe she liked to surprise me. Or maybe she was afraid I'd veto some of her more extravagant notions if I found out about them in advance. Either way, I was content. Especially since I'd found out she had a growing list of clients who paid her hundreds of dollars every December to do to their houses what she did to ours for free. And now that Michael and I had the boys, I focused a lot less on being independent and getting my own way and a lot more on making sure the boys had a fabulous holiday. And they seemed to like their grandmother's decorations.

The little hidden wireless speakers were playing "O Holy Night," and I hummed along as I followed Michael to the kitchen.

"Ham sandwich?" he offered.

"Not for me," I said. "Maybe just a slice of ham. I'm not doing the show house next year."

"Are we definitely having another show house next year?"

"If it makes a lot of money for the historical society and draws a lot of tourists, everyone will want to do another one," I said. "But I'm not doing it."

"We'll see," he said.

"I've even figured out who to dump it on instead," I said.

His mouth was full of ham sandwich, but he raised one eyebrow inquiringly.

"Martha."

"The bossy one?"

"She's perfect."

"I thought you found her really annoying and obnoxious."

"I do," I said. "But one reason she's so obnoxious is that she's really mad at the committee for not giving her a major room. She's taking it out on all the other designers. So if we put her in charge, she might be a lot less hard to live with."

"You could be right," Michael said.

"And if I'm wrong—at least she can get the job done, and I won't be there to be annoyed."

"Good plan. So have you figured out which of the designers did in Clay?"

"It's starting to look as if none of them did."

I filled him in on the rest of my day, including my success in figuring out alibis for all but one of the designers.

"Of course the chief's still checking them out, I suppose,"

I added. "But I feel a lot better, being reasonably sure I'm not hobhobbing with a murderer all day."

"Speaking of all day, the rehearsal for the boys' Christmas pageant is tomorrow at eleven. Are you going to be able to make it?"

"Is that tomorrow?"

"The pageant itself is on Christmas eve," he said. "And I hate to be the bearer of bad tidings, but that's only two days off."

"Don't remind me," I said. "I will make a point of coming to the rehearsal. And maybe we can grab a quick bite afterward. Are they still happy with the costumes?"

"Jamie is," he said. "And you know Josh."

Yes, I knew Josh.

Unfortunately, I hadn't made it to the parents' organizational meeting, or the first recital for the pageant. Michael was at both, of course, but I felt guilty that I hadn't been there. And I realized, only a few days ago, that he hadn't told me the important bit of information.

"We need new costumes," Josh had said one night.

"Can't you wear your costumes from last year?" I'd asked. "Or are they too small?"

Jamie had shrugged.

"Mo-om," Josh had moaned. "We were animals last year."

Actually, since they'd been dinosaurs last year, I'd have said they were reptiles. And extinct reptiles to boot. Although, as Grandfather was so fond of pointing out, technically, reptiles had just as much right to be called animals as any other living organism. Still, it was a long way from T. Rex to a sheep.

"Well, what do you want to be this year?" I'd asked. It wasn't as if there were a lot of choices in a nativity play.

Unless Robyn decided to spice things up and add scenes

not found in the original text. Based on the boys' prefer-
ences, I suspected a scene with pirates would go down well
with most of the participants. Perhaps instead of arriving
in Bethlehem on a donkey, the Holy Family could come by
boat, allowing Joseph to fend off pirates along the way. Or,
better yet, what if the Wise Men could encounter a party of
Imperial storm troopers—also bound for Bethlehem and
clearly up to no good—and repel the them with their light
sabers?

I'd abandoned that train of thought and dragged my
mind back to the immediate crisis.

"So if you're not animals, what are you?" I'd asked.
"Angels?"

"Mo-o-om!" I'd been hoping neither of them would
learn to roll their eyes like that until they were teenagers.
"*Girls* are angels. And little kids are animals. *Big* boys are
shepherds!"

As it turned out, Jamie would have been just fine with
being an animal. And he would have been quite satisfied
with Michael's plan for a shepherd's costume, which was to
cut a hole in a piece of burlap for the neck and tie the whole
thing together with a length of rope. Josh, however, had
demanded better, and his idea of proper shepherd garb
would have taxed the expertise of a Savile Row tailor, to say
nothing of my poor sewing skills.

It was December, so he'd wanted sleeves. Nicer sleeves.
And his tunic wasn't white enough. Could I wash it? The
hem was uneven. There was a loose thread. His belt was
too tight. His crook was splintery, could I make it smooth?
His sandals were too small.

And of course, I couldn't go to all that trouble for Josh
and leave Jamie as a ragged lump of burlap. In the end, I'd
managed to produce two passable tunics, with sleeves long

enough to keep them warm, especially when combined with a blue-and-white striped overcoat. Their crooks were polished till they shone; their belts were made of gold-brocade cord left over when Mother had gotten new curtain ties for her dining room, and we'd delighted them with long, fussy brown beards. It was going to look as if two of the members of ZZ Top were moonlighting in the hills outside Bethlehem.

"What do you think?" I'd asked them, when they finally tried on the finished costumes.

"It's okay," Josh had said. He still wasn't entirely happy with the sandals.

"This looks great, Mommy," Jamie had said.

Sometimes, just for a few moments, you're allowed to love one twin more than his brother.

Michael's voice brought me back to the present.

"Always a chance he'll find some kind of problem with his costume and pitch a fit today," he was saying. "But I think I can hold the threat of making Santa's naughty list over him."

"Or tell him that if he behaves, Grandma will give him some special passementerie to add to his costume on the night of the pageant."

"Will he know what passementerie is?" Michael asked. "Because I don't."

"It can be a surprise," I said. "And he'll be impressed with the five-syllable word."

"Well, that was satisfying," Michael said, as he finished off his sandwich. "Time we hit the hay."

We both pitched in to tidy up the kitchen, and headed upstairs, yawning.

"Is there really that much left to do on the house?" he asked.

"For me, yes," I said. "Tickets. Programs. Parking and shuttles. Schedules for the docents. Trying to get some more publicity so ticket sales will pick up. And keeping the designers from doing anything else to damage the house."

"But what about the designers? Surely they must be getting close to finishing?"

"I have no idea," I said. "I can look at a room and think it's perfect and if I say that, they look at me as if I'm an idiot. These are people who will repaint a room three or four times because the color doesn't work the way they thought it would. People who can spend five minutes plumping a pillow properly. If I hear the words, 'it needs . . . something' one more time, I might lose it. I think they're all going to keep tweaking and improving their rooms right up until the last minute. Beyond the last minute. I'm afraid that when the first paying guests walk in, Mother will ask them if they mind helping her rearrange the furniture."

"Well, it's only a couple more days," he said.

"True," I said. "I can survive anything for a few more days."

Chapter 15

December 22

As I was driving to the show house the next morning, my phone rang. It was an unfamiliar number. Could it be Boomer, reporting back already? I pulled over to answer it. Fortunately, I only said "Hello" rather than "Well, that was quick" or "I guess Rob was joking about how late you slept."

"Is this the Meg Langslow who's in charge of the Caerphilly Historical Society's Christmas Decorator Show House?" a male voice said.

"Yes," I said. "May I help you?"

"I'm with the *Richmond Times-Dispatch*," he said. "I'm supposed to come by to take some shots for a story in the paper. Would noon today be okay?"

I closed my eyes and contemplated how the designers would react if I arrived and told them a photographer would be arriving in four hours. Less than four hours.

"We don't actually open until ten a.m. on December twenty-fourth," I said. "And as you can imagine, the designers are still busy putting the finishing touches on their rooms."

"That doesn't matter to me," he said.

"But it will to them," I pointed out. "How about a sneak preview an hour before we let the public in on the twenty-fourth?"

"I'm tied up that day. Can we make it three today?"

We finally made it 10:00 A.M. on the twenty-third. Which was tomorrow.

Now to break the news to the decorators.

I stopped by the Caerphilly Bakery and picked up two dozen assorted doughnuts, bearclaws, and other breakfast pastries, to sweeten the news. And a couple of carryout carafes of coffee, to jump start their efforts.

Most of the designers were already there when I arrived. Sarah was carrying in boxes from her car. As was Violet. What were they up to? Now was time to be putting on finishing touches, not dragging in vast quantities of new stuff.

Mother was showing Tomás and Mateo exactly how she wanted them to put a light touch of gilding on the edges of some of the woodwork.

"Pastries?" she exclaimed. "How nice, dear."

She smiled indulgently as Mateo and Tomás abandoned their paintbrushes long enough to grab pastries. I carried the rest of the doughnuts and the coffee through to the kitchen. Eustace also had piles of boxes. Clearly it was a trend, and not one I was happy to see under the circumstances.

"Mind if I put these here?" I asked Eustace.

"Fine," he said. "Just how awful does this cabinet look? Be brutal."

I came around to where I could see the kitchen cabinets. He'd had all the cabinet fronts replaced with glass-paned doors in a sort of diamond-hatched pattern that looked vaguely Elizabethan. He'd even installed lighting inside the cabinets, the better to see the contents. And I noticed that he'd added—or, more likely, Tomás and Mateo had added—little flourishes of gold on the glass, curlicues and leaves and . . . well, squiggles. Evidently this was what had inspired Mother to commit retaliatory gilding.

And now he was arranging dishes in the cabinets. A really small number of dishes—especially when compared to the number of boxes he'd used to bring them in. One cabinet held nothing but a turquoise teapot and a matching teacup on the bottom shelf, two hand-painted goblets on the middle shelf, and a blue Fiestaware pitcher on the top one. At this rate, he'd need a lot more cabinets to hold just the dishes and glassware that were spread out along the counter, much less what lurked in the boxes.

"I'm not letting you anywhere near my kitchen," I said.

"But it's beautiful. They all are."

"Then why don't you want me near your kitchen?" he asked.

"Because I think those glass-fronted cabinets are fabulous, and you'd talk me into having them, and they just wouldn't work," I said. "We have too much kitchen stuff, and most of it's not decorative—at least not when you have to crowd it in to get all of it put away."

"Well, you're right, it's not practical," he said. "But it's beautiful, and people love to see it. Do you think I should switch the pitcher and the teapot?"

"I think you should ask Mother," I said. "I have no eye for this kind of thing. Meanwhile, I have news."

The assorted designers and worker bees gathered around the pastry looked up anxiously.

"They caught the killer?" Martha guessed.

"No, I haven't heard anything more about that," I said. "But a photographer from the *Richmond Times-Dispatch* is coming tomorrow morning to take pictures of the house!"

You'd think I'd announced my intention to have them all shot at sunrise.

"That'll never do," Martha said.

"We're not nearly ready!" Sarah wailed.

"Oh, great," Eustace said. "My rooms will be a disaster."

"Meg, dear, can't you possibly ask him to come a little later?" Mother said. "Christmas eve would be so much better. We could let him in before the general public."

"I suggested that, and he can't do it," I said. "He wanted to be here in about an hour. Just be glad I talked him into tomorrow morning at ten."

They all scattered—though not, I noticed, without taking their share of the coffee and pastries.

Eustace had stopped fiddling with his dishes and was looking around his room as if he'd never seen it before.

"Where to begin?" he muttered.

Out in the great room, Mother was standing in the middle of her room, hands on her hips, slowing turning around to survey it, and frowning, as if everything she had done needed to be ripped out and redone.

"Looks fabulous," I said as I passed.

She ignored me.

Throughout the house, all the other designers were performing their own variations on what Mother and Eustace were doing. Surveying their rooms as if they'd never seen them before—and evidently finding them wanting.

I stepped into the master bedroom. Which of all the rooms in the house was the one least ready for its close-up. Fat chance distracting one of the others from their pre-photo prepping, so getting it in shape would appear to be my job.

I texted Randall to remind him that we needed a new mattress for the room. And asked if I should buy sheets or if he was taking care of it.

Maybe I should talk to the designers, now that they'd had a few moments to absorb the news. Calm them down, if necessary. Find out if there was anything I could do to help them.

I went downstairs and was just stepping into Sarah's study when my phone rang.

"Hello," I said, as I stepped into the hall to avoid bothering Sarah if I needed to have a conversation with whoever was calling.

"He doesn't exist."

I pulled the phone from my ear and looked at the screen, which said only BLOCKED.

"Who doesn't exist?" I said into the phone.

"Spottiswood."

It had to be Boomer calling.

"He has to exist," I said. "I practically stumbled over his dead body two nights ago."

"Whoever the stiff was, he wasn't born Spottiswood," Boomer said.

Okay, that made sense. I'd always thought Clay's name was a little too good to be true.

"He showed up in Tappahannock five years ago," Boomer went on. "Here in Caerphilly two years ago. That's it."

"You tried all the variant spellings for Claiborne and Spottiswood?"

"Couple dozen. No dice. And the guy's not even filing income tax under any of those misspellings."

"What did you do, hack the IRS's databases?" I exclaimed. Silence.

"Forget I asked," I said. "Are you sure you checked every— never mind. Stupid question."

"Sorry," Boomer said. "If you get any other data—anything at all—I can keep trying."

"If I had any more information, I'd have given it to you," I said.

A soft voice from somewhere above my head spoke up.

"Clay Smith."

I looked up. Ivy was peering down over the railing from the upper hall.

"Hang on a sec," I said to Boomer. I took a few steps up toward Ivy.

"Clay Smith?" I said. "Claiborne Spottiswood is really Clay Smith."

She nodded.

"I heard that," Boomer said. "Clay Smith. What an unusual name. Won't be easy."

"Anything else you know about him?" I asked Ivy. Boomer was doing me a favor, so I decided to ignore his sarcastic tone.

"Tell your . . . investigator to look in New York City, fifteen to twenty years ago," she said. "He'll find the stories. It was in all the papers."

I relayed this to Boomer.

"I'll call you," he said.

I hung up and put away my phone. Ivy's head disappeared. I climbed the rest of the way up to the second-floor landing. She had gone back to painting one of her murals.

"It's Andersen's 'The Emperor's New Clothes,' you know," she said, without looking up from her work. "He's wearing the magic clothes the phony tailors have pretended to make for him—the clothes that are invisible to anyone unfit for his position."

"Nice," I said. Her mural showed a cobblestone street running along the length of the wall, lined on each side with townspeople in colorful medieval garb. Bits of snow flecked the cobblestones and covered the steep roofs of the buildings, so odds were the poor emperor would end his procession not only mortally embarrassed but probably also suffering from frostbite.

"So you knew Clay back then, in New York?" I asked, as I watched her carefully dabbing paint onto the cobblestones down which the emperor was strolling.

"Knew *of* him," she said, without looking up. "I doubt if he would've remembered me. He was an up-and-coming painter on the New York scene, and I was . . . not."

"Painter? As in fine art?"

"Oh, yes." She nodded absently, and hitched herself a little to the left, to reach more cobblestones. "He really was very good. A brilliant painter, and it didn't hurt that he was handsome and articulate and . . . larger than life."

"What happened?"

"What happened." She sighed. "Fame happened. He signed with a big gallery, and they started selling his paintings for a lot of money. But he was spending the money faster than he could paint. There might have been drugs involved. Or maybe he just went a little crazy. And unfortunately, he began to blame his financial problems on the owner of the gallery that represented him. Claimed the guy was a cheat."

"Blaming the gallery owner for his own mistakes?" I suggested.

"Oh, no. He was definitely right," she said, with a fleeting smile. "The gallery owner was cheating a lot of people. It came out at the trial."

"Clay took him to court?"

"No, Clay shot him."

"Shot him?"

"I don't think Clay meant to kill him," Ivy said. "Unfortunately, the fact that the man was cheating him only made Clay's motive look that much stronger. He was drunk at the time, and the gun belonged to the gallery owner, so a lot of people thought he should have gotten off with self-defense or justifiable homicide. Of course, other people thought he was lucky to have gotten off with manslaughter."

"So he went to prison?"

She nodded.

"For how long?"

"I don't know," she said. "Not life. Though however long it was, young as we were, I'm sure it seemed like a lifetime to him when they sentenced him. I suppose it must have been ten or fifteen years, since he's out now."

I stood and watched her paint for a while, mulling over what she'd said. And watching her paint. She was working on the emperor now. Most of his body was hidden by the onlookers lining both sides of the cobblestone street, but you could tell he was wearing nothing. And, in a sly touch, while most of the onlookers were cheering happily, every so often you'd spot one who couldn't quite keep up the pretense.

"Did you tell the chief about this?" I asked after a while.

"I expect he already knows by now," she said. "Clay's fingerprints would be on file, wouldn't they?"

"Probably," I said. "And if my investigator's right and he's not paying taxes under Spottiswood, he probably has paperwork at the house with his real name on it. The chief would have seen that by now."

"Yes," she said. "So I didn't think I needed to tell the chief. But if you think he needs to know, you can tell him. I don't mind."

As I watched, she was putting the finishing touches on the emperor's face. He looked a lot like Clay.

Chapter 16

I slipped away and left Ivy to work in peace. I stepped into Violet's bedroom. She was sitting on the floor, working on something.

"How's it coming?" I asked.

"Oh, just fine," she said. "I decided the shelves needed a little something."

I'd been thinking that for several days now, but then I knew better than to second-guess the designers. The twelve-foot back wall of Violet's bedroom had two windows, each fitted with a pink-cushioned window seat, and the rest of the wall was given over to shelves. I'd have called them bookshelves, but up till now Violet had only decorated them with a small assortment of pastel ornaments. A white vase containing dried flowers. A pink-and-lavender child's jewelry box. The overflow of pink, white, and lavender stuffed animals from the bed. A white ceramic lamb. A pink ceramic cat.

It all looked a little sparse to me, but I assumed it was the look she was aiming for. And at least she'd put up a few token holiday decorations. Nothing impressive—a few feet of silver tinsel garland, a few silver filigree balls. But at least she'd done something.

And I was delighted to see that she'd brought in books. Several tall stacks of books. From force of habit, I tilted my head to read the titles on the books.

A battered copy of *The Wind in the Willows.* A biography of Adlai Stevenson. A 1957 organic chemistry textbook. A lot of what I recognized as bestsellers from the forties and fifties.

"Oh, they're not interesting books," she said. "I just went down to the thrift store and bought a bunch that were the right size."

I glanced over and saw what she was working on. She was taking the dust jackets off the books and cutting new dust jackets out of pink, lavender, or white paper.

She was piling the dust jackets carelessly in the corner of the room.

I wasn't exactly a rabid bibliophile, but this bothered me.

"You're not using the dust jackets?" I asked.

"Oh, no." She wrinkled her nose slightly. "They're just so . . . gaudy. The books themselves are better, but the colors are all wrong for my room. This will be so much nicer, don't you think?"

Nicer as long as you had no particular desire to read any of the books. With her system, *Robinson Crusoe* and *The Life Cycle of the Dermestid Beetle* looked pretty much the same.

"Hey, could you save the covers for me?" I asked. "I have a project I could really use them for."

"Happy to," she said. "I was just going to throw them away."

"Great! Just stack them neatly in this box, and let me know when you've got a stack big enough that you want me to haul it away."

"No problem," she said. "You can take those now."

I set one of the boxes the books had come out of where it would be handy. Then I gathered up the twenty or so covers she'd already discarded, stacked them loosely, and carried them down via the back stairs, waving at the Quilt Ladies as I passed.

"You heard about the photographer at ten tomorrow?" I stopped to say.

"We'll be ready!" Vicky sang out.

Nice to see someone was optimistic. They did seem to be working frantically on something. A quilt in Christmassy fabrics of red and green, with a lot of gold metallic tracery on them. But whether or not the room looked exactly as they wanted it to, it should look fine in the photographs.

Down in the garage I found a box for the discarded covers.

"I don't know why I care," I muttered. There probably weren't any valuable books in there. Chances were, people who cared about dust jackets would turn up their noses at Violet's book collection.

But it bothered me, so if possible, I'd try to reunite them at the end of the show house.

Of course, there was always the chance she'd sell the books back to the thrift shop without the covers at the end of the show. Maybe I should talk her into donating them to the library, for the tax break. She'd probably go for that. And I could give our head librarian a heads-up that the dust jackets would be arriving separately.

Back into the house. Eustace had now put one or two dishes, vases, or bits of glassware on every shelf in his ever-so-many cabinets. I paused to watch him for a minute or two. He was now standing and studying the effect, pausing every once in a while to switch a couple of items, or adjust one a few millimeters in one direction or another.

"It's just not right," he said. "It's too much of a much-ness. What else can I put in these wretched cabinets?"

"Well," I said. "In my kitchen, a lot of that space would

be given over to food. Teas, spices, canned goods. But I don't suppose you want that gaudy modern supermarket look."

Eustace's face froze for a moment, then he beamed.

"You're a genius! Yes! Decorative tea caddies! Elegant spice jars! And perhaps a few vintage grocery items! I must go shopping!"

He grabbed up his coat, hat, and scarf and dashed toward the garage, presumably heading for the back door there.

"A genius," I murmured. "I like that."

In the great room, Mother was rearranging the logs in the fireplace into a more pleasing configuration while Tomás and Mateo dabbed little bits of gold on things.

In the dining room, Linda had assembled several dozen pieces of wooden or plastic fruit and was painting them all gold. Another theme. I should probably refrain from pointing out what happened to King Midas.

I grabbed my coat and hat from the coat closet. I didn't have to take off for the rehearsal for fifteen minutes or so, but with all the designers focused on something, now seemed a good time to make my escape.

"You heading out?" Randall appeared from the basement.

"Family stuff. Are you—"

My phone rang. It was Stanley Denton

"Remember that so-called charity you asked me to check out?" he said. "Designers of the Future?"

"So-called? What have you found out about it?"

"Not a whole lot, but enough to be very suspicious."

"Hang on," I said. "Let me put you on speaker so Randall Shiffley can hear."

"Okay."

"Hey, Stanley," Randall said. "What's up?"

"Meg had me look into the charity Clay Spottiswood designated to receive the proceeds if he won the contest," Stanley said.

Randall looked puzzled and glanced at me.

"Because I'd never heard of it, and someone told me Clay had founded it, and it didn't seem in character for him," I explained.

"Good instincts," Stanley said. "I can't quite prove it yet, but I have reason to believe it was pretty much a sham. I haven't been able to put my hands on any paperwork about the organization—"

"You think maybe there isn't any?" I asked.

"Good possibility," Stanley said.

"Didn't I give you the form he gave me?" Randall asked.

"You did," Stanley said. "But it's a forgery. The tax-exempt number on it belongs to the Vietnam Veterans of America."

"He's scum," Randall muttered.

"I talked to one of Clay's clients," Stanley went on. "A very wealthy man who doesn't want his name attached to any of this, but I believe him. Clay hit him up for a donation to his charity but he never did produce any paperwork. Nothing like a business plan or a budget. Only thing he could remember was Clay bragging about what a low salary he was going to pay himself for running the show, but my source didn't really think fifty thousand was such a bargain rate for an outfit that had no assets and no real hope of acquiring any."

"So Clay was trying to con us into putting half the show house proceeds into his own pocket," Randall said. "Meg, you're allowed to say 'I told you so' now."

"Did she predict Clay would try to pull something like that?"

"No," Randall said. "But she did tell me we ought to get

a lot more detailed contracts for these show house participants. Next year, I'll make sure I listen to her."

Probably not the best time to mention that next year I planned to make sure someone else was here doing the thankless job of riding herd on the designers.

"So does this have anything to do with Clay's murder?" Randall asked.

"I have no idea," I said.

"I'm going to fill Chief Burke in, just in case," Stanley said. "Because you never know what little bit of information will crack his case. See you later."

With that he hung up.

"And before you ask, I'm off to fetch the mattress for Clay's room," Randall said as he strode down the hallway. "And the sheets."

As I was standing in the foyer, putting my coat on, Sarah appeared in the doorway of her study.

"You're leaving?"

"Important family stuff," I said. "Back in a couple of hours. How's it going?"

"Getting close," Sarah said. "I decided I needed a lot more books on the shelves. After all, it's a study."

I winced, and stepped farther into the room so I could see what she was doing to her books, and whether I needed to rescue another flock of unloved dust jackets.

But to my delight, Sarah was filling her shelves with real books in their natural state. Many of them had dust jackets, and I had to admit that some of the individual dust jackets were gaudy. But once she arranged them on the shelves, the individual jackets blended into a pleasing mosaic. And some of the books were jacketless, shabby, and obviously much read, but they also blended in and added to the patina.

I found myself remembering a period, from when I was nine or ten until I went off to college, when Mother and Dad would often take me with them to Virginia's Garden Week or any other event that opened other people's homes for tours by the paying public. Mother was interested in the décor, of course, and Dad went along because many of the houses had beautiful gardens. He was prone to complaining in the car afterward if not enough of the houses had landscaping worth looking at. I wasn't that keen on any of it, though I did find it rather interesting to snoop into how other people lived. I only came along because I didn't want to be left home with Rob and the babysitter—or later, as Rob's babysitter. Mother always said that if she lost track of Dad and me in one of the houses, she'd think back over the rooms she'd seen. If one of them had books in it, she'd head back there, and would find the two of us standing side by side in front of the shelves, browsing the books— both of us with our hands clasped behind our backs, because you weren't supposed to touch anything, and leaning forward to read the titles. And if there weren't any books, we'd be outside, kicking our heels till she emerged.

Sarah's books would have kept Dad and me happily occupied for however long Mother wanted to spend in a house.

"Nice selection," I said, adopting the traditional posture with my hands clasped behind my back and my body leaning toward the shelves. "You must patronize a better class of thrift shop than Violet."

"Actually, I brought in some of my own books," she said with a laugh.

Better and better. I saw a lot of my own favorites, both childhood and adult, and Dad would have been gratified by the large selection of crime fiction. And she had interesting tastes in history and biography.

"I admit, I left my small collection of first editions at home," she said. "And I'm sort of arranging these by color, which I wouldn't do at home. I'm strictly alphabetical there."

"Michael and I do alphabetical within subject," I said. "Although we recently pulled together all the kids' books that we want the boys to find and read over the next few years, and put them on shelves in their rooms. And we also decided to get a few locked bookcases for the stuff we didn't want the boys to get their hands on for a couple of decades."

"Good idea." She took a few steps back, tilted her head, and squinted to see what effect she'd created. "So is my library more interesting than Violet's?"

"No idea," I said. "She's covering all her books with pretty pastel paper."

Sarah winced. She was a reader. She got it.

I made a mental note to come back later and peruse Sarah's shelves.

"So is this photographer really coming to see the house?" Sarah asked. "Or is he coming to see the place where a murder took place?"

"Your guess is as good as mine," I said. "But who cares, as long as it gets the show house some publicity?"

"And if he shows up and only wants to take pictures of the crime scene?"

"Then I'll tell him that I have to get permission from the police to let him do that, and in the meantime, would he like to take some pictures of the other rooms."

"I like the way you think," Sarah said. "And if he doesn't bother with our rooms—"

"Then the chief won't give his permission." My phone had started ringing, so I nodded to Sarah and stepped out into the hall to answer it.

"Do you put marshmallows on your sweet potatoes?" Michael's mother again.

"I don't, because I never make sweet potatoes," I said. "And I have no idea what Mother does, because I dislike sweet potatoes and never eat them. You could make some with and some without."

"But what's your family tradition?"

"I'll ask Mother," I said.

I stuck my head into the great room.

"Mother! Sweet potatoes! With or without marshmallows?"

"Well, I prefer them without," she said. "But your father and your brother love marshmallows. And while I don't know about—"

"Some of each," I said to Michael's mother. "Gotta run."

The relief I felt at getting out of the show house for an hour or two was a little preview of how happy I was going to feel when it had opened. Better yet, when it was all over but counting up how much we'd raised for the historical society.

Chapter 17

Downtown, the sidewalks were full of shoppers—the sidewalks, and in a few places, the streets, where residents and business owners hadn't yet done a good job of snowplowing. A lot of unfamiliar faces, so it looked as if Randall's annual Christmas in Caerphilly tourism campaign was working.

Last year, Randall had had to scale back his plans when the county council had balked at any major expenditure. But after seeing the dramatic increase in revenue from local shops, restaurants, and lodgings generated by Randall's relatively modest efforts, the council had authorized a much more ambitious plan this year. Nearly every building in town had been decorated to the hilt and the street swarmed with low-paid or volunteer reenactors in Victorian costume. The clothing shops featured bustles and top hats in their front windows. The toy store displayed wooden toys and elaborately painted nutcrackers. The candy store featured rock candy, candy canes, and old-fashioned taffy.

Volunteers in thick Victorian greatcoats lurked on every third corner, ringing bells and collecting funds for Caerphilly Cares, a consortium of local charities. Parties of carolers roamed the streets in hoop skirts and frock coats, serenading the crowds with Victorian-era carols. Chief Burke had drawn the line at forcing his officers into old-fashioned London policemen's outfits, so Randall had recruited a volunteer security force who strolled about the town wearing their distinctive custodian helmets and twirling realistic looking truncheons. And some of the more enterprising shopkeepers had begun showing up in costume and claiming it increased sales.

About the only holdout to the Victorianization of Caerphilly was Muriel's Diner, whose owner was so firmly entrenched in her attempt to maintain its original 1950s décor that even Randall couldn't sway her. But she'd decorated the building with so many garlands, bows, angels, holly branches, and "Merry Christmas" banners that you couldn't see the chrome and vinyl booths until you actually stepped inside, so no one minded.

My route to Grace Episcopal took me past the town square, where the Christmas tree—"just a smidgen shorter than the National Christmas Tree," according to Randall— was beautiful, even though a lot of the ornaments were presently obscured by snow.

The Methodists, who would be hosting the annual live nativity on their front lawn tomorrow night, were busy. They'd decided not just to build their usual manger but also to surround it with a cluster of houses to represent the rest of Bethlehem. And they'd set up a tent to represent one that the wise men might have slept in during their travels from the east across the desert. The original idea had been to exhibit the camels from Grandfather's zoo there on warm days, but so far we hadn't had any. So the camels stayed indoors, and there was just the tent, its intricate painted decoration—done as a Christmas project by the Methodist children's Bible study classes—also, alas, obscured by the snow.

But the Methodists were getting busy for tomorrow's big event, shoveling the area around Bethlehem and the wise men's tent—and with luck, once they dug a path to it they'd clear off the tent as well.

I arrived at Grace Episcopal in plenty of time for the rehearsal. I waved at Robyn, the rector, but I'm not sure she saw me. She had her hands full. There were at least twice as many children appearing in the pageant as last year, which spoke well for Robyn's efforts to recruit new members and get the existing ones more involved. But as any parent can testify, doubling the number of children in any given situation quadrupled the amount of noise and confusion.

I wondered briefly if any of the children came from the women's shelter. I thought I recognized one small sheep as the child Vermillion had been carrying. What if—

And then I shoved Vermillion and the shelter and the show house and the murders out of my head and tried to concentrate on enjoying the pageant.

There were several mothers helping, and I needed a break from my own set of rambunctious and badly behaved charges—by which I meant the designers, not Josh and Jamie—so I just sat with Michael in a pew a few rows back from the temporary stage and braced myself to leap into the fray if either of our angels did anything particularly heinous.

The church was beautifully decorated, as usual, with spruce and fir garlands, clusters of holly, and banners along all the walls in red, green, gold, and purple—since we'd all figured out that purple was Robyn's favorite color. The bracing evergreen smell that permeated the whole sanctuary lifted my spirits and cleared my sinuses, all at the same time.

And one of Robyn's innovations for this year was an actual curtain, to make the altar end of the church, where the play would take place, even more like a real theater. The curtain was made of deep-blue plush material, representing the night sky, with sparkling stars all over it, and there were a few palm trees on the far right and left sides.

The pageant began, as always, with Mary and Joseph entering the back of the church to wend their way down the center aisle to Bethlehem. In another of Robyn's innovations, Mary was going to be riding a real donkey, lent by a local farmer who certified him docile and highly reluctant to answer any calls of nature if he wasn't in his favorite spot in his own back pasture. But Robyn had decided not to push our luck by having the donkey in rehearsals, so the boy playing Joseph appeared to be leading his wife down the aisle with a rope around her wrist, while Mary, with a sullen expression on her face, slouched along, chewing her gum and occasionally blowing a small bubble. The organist played "O Little Town of Bethlehem," to mark what the choir would be singing at the real performance, and Mary and Joseph eventually climbed up the shallow steps onto the sanctuary/stage—was the donkey going to be able to do that?—and ducked behind the blue curtain.

Cut to the shepherds, who filed out from behind the curtain to abide in their fields by night—the fields being represented by the area in front of the curtain and a potted palm tree. Josh seemed to think that abiding meant walking up and down at the front of the stage with his crook over his shoulder like a sentry's rifle, glowering at any sheep who even thought of leaving his or her assigned piece of turf. Jamie took a milder view of his duties, and was happily sitting in the midst of the sheep, his head barely visible over the sea of woolly forms.

It was at this point that I deduced that Jamie and Josh's promotion to shepherd had occurred not because they were so much older and wiser but because, thanks to the new influx of families, the church had an overabundance of children even younger.

I caught a glimpse of Robyn, looking harried, peeking out from behind the curtain. It occurred to me that she was filling much the same cat-herding role for the pageant that I did at the show house. Though at least her charges had an excuse for behaving immaturely. And so far none of them had slaughtered each other, though if Josh kept waving his crook about wildly that, too, was a possibility.

I was about to hiss a cease-and-desist command at Josh when the angel of the Lord appeared stage left, causing Josh to leap to the defense of his flock. Some of the smaller sheep, startled by the angel's sudden appearance, cried a little and huddled closer to Jamie for protection. But the angel ignored Josh's dramatic flourishes of his crook and mimed speaking while Michael intoned the relevant verses from Luke.

And when Michael read out that a "great company of the heavenly host appeared," a dozen assorted preteen angels shuffled out from the wings and put their hands together as if in prayer. Most of them weren't in costume yet, but they were all wearing their wings, because not putting each other's eyes out with the wings was the tricky part that they needed to rehearse. Along with not knocking each other down and not stepping on the sheep as they lined up between the sheep and the curtain. Robyn took them through their entrance half a dozen times, to the great displeasure of the sheep, who were impatient to get to their favorite part of their roles, singing "Gloria in Excelsis Deo" along with the choir.

But eventually the angels managed their entrance to Robyn's satisfaction, and then we all sang the carol together, sounding almost as good as we would when the full choir joined in. After that, the curtain opened, and Josh and Jamie and a third shepherd herded the sheep past the stable and settled them on one side of the stage—except for one very small sheep who was discovered to be in dire need of a diaper change and was handed down to his waiting mother.

Then the wise men entered. In spite of Grandfather's offer to lend her three of the camels from his zoo, Robyn had decided not to risk it. So the wise men entered stage right, afoot, while one of the older boys stood in the wings and played a recording of Grandfather's camels making their characteristic moaning and groaning sounds. Perhaps by Christmas eve someone could help him edit out the part where an adult male voice yelped and then said, rather loudly, "let go of my hat, you smelly beast!"

Then we took another break in the action to sing "We Three Kings," after which the three wise men presented their gifts—represented, at the moment, by a popcorn tin, a shoe box, and a coffee pot, since the church's traditional gold, frankincense, and myrrh props had been repainted at the last minute and were not quite dry yet.

A final rousing rendition of "Joy to the World" ended the pageant, and the players all scattered to join their parents and hurry back to the room where the buffet lunch had been set up.

"Mommy," Josh asked me during lunch. "Do you like frankincense and myrrh?"

"Frankincense and myrrh are for babies," Jamie said scornfully.

"No, they're not," Josh said.

"Then why did the wise men give them to Baby Jesus?"

"No one had invented Xboxes yet," Michael said.

"Actually, I think I might be allergic to frankincense and myrrh," I said.

Josh looked disappointed.

After lunch, Michael headed off to take the boys sledding, and I was walking out to my car, planning to head back to the show house, when I got a text from a vaguely familiar phone number. It said simply "Check e-mail for Smith info."

I opened my e-mail and scrolled down till I found one from boomer@mutantwizards.com. I opened it and found it consisted of page after page of links. E-mail worked on my phone, but for links, I'd need to be at my computer. I closed it and was getting into my car when my phone rang. Chief Burke.

"Meg, are you very busy right now?" he asked.

If anyone else had asked me that, I'd have given them chapter and verse of everything waiting for me back at the show house. Somehow I didn't think it was a good idea to be so blunt with the chief.

But while I was struggling for a tactful answer, he figured this out.

"Of course you're busy," he said, with a sigh. "What I meant was, can you possibly break away for a few minutes to take a look at something here?"

"Where's here?"

"Mr. Spottiswood's house—1224 Pruitt Avenue."

Suddenly leaving the show house to fend for itself for a while seemed like an awesome idea.

"I'll be right there."

Clay's house surprised me. I'd expected something imposing, expensive, and decorated to the nines in taste that was utterly different from mine. But 1224 Pruitt Avenue turned out to be one of a nearly identical row of town houses, in a subdivision full of such rows. I suspected most of the town houses were rented by pairs, trios, or quartets of young singles. There were no toys in any of the yards, very little landscaping, and even though every house had a garage, both sides of the street were lined with parked cars, bumper to bumper. I had to park over a block away.

When I showed up at the doorway, Sammy Wendell came out to meet me. His deputy's uniform looked disheveled, as if he'd been working several shifts without a break.

"This way." He led me through a living room decorated with mismatched and slightly battered articles of furniture that looked as if they belonged in larger and more imposing rooms. The only things that didn't look like castoffs from some of Clay's decorating projects were the paintings—a dark, moody landscape over the mantel, an equally dark and moody bar scene over the sofa, and a huge cityscape filling all of one otherwise empty wall. Were they Clay's own paintings? Probably. I could see a signature in the corner of each that looked rather like a stylized *CS*.

"It's this way," Sammy said, interrupting my study of the art.

I followed him through a kitchen decorated only with dirty dishes. And finally into the garage.

Chief Burke was standing in the garage, looking down at a collection of twenty or so boxes. I could see my cousin Horace squatting down beside the boxes, writing something down in a notebook. His uniform also looked a little the worse for wear.

"What's up?" I asked.

"You tell me," the chief said. "Horace?"

Horace stood up and pointed to a stack of four boxes. I

squatted down and looked at them. They were all addressed to Mother at the show house address.

"These are Mother's," I exclaimed. "What are they doing here?"

"A good question," the chief said. "You can think of no legitimate reason for them to be in Mr. Spottiswood's possession?"

"All four of these packages are ones Mother thought were lost in transit," I said. "Three of them she had to have shipped again. She's been bugging me for two days to find this one."

I held up a small, flat parcel from The Braid Emporium.

The chief turned to Horace.

"And what did the UPS tell us about these packages?"

Horace looked down at his notebook.

"These two were drop shipped," he said, touching two of Mother's parcels. "No signature required. These two were signed for."

"Who signed for them?" I demanded.

"This one was a W. Faulkner," Horace said. "The Braid Emporium one went to a C. Dickens."

"We also have signatures from T. Capote, F. S. Fitzgerald, and D. Hammett," the chief added. "The manager of our local UPS facility will be having a word with the driver responsible."

"That jerk," I said. "Clay, I mean. Ever since the designers started working in the house, we've had problems with packages taking longer than expected, or getting lost entirely. I assumed someone had figured out that a lot of expensive stuff was being left at a house where no one lived, and was pilfering packages. So a week ago I told everyone that I'd rather they ship stuff to their own offices, but if they had to ship to the house they had to require a signature. We still had a few problems with packages, but not nearly as many."

"That makes sense," the chief said. "Most of these packages would have been delivered between ten days and three weeks ago."

I glanced through the other packages. They came from fabric and trim companies, glass and china vendors, antique stores—all the kinds of vendors the decorators would have used.

"That jerk," I said. "He's been sabotaging everyone."

"That makes you angry," the chief observed.

"Damn right it does," I said.

"I imagine the designers themselves would be even angrier," he said.

"Angry enough to kill him? Is that what you're asking?"

The chief raised one eyebrow and waited.

"How should I know?" I said. "Maybe. I can't see killing someone over a bit of braid, or a few yards of fabric. But if one of them realized Clay was deliberately sabotaging them, and had been for weeks? Can I see someone losing it and lashing out in anger? Yes. Don't ask me who, though." I waved at the stack of packages. "He's got at least one from everyone."

"If Mr. Spottiswood had been stabbed or bludgeoned by something that could readily be found at the crime scene, I could more easily accept the theory that someone lashed out in anger." The chief leaned back in his chair and steepled his fingers. "But he was shot. Someone had to bring a gun to the scene. Which looks more like premeditation. Unless, of course, Mr. Spottiswood had the bad luck to enrage someone who happened to be carrying a firearm. Were you aware that any of the decorators were armed?"

"If any of them were, it's news to me," I said. "Apart from

the gun Sarah's partner Kate tried to get her to take. I assume you heard about that."

The chief nodded.

"Given the amount of arguing, backbiting, and general nastiness going on in the house, if I'd known any of them were packing, I'd have ordered them to leave their guns at home, on pain of expulsion from the house. Remind me to suggest to Randall that we make that a rule for next year. No guns at the show house. New rule number two."

"What's new rule number one?" the chief asked. "No murders at the show house?"

"No packages sent to the show house," I said. "The amount of bickering and backbiting those stolen packages have caused . . . Incidentally, I'd already planned to come and see you this morning to see if you could do anything about the thefts. I wasn't sure any of the designers paid any attention when I told them to make a police report."

"Two of them did," he said. "Mrs. Martha Blaine and Mrs. Linda Dunn."

The other Martha and Our Lady of Chintz.

"But I didn't have enough officers to stake out the house, as Mrs. Blaine suggested," the chief went on. "And as I pointed out, a stakeout wouldn't do much good if, as they suggested, the thefts were an inside job."

"Did they suspect Clay?" I asked.

"Mrs. Blaine, rather presciently, did," the chief said. "Mrs. Dunn was more suspicious of the various workmen who frequented the house, particularly Mr. Cruz and Mr. Torres, who worked for Mr. Spottiswood."

"Tomás and Mateo?" I said. "I don't believe it. And do you really think two guys who speak little or no English would forge William Faulkner's and Charles Dickens's signatures on the UPS forms?"

"We were aware of that implausibility," the chief said. "We thought it was neighborhood juvenile delinquents."

"Very erudite delinquents," I said.

"The same ones who had been vandalizing the house this fall," Horace added.

"Vandalizing it how?"

"On several occasions, neighbors called us to report that there was activity in the house," the chief said. "We found wallboard ripped away from the walls, floorboards pulled up. As if someone was trying to destroy the house from the inside out. We were keeping our eyes on several neighborhood juveniles with troubled histories. So you can imagine how pleased the bank was when Randall Shiffley approached them offering to fix up the house if it could be used for the show house. Apparently your mother thought she had a house lined up, but it fell through at the last minute."

"She was planning to use our house," I said. "And it didn't fall through at the last minute. When she told us what she was planning, months ago, Michael and I both put our feet down. It just took her till the last minute to believe we were serious. That's the reason the show house didn't open up so people could tour it in the weeks before Christmas, which would have made a lot more sense. By the time Mother got it that she couldn't use our house, there wasn't much time for Randall to get this house ready."

"I see." The chief was trying to hide a smile and failing. "Would that have anything to do with your taking the job as coordinator?"

"Everything to do with it," I said. "I said I would do anything else she wanted, but if any decorators invaded our house, we'd set Spike on them."

"Very sensible," he said. "Some of the things they're doing to that house are mighty peculiar. Like gluing moss to the ceiling."

"Moss?" I repeated. "To the ceiling? Which room?"

"The one that looks like Dracula's lair," Horace said. "She's got Spanish moss hanging all around the edge of the room, and from the chandelier, and—"

"Good grief," I said. "Well, as long as she either takes it down when the house closes or reimburses us for doing it. But getting back to—"

"Where is he?" a woman was shouting in the main part of the house. "Where's Clay? I need to see him."

Chapter 18

The woman's words grew louder, and I could hear Sammy trying to calm her down and hold her back. With no success. She burst into the garage and looked around, puzzled at seeing us there. She was petite, buxom, redheaded, and probably attractive when she wasn't hysterical. She focused on me and her face contorted with rage.

"Who the hell are you and what are you doing here?" she shrieked, and launched herself at me, fingernails poised to attack. Horace and Sammy both grabbed her and held her back, taking damage in the process.

"Madam!" the chief roared.

The woman stopped struggling and fixed her gaze on him.

"I am Henry Burke, chief of police here in Caerphilly. Ms. Langslow is assisting me in an investigation. You have already opened yourself to charges of assaulting a police officer in the performance of his duties."

"*Two* police officers," Sammy corrected.

The chief favored him with a withering glance.

"Kindly cease this ridiculous behavior and tell me who you are and what you're doing here," the chief went on.

"My name is Felicia Granger, and Clay is my . . . my friend." She pulled herself up and stood still. Sammy and Horace let go of her, but stood ready in case she backslid.

Granger—she was probably the wife of the man who'd been following me the night before.

"And your purpose in coming here?" the chief asked.

Felicia seemed to wilt.

"We were supposed to see each other last night," she said. "He never showed up, and never returned my calls, and—did something happen to him?"

"I'm afraid Mr. Spottiswood is dead," the chief said, very gently.

Felicia uttered a shriek and fell in a small heap on the floor.

The chief and his officers seemed taken aback by the violence of her grief, and I ended up being the one to help her up, lead her back to the living room, plunk her down on the couch, and say "there, there" as she cried on my shoulder.

The chief had the presence of mind to send Sammy for a glass of water and Horace for a box of tissues, and then ordered them to get back to work searching Clay's house.

After a while, when Felicia's sobs finally subsided, she sat up, wiped her nose on the back of her hand, and looked over at the chief.

"How did he die?" she asked.

The chief paused, obviously weighing the effect of what he was about to say, before he answered.

"I'm afraid he was shot," he said.

"Oh, my God!" Felicia turned pale and clapped both hands over her mouth. "He did it! He really did it!"

"Who did it?" The chief sounded irritated. I could tell Felicia was wearing on his nerves. He wasn't the only one.

"My husband," she said. "Ex-husband. Well, not quite ex yet, but we've been separated for two months. And he hates

Clay. He said he'd kill him if he didn't leave me alone. Lots of times."

"That would be Mr. Gerald Granger?" the chief asked.

"Yes," she said. "Jerry's been threatening to—"

The door flew open, and Jerry himself burst in.

"Aha!" he exclaimed. "Caught you red-handed! I'm going to—what's going on here?"

"That's him," Felicia said, pointing to the new arrival. "That's Jerry."

"I have already met Mr. Granger," the chief said. "Sit down!" he snapped at the newcomer.

Mr. Granger flinched at the chief's fierce tone and scuttled over to the chair with surprising meekness. The chief scowled at him for a few moments, as if making sure he was planning to stay put. Then he turned back to me.

"Meg," he said. "Take Mrs. Granger to the garage and ask Sammy and Horace to keep an eye on her. I need to have a few words with Mr. Granger about his violation of the restraining order against him."

"You're going to arrest him, aren't you?" Felicia said, as I pulled her to her feet and started steering her toward the kitchen. "Because he did it."

"Somebody did the world a favor," Jerry said. "But it wasn't me."

"You bastard!" she shrieked. She tried to launch herself at him, but unlike Sammy and Horace, I had considerable experience dealing with juvenile tantrums. She wasn't a particularly large woman, so I slung her over my shoulder in a fireman's carry and hauled her out to the garage, still kicking and shrieking. Sometimes it comes in handy being not only taller than average but, thanks to my blacksmithing work, a lot stronger than most women.

"The chief says keep an eye on her," I said to Sammy and Horace, who looked alarmed at her return.

"Bitch," she said to me, but she seemed to have calmed down.

"What happened?" Sammy asked.

"My husband happened." Felicia grabbed Clay's recycling bin, turned it upside down to dump the contents on the garage floor, and sat on it, with her elbows on her knees and her head in her hands. "He killed Clay Spottiswood."

"He's a suspect," I said. "How did you and Clay meet, anyway?"

"He decorated our living room." Felicia shook her head. "You want to know the ironic thing? I didn't want to hire him in the first place. I actually preferred one of the other designers who gave us a proposal. But Jerry liked Clay's designs. Said he wanted a masculine look in the living room, not a lot of female frippery." She chuckled mirthlessly. "Bet now he wishes he'd picked Martha Blaine's design."

Interesting. Of course, I'd already figured out that in Caerphilly's relatively small interior design community, the major players all knew each other, and had done battle over potential clients many times. But given the antagonism I'd already seen between Clay and Martha . . .

"She tried to poison me against him, you know," Felicity said.

"Martha?"

"Yes. Tried to tell me all sorts of wild stories about him being a criminal or something. She's a piece of work. If Jerry wants to hire her to redo the room Clay decorated— well, at least I won't have to deal with her."

"So now what happens?" I said aloud. "With you and Jerry."

"Now that Clay's dead, you mean?" She shrugged.

"You don't think you'll get back together?"

"No." She shook her head. "Clay wasn't my true love. Just my exit strategy. I'm not going back to Jerry. I'm tired of him knocking me around."

But she looked so bleak that I wondered if she'd stick to that. I wouldn't want to bet against the notion that by next Christmas, she and Jerry would be back together.

Assuming neither one of them turned out to be Clay's killer.

"So where have you been staying?" I asked. "At the local women's shelter?"

"I didn't know we had a local women's shelter," she said. "And no, I've been staying with a friend in Westlake."

Westlake was one of the posher local suburbs, the sort of place where people who could afford decorators were apt to live. Her tone implied that people with friends rich enough to live in Westlake had no need of a women's shelter. I hoped she was right. Though I suspected the women I'd seen last night at the shelter were there out of fear, not economic need.

The chief stuck his head in.

"Mrs. Granger? We'd like you to come down with us to the station."

"Great," she said. "What did Jerry tell you?"

"Nothing yet," he said. "I'd rather talk to both of you down at the station."

She heaved herself off the recycling bin and headed toward the door. The chief stepped aside to allow room for her to pass. Sammy followed her.

"Horace is going to process those packages," the chief said. "And then he'll bring them back to the show house. We'd like to talk to each of the people whose packages were stolen."

"Okay." I nodded. "I gather Mr. Granger got out on bail this morning."

"Yes," the chief said. "But he won't be for long. Last month Judge Shiffley granted his wife a protective order against him. He violated that by showing up here. And it's his third violation, which means a mandatory six-months sentence."

"And what are the odds Judge Shiffley will let him make bail twice in less then twenty-four hours?" I asked.

"Slim." The chief smiled slightly. "We'll also be charging him for everything he got up to last night. Should hold him for a while."

"Long enough for you to figure out if he killed Clay?" I suggested.

The chief didn't answer, but his face wore a look of satisfying anticipation, like a cat who had a mouse cornered and was looking forward to playing with it.

"So did you figure out why Mr. Granger was following me last night?" I asked.

The chief frowned.

"I'm afraid that's partly our fault," he said. "I had him in for questioning yesterday—Martha Blaine suggested him as one of Mr. Spottiswood's clients who might have reason to dislike him."

"That's the understatement of the year," I muttered. And I suspected Martha had enjoyed having a chance to get back at the Grangers for choosing Clay over her.

"And while he was down at the station," the chief went on, "it appears he overheard several of my officers discussing their inability to locate Mrs. Granger for questioning. One of them suggested going over to the show house to ask someone with a connection to the Caerphilly women's shelter if Mrs. Granger had taken up residence there. Apparently, after spending some time observing the comings and goings at the show house, Mr. Granger decided that you were the connection."

"Based on what?"

"He was unable to articulate his reasons," the chief said. "He'd ingested a considerable quantity of alcohol. He was well past the legal limit when we administered the Breathalyzer."

"I should get back to the house," I said. I followed the chief back into the living room. Which was empty of feuding Grangers; I could see Sammy escorting Felicia to his cruiser. Another cruiser was pulling away, presumably with another deputy escorting Jerry.

"Now that he's safely locked up, I'm rather glad Mr. Granger showed up," I said. "After all, it's starting to look as if everyone in the house is alibied, and if none of the designers did it—"

Oops. Probably not the smartest thing in the world to let the chief know I'd been poking around behind his back. He was frowning.

"Sorry," I said. "But we're all there together all day. The designers talk to each other—and to me. Everyone who has an alibi is thrilled, and wants everyone to know all about it."

"Mr. Granger is only a suspect at this point," he said. "And the designers are not all completely alibied. Unless you know differently."

That sounded like an invitation to share.

"Well," I said. "Mother was with family, and Martha was serving as designated driver and chief nurse for Violet, who was soused, and the Quilt Ladies were at Caerphilly Assisted Living, and Eustace was with his AA sponsee—"

"Ah," the chief said. "That explains why he said he'd have to get back to me with his alibi."

"Oh, dear," I said. "I hope I wasn't supposed to keep that part a secret. Don't tell him I spilled it. And he didn't tell me the name. And Sarah was neutering cats—"

"Doing what?"

"Neutering cats. Feral cats. With Clarence."

"I think I could have lived without that image," he said, shaking his head. "She only told me she was working at the animal shelter."

"Who does that leave? Oh. Ivy. I don't know about Ivy."

"Home alone with a migraine, which doesn't prove much," he said. "But it's possible the snow will alibi her."

"The snow?" I had a brief image of the chief with his pen poised over his notebook, attempting to interrogate a falling flake.

"One of her neighbors is an avid amateur photographer," the chief said. "And particularly fond of snowy landscapes without a single footprint in them. Apparently, due to her headache, Ivy did not emerge to shovel until sometime in the afternoon, and the neighbor took a great many pictures of the virginal snow in her front and backyard. Horace is analyzing them, and thinks it likely that she'll be alibied."

"Oh, good," I said. "And did Our Lady—did Linda talk to you about her alibi?"

"Also home alone," he said.

"Home alone, but online," I said. "You got my e-mail about that, right? Because while I don't understand it myself, I gather if she really was online, it might be provable."

"I've already spoken to our department's computer forensic consultants," he said.

"And Vermillion was with the Reverend Robyn, at the

women's shelter. The location of which I'm busily trying to forget."

"I don't actually know it myself," the chief said. "I suppose they let you in on the secret because of your gender."

"They didn't let me in on the secret," I said. "Vermillion has absolutely no idea how to be discreet and furtive. She might as well be driving around with a neon sign on her car saying 'Please don't follow me! I'm going someplace I don't want anyone to know about.'"

"I'll speak to the Reverend Smith," the chief said, with a smile. "Offer to give her couriers some lessons on defensive driving. I used to be pretty good at it, back in my undercover days in Baltimore. I don't think I've quite forgotten everything I used to know. And I feel I owe them something, after my department inadvertently alerted Mr. Granger to their existence."

"That would be great," I said. "But anyway, with so many of the designers alibied, it must be very satisfying to find some fresh, juicy suspects."

"I'd rather just find the killer," he said. "But yes, Mrs. Granger and her jealous husband bear looking into. As does the disgruntled client Stanley told me about, the one who was suing Mr. Spottiswood. Meanwhile, there's another small matter you can help me with."

"Glad to," I said.

"That student reporter you mentioned—the one who was visiting the house the day Mr. Spottiswood was killed."

"And was wandering around for quite a while, taking photos. Yes."

"I wanted to follow up on your suggestion that I look at her photos. What was her name again?"

"Jessica," I said. "Sorry—I can't remember her last name. You can probably find her through the paper."

"But you're sure it was Jessica?"

"Yes—why?"

"I dropped by the student paper office today," he said. "Only one person there holding down the fort, since the college is on Christmas break. But she didn't remember anyone sending a reporter over to do a story on the show house. And they don't have a Jessica on staff. She looked through all their files."

He let me ponder that for a while.

"Maybe Jessica's trying to wangle a spot on their staff by coming up with a good story," I suggested at last. "Maybe she's off writing up her exciting account of the show house where one of the designers was murdered. The paper's on hiatus until classes start up again, so she'd have no reason to turn it in yet."

"Maybe." He didn't sound as if he found the idea too plausible.

"Damn! I didn't ask her for any credentials." I was getting angry now. "I sent a press release over to the student paper, and a week later, someone shows up saying she's here to write a story. I fell for it."

"It's a natural mistake."

"She played me."

"So let's find her. Ask her what she was up to."

"How?"

"I've called the student records office," he said. "They have photos of all the students in their files. Go down there and they'll show you all the Jessicas."

"All the Jessicas? You think they'll have a lot of them?"

"Did you know that between 1981 and 1997, Jessica was either the number one or number two most popular name in this country? And it hasn't been out of the top two hundred since 1965."

I closed my eyes and sighed.

"So yes, there are quite a lot of them. And if none of the Jessicas look familiar, they're going to let you thumb through the whole student photo file. Women students, anyway."

"If she's there, I'll find her," I said.

"And meanwhile, in case she's not there. I'm arranging to bring in a sketch artist," he said. "So call me as soon as you identify her . . . or when you've looked through all the records."

So much for having a productive day.

Chapter 19

I drove over to the campus and prowled around until I found a parking space reasonably close to the administration building. If classes had been in session, I might almost as well have walked from Clay's house, but most of the students were gone now. And the administration building wasn't all that close to any of the shops and restaurants being overrun by holiday tourists and locals alike.

The student records office was festively decorated with tinsel and evergreens and a small tree in the corner, but I detected no signs of Christmas spirit in the single glum staffer sitting behind the information counter.

"You must be the one here for the Jessicas." She stood up and walked over to open a little gate and let me behind the counter that separated visitors from staff. "We've got all the student photos in a database. Should be online, really, but our IT guys are always too backed up to get to it. I've got you set up here at this computer."

She pointed to a desk toward the back of the room.

"Thanks," I said. "Please tell me you're not here right now just to let me in."

"No," she said. "My boss insists that we have someone here any day that's not a federal holiday. I drew short straw this year. I'm Jen, by the way."

"Meg."

We shook hands. She showed me how to page through

the photos. Then she drifted back to her desk, picked up her coffee mug, and came back to sit on the file cabinet beside me, where she could watch as I paged through the photos.

"Why are you looking for this kid, anyway?" she asked after a while.

"She pretended to be a reporter from the student newspaper," I said. "But they don't have a Jessica. And she might have information relevant to a case Chief Burke is working on."

"The murder," she said, nodding. "Is she a suspect?"

"No idea. Is this all the Jessicas you've got?"

"Guess she was using a fake name. I can show you the rest of the women students. Hang on a sec."

She leaned over, punched a few keys. Large numbers of men and women students appeared on the screen. Another few keystrokes and the men disappeared.

"Help yourself," she said.

It took an hour, during which I found out all about the family Christmas revels Jen's boss was keeping her from enjoying, and her plans to look for a new job after the holidays.

Michael's mother called me once, right in the middle of my search.

"What's your family's gluten situation?"

I looked at the phone in dismay.

"I had no idea we had a gluten situation," I said finally. "What kind of situation?"

"I meant, are a lot of your family going gluten free, or is it safe to have rolls and a bread-based stuffing?"

"I think it's safe to have rolls," I said. "As long as you don't force anyone to eat them at gunpoint. But I have no idea how many people are avoiding gluten. Maybe a gluten-free stuffing would be best."

"I'll do both, then," she said, and hung up.

"Mother-in-law," I said to Jen.

"Tell me about it."

I persevered to the end, from the Abramses and Addisons all the way to the Zooks and Zuckers, but finally I had to admit defeat.

"She's not here," I said.

"Could be a townie," Jen said. "A lot of townies pretend to be students at the college. Especially if they're trying to get into bars."

"Yeah, but this one wasn't trying to get into a bar. She was touring a half-completed decorator show house."

"Was there anything missing after she left?"

"Good question," I said. I wasn't about to mention the gun that might have gone missing.

"You should check carefully," she said. "We've started seeing a lot of it. Crooks in their teens or early twenties. They come here and they just blend in. Everyone looks at them and sees students. If you don't know them you just figure they're transfer students, or students in a department whose building is on the other side of campus. It's not like a neighborhood where people get to know each other and call the police if they see a stranger hanging around."

"You're right," I said. "Unfortunately, there's not much we can do in hindsight."

We wished each other a merry Christmas and I left. She seemed sorry to see me go. Clearly her boss's desire to have someone in the office wasn't motivated by a heavy workload. I suspected I had been the highlight of an otherwise boring day.

I waited till I was outside again to call the police.

"No dice," I said. "Jessica was definitely not a student."

"Blast," he said. That was usually as close to cursing as the chief went, so I knew he was seriously frustrated.

"I'm heading back to the house," I said. "Unless you need me to do anything else."

"Just be careful," he said.

As soon as I stepped in the door of the show house, Sarah and Violet came running to meet me.

"Did you hear?" Sarah said. "The police found all our packages."

"Clay did have them after all," Violet said. "What a horrible man!"

"Martha was livid," Sarah said. "If he wasn't already dead, I think she'd probably strangle him over this."

"And I'd probably help her," Mother said from the doorway of her room.

I was still taking off my coat when Randall pulled up in a panel truck.

"Got that new mattress for Clay's room," he said, as he came in the front door. "Can anyone help me haul it in?"

Eustace said a few words in Spanish to Tomás and Mateo, and they raced out the door.

"And I found some black sheets and a bedspread to replace the damaged ones," Randall went on, handing me a bag from a well-known discount chain. "Had to send my cousin Mervyn down to Richmond for them."

"Excellent," I said, pulling the package of sheets out of the bag.

"These are cotton polyester blend," Eustace said, in a tone of utter horror.

"Yeah," Randall said. "That's what Mervyn could find down in Richmond. Not a hot item in the River City, black sheets."

"Clay's were Egyptian cotton with a fifteen hundred thread count," Eustace said.

"And now they're locked up in the Caerphilly Police Department's evidence room," Randall said. "And even if the chief let us have them back, between the bloodstains and damage from the ax the killer used to wreck the room, they don't look so pretty."

"I seem to remember Clay saying he had to special order the sheets from somewhere," I said. "And they took forever to get here. Even if we knew his source, it's not as if we have the time to order them all over again."

"And it's also not as if the people coming through the house are going to wallow on the sheets," Randall said. "We'll probably have a docent in here to make sure no one touches a thing."

"Well, go ahead," Eustace said. "Who knows? If you actually put those sorry things on the bed in Clay's room, he just might rise from the dead to smite you, and save Chief Burke the trouble of solving his murder."

With that he strode majestically back to his own room.

"Do you really think anyone will notice?" I asked Mother. "Or care?"

"If anyone does, we can tell them it was a deliberate design decision on Clay's part," Mother said.

I suspected this was a subtle attempt to sabotage Clay's posthumous reputation, but I didn't really care.

Tomás and Mateo appeared at the front door, carrying the mattress. I followed them upstairs and watched as they efficiently put it in place and left, taking the packaging materials with them.

I opened the package of sheets—okay, they weren't the softest I'd ever felt, but they looked fine. I made the bed, and topped it off with a matching black coverlet.

And someone had responded to my pleas for design assistance and added a few token Christmas decorations. The dresser now held a red bowl filled with gold-painted magnolia leaves, flanked by two red candles in black glass holders. Not my idea of a proper Christmas decoration—it was beautiful but cold and uninviting, and I couldn't help comparing it to our house, where Mother had achieved beautifully decorated rooms that seemed to welcome friends, toys, dogs, carols, cups of hot chocolate, and Christmas cookies. But I had to admit that the bowl and candles looked like precisely what I'd have expected of Clay.

Mother, Eustace, and Martha appeared in the doorway as I was surveying the room.

"Very nice," Mother said.

"I suppose it will have to do," Eustace said.

"My thanks to whoever brought in the decorations," I said.

"Seemed like his kind of thing," Martha said.

"The room still needs something," I said. I winced as soon as the words left my mouth. How many times had I heard the designers say that about a room that looked just fine to me. But in this case, I thought I was right. "The walls look pretty bare."

"He might have been planning to leave them that way," Eustace said. "His rooms always looked a little bare to me."

"I think Clay would have used the words 'uncluttered' and 'clean' and 'minimalist' to describe his work," Martha said.

I glanced over in surprise. She sounded almost melancholy.

"But I think Meg's right about the room needing something," she went on. "Not a lot—just a few well-chosen pieces of art on the walls. The problem is, without him here to do the choosing, I don't see how we can possibly decide what."

"Didn't Randall find his design sketches, dear?" Mother asked. "What do they show?"

"They show art there, and there, and there." I pointed to

the three biggest bare spots. "But the art is indicated by a rough rectangle. Nothing in his almost nonexistent notes gives me any idea what he had in mind."

"You see?" Martha said. "Impossible. We shouldn't even try."

"So while the room may need something," Eustace said, "I think its needs will have to remain unfulfilled. You can't always get what you want."

"Martha, dear, I think you're in a lot better position to decide what that something is than we are," Mother said. "You're so good at that elegant simplicity he was clearly trying to emulate. Much better than Clay, actually."

Nicely flattered, I thought.

"Yeah." Martha did look pleased.

"And you've known him longer than any of us," Eustace added.

Martha didn't like that as much.

"Don't remind me," she said. "Well, I'll think about it. By the way, I was right, wasn't I?"

"Right about what?" I asked.

"Clay was the one stealing the packages," she said. "You didn't believe me."

"I didn't disbelieve you," I said. "But without any kind of proof—"

"Well, it's water under the bridge now," she said. "The bastard won't be doing it again. I've got work to do."

She strode out.

"Which means she's going to ignore my request for help with the room," I said. "Because if she did a really good job on Clay's room, it would reduce her already small chance of winning the best room contest."

"Her rooms are very nice," Mother said.

"Yeah, but they're two bathrooms and a laundry room,"

I said. "You really think the judges are going to be that impressed?"

Mother nodded as if conceding my point.

"Look, you guys are busy," I said. "I'll take care of it."

"You, dear?"

"Is my taste that awful?"

"No, dear, but Clay's room isn't very much to your taste, is it?" she said.

"True," I said. "I thought I'd ask Vermillion for some help. They've both got that black-and-red color thing going on."

Mother and Eustace both froze.

"I think she's kidding," Mother said, after a few moments.

"I certainly hope so," Eustace muttered.

"I was," I said. "Actually, I know exactly what to hang there. Clay's own paintings."

Mother and Eustace were silent, and obviously startled. But they didn't ask, "What do you mean, his own paintings?" Interesting.

"I suppose that would work," Mother said.

"Assuming you can find any of his paintings," Eustace said. "It's not something he'd ever have done, though. I think he was trying to forget his old life."

"If he was trying to forget it, then why did he have some of his paintings hanging in his living room?" I asked. "At least I'm pretty sure they're his. I saw them when the chief called me over to look at the packages Clay stole—you heard about that, right?"

They nodded.

"I don't think he was trying to forget his old life," I went on. "Just trying to hide it from the rest of the world."

"Which means he'd definitely never have hung his own

paintings in the show house," Eustace said. "But now that he's gone—why not? Can't hurt him now. And it's about the only thing I can think to put there that would be absolutely, undeniably his work."

"Yes," Mother said. "A good idea."

"Just out of curiosity," I went on. "Does everyone know about Clay's checkered past?"

They exchanged a look.

"People will talk," Mother said.

"Martha will talk," Eustace said. "And she's not exactly an unbiased source. I assumed she was just spreading lies about Clay until I checked with a friend who runs a gallery in New York."

"And he confirmed her story?" I asked.

"He told me the facts, which were a lot less damning than Martha made them out to be," Eustace said. "To hear her talk, you'd think he was a serial killer who'd gotten off with a slap on the wrist."

"Well, she had considerable provocation," Mother said.

"To slander the guy?"

"Slander is a little strong, don't you think?" Mother murmured.

They went back to their rooms, still amicably debating whether Martha's dislike of Clay had motivated her to judge his past actions too harshly. I left them to it.

I pulled out my cell phone and called the chief about getting back into the house to borrow Clay's paintings.

"I have no objection," he said. "But I think you should get permission from the estate first."

"Do we even know who inherits?" I asked.

"A brother in Richmond," the chief said. "Runs a used-car dealership there. I can give you his number."

"Do you think it's okay to call so soon after Clay's death?" I asked.

"I didn't get the feeling he was too distraught," the chief said. "They hadn't seen each other in five years."

The brother was, at first, baffled by my request.

"Sure I can sell you the paintings," he said. "If we can agree on a price. But not till we finish probating the estate, and who knows how long that will take."

"I don't want to buy the paintings," I said. "I want to borrow them. To display in the show house, in the room Clay decorated."

"Show house?"

"The last project he did before his untimely death," I said. "As a memorial to his life and work."

I was laying it on a bit thick, but the brother didn't seem to be grasping the concept.

"I'm not sure we want to do that," he said. "They could be worth something. Not my cup of tea, but for a while there he was getting a pretty high price for them."

"Yes, but he's fallen off the radar in the last fifteen years," I said. "An artist needs to keep producing new work to keep people interested, and I got the impression he hasn't been painting these last few years."

"Not since he went off to prison," the brother said. "He came and stayed with me when he got out. I thought maybe he'd start up painting again, but he never did. Just hung around moping until I told him he had to get a job or get out."

"What happened then?" I asked.

"He managed to get a job working for a woman decorator," he said. "Old girlfriend of his."

"What was her name?" I asked.

"Martha something," the brother said.

Interesting. Clay wasn't just Martha's hated rival. He was also her hated ex.

"He knew her from high school, I think. Moved out of my basement and into her fancy West End house. And the next thing I knew, he's a *decorator* himself."

Heavy sarcasm on the word "decorator." Was he implying that his brother wasn't much of a decorator? Or indicating that he didn't think much of decorating as a career choice?

"You didn't approve?" I asked aloud.

"More like he didn't approve of me. Didn't want to have anything to do with a used-car salesman. We weren't getting along when he left, and I haven't heard much from him since. I'm just hoping he hasn't left a whole bunch of debts for me to take care of."

I saw my opening.

"Well, if he has left debts, selling the paintings could help out, couldn't it?" I said. "Assuming you can get his name out there again to raise the price. Displaying the paintings in the show house will help make him visible again. Hundreds and hundreds of affluent people will be going through that house, seeing the paintings in the best possible setting. And if anyone asks if they're for sale, we can steer them to you. When you combine that with the publicity that's bound to follow when the media find out his real name—well, I wouldn't be surprised if the price you can get for the paintings went up considerably."

"Ah," he said. "Well, that might be something we could think about doing."

"And we'll post a cash bond for the appraised value of the paintings, to ensure their safe return, and give you credit in the program as a major sponsor."

"You've got a deal."

Okay, we had a deal, but it took a little while to hash out

the terms. Program credit turned into an ad for the brother's car dealership, but he agreed to fax me permission to borrow as much of Clay's artwork as I wanted.

"Not just a former boss but a former girlfriend," I muttered after I hung up. Should I tell the chief about this, or would he already know it? Of course, Martha had an alibi—unless the chief had found a problem with it. But what if one of Clay's more recent flames found out about their shared history and thought they were rekindling their old romance? I'd have thought they were more likely to rekindle the St. Valentine's Day Massacre, but who knows what crazy ideas someone who hadn't seen them together might get. Someone like Felicia Granger, for example.

I'd figure out how to share this with the chief later. Right now I had work to do. I called Randall to saddle him with the job of arranging for the appraisal and the bond. I called the program designer and told her to figure out a way to work the ad in before she delivered the program to the printer today. And then I called the chief to ask if he could let me into Clay's house.

"Can you meet Deputy Butler over there in fifteen minutes?" he asked.

"I'm already out the door," I said. "By the way—Clay's brother seems to think that he and Martha were an item at one time."

"Does he now?" the chief said. "Thanks."

So much for finding out whether the chief already knew.

Chapter 20

While I was driving over to Clay's house, my phone rang. Michael's mother again. Probably more cooking questions.

Sure enough, when I pulled up in front of Clay's house, there was a voice mail.

"Meg? Are you there? Your brother told me there was a pie your family always likes to have at Christmas. Could you call to give me the recipe?"

"Later," I muttered, as I scrambled up the walk to meet Aida Butler.

"Girl, are you okay?" she asked. "You look frazzled."

"Gee, thanks," I said. "I feel frazzled. I cannot wait till this show house is over."

"And these paintings you're picking up are part of that?"

"A big part."

She opened up the door and I followed her in.

"Stay here while I check the house," she said. She didn't pull out her gun, but she was clearly not just going through the motions. I reflected that since Aida was even taller than me and entered Ironman competitions in her spare time, she was probably at least as good a bodyguard as anyone on the force.

I waited in the living room, trying to be alert for sounds around me. And studying Clay's paintings, trying to imagine how they'd look in the house.

"All clear," she said, returning to the living room.

"Was that just standard procedure?" I asked. "Or do you have reason to worry that someone might be in here?"

"The killer's still on the loose," she said. "And more to the point, this is a house known to be unoccupied. Open invitation to vandalism. These the paintings you want?"

I nodded.

"They're good," Aida said. "But I'm not sure I'd want any of them on my wall. Looking at those things day-in day-out could make you slit your wrists."

I could see that. They were dark and bleak and uncompromising. And as far as I could tell, very good. I wouldn't want them on my wall, either, but if they were in a museum I could see going back to visit them more than once. Why would anyone who could do something this good ever stop?

I could worry about that later. For the moment, the important thing was that, as I'd remembered, they were the right sizes for the blank spaces in Clay's room. And they were painted mostly in black and gray, with a few muted browns and greens and the occasional stark splash of white or red. They'd fit in perfectly with the décor in his room.

"Help me get this thing down," I said, indicating the cityscape.

The canvas was huge, at least four by five feet, and heavier than we expected. As we were easing it down to the floor, Aida lost control of her end and it slammed down on her foot.

"Owwwww!" she shrieked, and began hopping around on her good foot. "Rainbows! Rainbows!"

"Are you okay?" I asked. Rainbows? Was she becoming delirious?

"No, I'm not okay," she moaned. "That thing hurts like a son-of-a—rainbows! Rainbows! Dammit, *rainbows!*"

She pulled off her heavy shoe and her sock and we

looked at her foot. Apparently the corner of the painting had landed on her big toe. The nail was turning black, and the whole toe looked bruised.

"Only time I've ever been grateful for these plug-ugly shoes they make us wear," she muttered. "That thing could have taken my whole toe off."

"You probably broke it," I said. "Go down to the ER. And what's with the rainbows?"

"Trying to clean up my language," she said. "You know our new civilian employee? That prissy little twerp who just started helping out at the front desk? He accused me of creating a hostile work environment, just 'cause I dropped the F-bomb a few times when I was ticked off about something. And the chief said he wouldn't discipline me, but could I please find something else to say."

"And how can anyone object to the word 'rainbows'?" I said, laughing.

"Well, it's starting to make the twerp really nervous whenever I say it," Aida said. "But he hasn't complained, so that's something. Did we damage the painting?"

We hadn't. I suspected Aida was a little disappointed at that. She stared at it balefully while putting her sock and shoe back on.

"No way that thing's ever gonna fit in your car," she said. She stood up and winced a little.

"You're right." I pulled out my phone and punched one of my speed-dial numbers. "Randall," I said. "Can you spare a truck?"

Aida and I wrestled all three paintings off the walls and into the foyer.

"Did you see any signs that he was still painting?" I asked while we were waiting for Randall.

"You mean like an easel?" she asked.

"Or unfinished canvases. Or paints."

"No, but I wasn't looking for that. Let's take a look."

It didn't take us long. Clay wasn't into clutter. In fact, he wasn't into much of anything that we could see.

"Likes to travel light," Aida said. "I hear it happens sometimes with ex-cons."

And no sign that he was painting.

We did find an unfinished painting in his attic—a nude study of a blond woman. Her voluptuous body was rendered in minute detail, but the head was sketchy, merely a flesh-colored patch on the canvas with the barest suggestion of features. From the amount of dust on it I deduced he hadn't abandoned it recently.

"Not bad," Aida said. "But if you're thinking about putting that in the show house, I'd think again."

She had a point, and not just because the painting was unfinished. It wasn't just sensual—it was lascivious. Provocative. Way too controversial for our small-town show house.

I took a couple of pictures of it with my phone, and then we put it back where we'd found it—shoved away in a corner of the attic—and went downstairs again.

"You're right," I said. "Not a good idea to use that painting. But damn, it's good. I didn't like Clay, and I can't say I'll miss him all that much, but I'd like to have seen what else he'd have done if he'd started painting again."

"Maybe he was planning to," Aida said. "Isn't this a sketchbook?"

She picked up something sitting on the coffee table and handed it to me—an eight-and-a-half by eleven notebook bound in black faux leather. I opened it to the first page and found myself looking at a sketch of a nude woman. Recognizably Felicia, though a lot more voluptuous than I remembered her as being. Maybe Clay was trying to flatter her.

"Okay," Aida said. "I see why Jerry Granger might be a bit put out if he caught sight of that."

Just then we heard a heard a knock on the door.

"I'll get it," Aida said. "Just in case it's not Randall."

I flipped through a few more pages in the sketchbook. Several more flattering sketches of Felicia. A distinctly unflattering but highly recognizable one of Jerry Granger. Until I saw Clay's sketch, I hadn't quite realized how large Jerry's jaw was, or how Neanderthal it made him look.

On the next page was a sketch of Ivy. Ivy in the show house, hunched over in a corner of the hallway with a paintbrush in her hand, peering at the wall she was painting. He'd exaggerated the height of the walls looming over her, so she looked more like a mouse than a human. But unlike the one of Jerry, this sketch didn't feel unkind or mocking. More . . . bemused.

I kept turning the pages. Apparently this was a very recent sketchbook—all the denizens of the show house were there. I could tell he didn't like Mother—he'd sketched her looking at Ivy's Snow Queen mural, and made the Snow Queen look the warmer of the two. He didn't like Eustace either, but about the only unflattering thing he did was exaggerate Eustace's neat little paunch into a huge Santa-like belly.

He had a wicked take on Linda, showing her in her room, not only surrounded by chintz but even dressed in it, and when you looked at her feet you saw that she was gradually being sucked in, as if the chintz were quicksand and she its unwary prey. And of course he'd turned Vermillion into a stereotypical vampy figure reminiscent of Morticia Addams, which showed he hadn't looked too closely at her.

I was surprised that the sketches he'd done of me were pretty accurate and made me look reasonably good. Violet and Sarah came off pretty well, too. And he had a sketch of

Martha that was downright flattering. Flattering and noticeably younger than she was.

One sketch stopped me cold—a sketch of Clay himself. He'd been a handsome man. Not my type—too brooding and saturnine. But handsome. Probably a real heartbreaker when he was in his twenties, back in his New York art world days. Funny that I couldn't remember noticing his good looks when I'd first met him, probably because he'd barged into the middle of a conversation I'd been having with Sarah, intent on bullying me into something or other, and after that it was all downhill. Looking at his sketch made me sad. It was accurate enough, but somehow not the least bit flattering. I hadn't liked Clay, but I felt sorry for the man who'd drawn himself with such mockery, self-loathing, and pitiless honesty.

I couldn't understand why anyone with Clay's talent would give up his art. And I couldn't decide who to be angrier with: Clay, for doing so, or the killer who'd removed any hope that he'd ever change his mind.

The sketch of Clay was the last one in the book. No, wait—I flipped past several blank pages and came across another one.

Martha. But not the flattering version that had appeared earlier in the sketchbook. This one was a nude that showed every blemish, bulge, and bit of sagging skin with cruel precision. And her face didn't have the pleasant, almost dreamy look of the first sketch but a look of utter fury, as if he'd imagined how she'd react if he showed her the sketch. Imagined, or maybe seen?

And the pose—wasn't it curiously similar to the one in the unfinished painting in the attic? I pulled out my phone to check. No, not just similar. Exactly the same pose. Only with fifteen or twenty years added—that, and a whole lot of anger.

"Meg?" Aida called. "You coming?"

"On my way."

If this were my sketchbook, I'd have torn out that last drawing. No one deserved to see that kind of hateful picture of herself. But it wasn't mine, so I tucked the sketchbook into my tote. If anyone challenged me on it, I could say that I was keeping my options open in case one of the paintings proved too big for its space. My permission form from the brother did say as much artwork as I needed, not just paintings. And in the meantime I could glance through it and learn more about Clay. And of course, I could always take it to the chief if I thought any of the sketches had any relevance to the murder case.

Out in the foyer, Randall was standing with his arms crossed, staring at the paintings.

"Someone wasn't taking his Prozac." He shook his head as if throwing off a baneful influence. "I brought some furniture pads to wrap them in."

Randall and I hauled the paintings back to the show house, and he helped me hang them.

"Looks good," Randall said. "Not that I like the paintings all that much, but they look better here in this room. The red walls sort of keep them from being such a downer."

"They're still a downer."

Martha was standing in the doorway, glaring at us. She stepped into the room and did a quick survey. Was I only imagining it or did she relax just a little when she'd seen all three paintings. Did she know about the unfinished painting that was probably of her?

"Why'd you pick these paintings, anyway?" she asked.

"I didn't exactly pick them," I said. "These three were the only ones he had." At least the only paintings that were complete, and framed. It wasn't such a big lie.

"Seriously?" Martha asked.

I nodded.

"Damn," she said. "I wonder what happened to the rest of them. He was prolific, once upon a time." She made "prolific" sound like a put-down.

"Maybe he sold them all," I suggested.

"No." She shook her head. "Not a lot of his work is out in the market. Whoever owns these will make a mint on them, now that he's dead."

"His brother will be happy to hear that," I said. "It seems he's inherited these."

"There could be others out there," Martha said. "The chief should look into that. Follow the money. See if someone, like his dealer, has a stash of them ready to put on the market."

"I thought Clay murdered his dealer," I said.

She looked startled at that. Was she surprised that I knew? Or just surprised at my bluntness?

"True," she said. "No use trying to contact his original dealer. But he could have gotten another one."

"Unless he gave up painting entirely," I suggested.

"Maybe he did." She was staring at the cityscape now. "What a waste. All that talent gone."

She didn't look as if she were sad over the waste. She looked as if she couldn't decide whether to feel envious of the talent or triumphant that its owner was dead.

"He was very talented," I said.

"Yeah," Martha said. "Always thought he was a cut above everyone else because he was an artist. And look at him now. He's dead, and the used-car salesman gets his precious paintings."

She said it with such venom that I was speechless.

"Well, life goes on," she said after a few moments. "And my rooms aren't going to finish themselves."

She left.

"If you ask me," Randall said, "she's lucky her alibi checks out."

"You're sure it does?" I asked.

"The chief seems pretty focused on the Grangers right now," Randall said. "And he's checking out the possibility that the killer was someone blackmailing Clay over his prison history."

"That doesn't make sense," I said.

"Does to me," Randall said. "I'm not sure how all those rich clients of Clay's would feel if they found out they were hiring an ex-con. And a convicted murderer, no less."

"Yeah, but why would the blackmailer kill Clay?" I asked. "Clay killing the blackmailer, maybe. But why would the blackmailer kill the goose that's laying golden eggs?"

"Clay had a temper," Randall said. "Maybe they quarreled, and the blackmailer killed him in self-defense."

"Maybe," I said. "Anyway, not our problem. I hereby declare this room finished. And in the nick of time."

"Today's not the nick of time," he said. "That would be tomorrow morning, when the photographer rings the doorbell."

He picked up his tools and tarps and headed for the door.

"I bet you'll be glad to work on something other than this house," I said, as I followed him downstairs.

"Will I ever," he said. "But that's water under the bridge. If we can just keep from having any fresh disasters, maybe we can make us some money for the historical society."

I noticed he tapped lightly on the woodwork as he said it.

"Assuming anyone wants to come to a show house where someone was murdered," I said.

"Oh, they'll come all right," he said. "It's the notoriety. Like having our shindig in Lizzie Borden's old house."

"Lizzie Borden's a lot more famous than whoever killed Clay will ever be."

"Yeah, but we've got recent and local on our side," he said. "No, I'm not worried about people coming to the show house. Now, the bank's a little worried about who's going to buy the house. It's one thing to visit a famous murder scene and another to live in it."

"Fortunately, not our problem," I said.

"Fortunately," he agreed. "I expect someone will buy it sooner or later, given the housing shortage here in town. And I have to say, it's been an interesting house to work on."

"With all these different personalities, you mean?"

"And interesting in and of itself," he said. "Didn't I ever tell you about all the hidey-holes we found?"

"Hidey-holes?"

"Secret compartments all over the house. Like in the back of one of the kitchen cabinets there was a false panel you could slide up to find a little hollowed out place between the studs. And in the master bath, if you took the drawers out of the vanity you'd find a door to another hiding place under the eaves. And in the front bedroom, the one that now looks like Dracula's castle, one on either side of the window seat. Someone had fun with it, making secret compartments every place where most houses would have little pockets of dead air and lost space. And there were a couple of places you could lift up floorboards to find secret compartments. All told, a couple dozen hidey-holes."

"What was in them?"

"Nothing," he said. "We'd get excited every time we found one. Me and the boys spent hours, poking and prodding to find every single secret hidey-hole. But not a single one of them had anything inside but dust."

"Not by the time you got to them," I said slowly. "But what if there was something in them at one time?"

"I'm sure there was, sometime or other," he said. "I was thinking most likely a drug dealer built them to hide his stash."

"Or a miser who didn't trust banks," I suggested. "Or a woman who wanted to keep her jewelry with her instead of putting it in a bank vault. Or maybe just someone who thought they were cool and would amuse the kids by hiding toys and candy in them."

"That's an idea," he said, chuckling. "Make it sound all romantic. Maybe the bank will have an easier time selling the house if people think there's gold and jewels hidden away inside it."

"Maybe that's the reason for all the vandalism that happened in the house this fall," I said. "Maybe it wasn't really vandalism—maybe someone suspected there might be secret compartments and broke into the house to look for them."

"Well, they did find a couple of the compartments," he said. "Looked like an accident to me, though. And a lot of the damage wasn't to anything that could possibly have a secret compartment in it. Just pure meanness."

"Maybe that's what you were meant to think," I said. "If I didn't want anyone to know I was breaking down a wall to find a secret compartment in it, maybe I'd just do a lot of random damage all around."

Randall looked thoughtful.

"They were pretty persistent," he said. "Kept trying to break in even after Chief Burke put on extra patrols in the area. I suggested putting in a security system—the bank wasn't too crazy about the expense, but I think they'd have gone for it eventually. Then the idea of the show house came up, and I figured whoever was doing it was scared off by all the activity—first me and my workmen, and then all the decorators."

"Who used to live in the house?" I asked.

"Nobody," he said. "Like I said, it's been vacant—"

"For six years, yes," I said. "But before that?"

"Family named Green," he said. "Not from around here, and they moved away after the bank took their house. Why?"

"What if one of the Greens is trying to find something they left here?" I asked. "In one of those hidey-holes?"

"Something that's still here after six years?"

"What if Clay wasn't killed because anyone had a grudge against him but because he was unlucky enough to be here when the prowler broke in?"

He thought about it for a few moments.

"No crazier than some of the other stuff I've seen lately. Tell the chief, and maybe he can track down the Greens."

"Randall?" It was Mother. "Could I borrow you for just a moment?"

"Later," he said to me as he followed Mother.

I went upstairs and looked around the master bedroom. I brushed a few specks of dust off the glossy black dresser and plumped the pillows on the bed. I was starting to feel a little bit proprietary about the room.

What would I do if I walked in and found someone hacking at its walls with an ax? I liked to think I'd retreat to safety and call 9-1-1. But Clay had a hot temper.

"We need to find out more about the Greens," I murmured.

Chapter 21

I was sure the chief could easily track down the Greens if he wanted to. But he might be too busy interrogating the Grangers right now. Which was fine if either Felicia or Jerry turned out to be the killer, but I wasn't sure I believed that. Or maybe he was looking for whoever had been black-mailing Clay, but I wasn't sure I believed that either—at least not as a motive for the murder.

It occurred to me that while it would be up to the chief to track them down, I might be able to find out a little bit about the Greens. All I needed to do was find a neighbor who'd been living here six years ago.

I stepped outside, went down the front walk to the edge of the street, and looked up and down.

Which house to try first?

I started with the house directly across the street. It would have the best view of the former Green house. There weren't any cars in the driveway, but some people do keep their garages tidy enough to have room for cars. But after several minutes of knocking and waiting, with no answer, I gave up and strolled back to the sidewalk to try again.

The house to the left of the one I'd just tried hadn't even had its front walk or driveway plowed, so I marked that off my mental list. But the one to the right had a shoveled walk and driveway. It was smaller and older than most of the houses in the neighborhood. I decided to try it.

I was delighted when the door opened to reveal an alert old lady wearing a purple velour top and matching leggings.

"Good morning," I said. "I'm Meg Langslow, the organizer for the show house the historical society is putting on across the way."

She cocked her head slightly, as if curious, but took my offered hand.

"Emily Warren," she said. "What can I do for you?"

"Mrs. Warren, did you know the people who used to live in the show house?"

"Emily," she said. "And yes, I did. In the neighborhood, we still call it the Green house. Would you like to come in?"

I followed her into a neat living room. The furniture was faded and well-worn, but both the television and the exercise bike in front of it were shiny and new, and from the size of her framed photo collection she must have had at least a dozen assorted grandchildren.

She sat down in what I suspected was her customary end of the sofa, surrounded by her TV remote, a half-completed crossword puzzle, and a tote bag full of knitting. I took the chair at right angles to it.

"Quite a lot of excitement thanks to you folks," she remarked.

"Not the sort of excitement you want," I said. "I'm sure it's quite upsetting for everyone, having a murder in the neighborhood."

"Well, it's not as if he lived here, and from what I hear, he was a wrong 'un. Not that that's any excuse for killing another human being, but in this life we reap what we sow, don't we?"

I could get to like Emily.

"Chief Burke was over here yesterday, asking me if I'd

seen or heard anything that night," she went on. "But I go to bed early, and I take out my hearing aids, so I was of no use to him."

"I was actually trying to find out some information about the Green family," I said. "It only just occurred to me that some of the people who come to see the house might want to know about the family that used to live there, and so far I haven't found anyone who knew them."

"I knew them," she said. "Not well, but probably as well as anyone who's still living here. They moved in—let's see. Twenty years ago this summer. Bob and Carol Green. In their thirties—seemed like a nice couple. They had a little boy when they moved in, and the little girl was born shortly afterward."

"What were the children's names?" I asked. Not that the children's names seemed at all relevant, but I needed to keep up the pretense of working up a short history of the house.

"The boy was Zachary," she said. "Nice when old-fashioned names come back in style, isn't it? And the girl was Jessica."

"Jessica? You're sure?" I had to struggle to conceal my excitement at this bit of information.

"Quite sure," she said. "I always liked the name. On account of Jessica Tandy. You remember her."

"The original Blanche Dubois in *A Streetcar Named Desire*," I said. "Of course."

"Very good, dear," she said. "Most people only remember her as the old crone in *Driving Miss Daisy*."

"My husband's in the drama department at the college," I said.

"That explains it. Yes, the little Green girl was Jessica. Popular name—we had two or three other Jessicas about the same age. And at least one boy named Jesse. But I could keep Jessica Green straight because she was a redhead, and half the time her mother dressed her in bright green, to match her eyes."

I couldn't wait to tell Chief Burke that I'd probably identified the fugitive Jessica.

"When did they move away?" I asked.

"Six years ago—it'll be seven in March," she said. "And they didn't just move away—there was quite a to-do! Bob Green did something in the stock market, and they always seemed quite well off. I half expected them to move into one of those starter castles over on the other side of town— you know the ones I mean?"

I nodded.

"They had three or four cars, and a boat, and they were always giving elegant, catered parties." Emily went on. "They kept horses in the field behind the house. They even broke ground for a pool in the backyard. But then something happened, and the pool stayed a hole in the ground, and the horses left, and the fancy cars were replaced with more practical ones, and the caterers stopped coming. One day they were gone. I heard the bank foreclosed on the house. And I got the feeling a lot of people in the neighborhood weren't too happy with Mr. Green. People who'd invested with him."

"I guess the bank had the half-finished pool filled in," I said.

"I expect the insurance company insisted," Emily said. "And the stable was practically falling down, too, so they tore that down as well. Frankly, a lot of us in the neighborhood were glad to see your lot show up. We were starting to worry that the bank would just wait till the house fell apart so they could tear it down and sell the land for condos."

"So there's no one here who really resents the designers, then?" I asked.

"A few people aren't keen on all the traffic that's going to happen when the house opens," she said. "But even they know that's short term, and if fixing up the house and having people tromp through helps sell it, all the better. It's bad for the neighborhood, having an abandoned house. An open invitation to squatters, or mischievous teens. Ask Chief Burke—we have a recurring problem with break-ins over there."

"Recently?"

"Not since your people came," she said. "But four or five times this fall."

"That matches what I've heard," I said. "Emily—do know know anything about all the secret compartments in the house?"

"Secret compartments?" She tilted her head as if not sure if I was serious.

"Randall Shiffley calls them hidey-holes. Secret compartments built into the walls or the floor. A lot of them. A couple of dozen, all through the house. He found them when they were repairing the house."

"I never heard about any secret compartments," she said. "Of course, I didn't get invited over there much. I was never what you'd call socially prominent, and they were trying to be. But I think I'd have heard if anyone in the neighborhood had seen secret compartments. Maybe that's what happened to all the money people are supposed to have lost with him."

"I thought he lost it in the market," I said.

"Maybe he only told his investors that," she said. "Maybe instead of investing their money he converted it into Krugerrands, and hid them in the secret compartments until he was ready to run away."

"Kruggerrands?"

"You know, those South African gold coins—very popular with these shady criminal types, I hear, if they're planning to make a fast exit. Or diamonds. Although you'd think if they had any diamonds they'd have managed to finish the pool."

"I'll share that theory with Chief Burke, if you like." I probably would. It wasn't any crazier than some of the theories I'd come up with.

"Well, I should let you go," she said, glancing at the clock. And then at her TV remote, so I deduced that something she wanted to watch was about to start.

"Thanks for the information," I said. "We'll have to figure out how much to say about the Greens in our tours."

"Probably as little as possible," Emily said. "People like that always come out of the woodwork and threaten to sue if you say the least thing against them."

"If you're interested in seeing what the designers have done to the house, drop by," I said. "I'll leave a ticket for you."

"Thank you, dear." Emily's eyes gleamed with real enthusiasm. "I do love house and garden tours—nothing more fun than peeking in on how other people live."

She ushered me out and waved a cheerful good-bye from the doorway.

I headed back to the house with an interesting new theory. And I knew the minute I walked back into the house, I'd get caught up in the madness. So I stopped by my car, leaned against the bumper, and called the chief.

"Something wrong?" he asked.

"Something right, I hope," I said. "I have an idea who Jessica, the fake reporter, really is."

"I'm listening."

And listening rather irritably, by the sound of it.

"You know the people who used to own the house before the bank foreclosed on it? The Greens?"

A small pause.

"I know *of* them," he said. "I never met them, and I understand they're no longer living in town. Haven't been here for six years. Do you think they had something to do with the murder?"

"I talked to a little old lady across the street. Emily Warren."

"The one-woman neighborhood watch," he said. "I know Mrs. Warren."

"She didn't know the Greens that well," I said. "But did remember that they had a daughter born shortly after they moved in. A redheaded daughter named Jessica. She remembered the name particularly because of Jessica Tandy."

"Jessica Tan—oh. *Driving Miss Daisy*. One of Morgan Freeman's finer roles. The fact that that he didn't win an Academy Award for that role—but I digress. So you think the Jessica who pretended to be a student reporter was Jessica Green?"

"It makes sense," I said. "And I remember something—Jessica was very upset when she saw what Vermillion was doing. I thought she was creeped out by all the Goth stuff, but maybe that wasn't it. She talked about it being a perfectly nice bedroom and Vermillion was turning it into something out of the Addams Family. What if she was upset because Vermillion had done such a drastic remodel to her childhood bedroom?"

"I don't think you need to have grown up in the house to find Miss Vermillion's décor peculiar," the chief said. "But go on."

"And she was there at the house when Violet lost her key again—Violet was always losing keys. What if Violet didn't lose her key that day? If Jessica picked it up, she'd have a perfect way to get back into the house that night. And she was also there when we were all dragging stuff out of Sarah's room. She helped. She could have picked up the hidden gun."

The chief said nothing for rather a long time. I was sure he was about to weigh in and demolish my suspicions with some bit of evidence he hadn't shared with the public. Or announce that one of the Grangers had already confessed.

"I was already eager to talk to the missing Jessica," he said. "She has just risen to the top of my priority list. I'm going to see what's taking that sketch artist so long. I'll call you as soon as he gets here."

"I'm going to have Randall arrange to have the house rekeyed," I said. "The designers have been strewing keys around like confetti for weeks now. I'll feel a lot better if we know that Jessica can't just waltz in with her own key."

"Good thinking," he said. "And read the riot act to everyone in the house about locking up."

"Will do."

Randall was still in the living room with Mother, helping Tomás and Mateo with something.

"Mother, I hate to interrupt, but we have an urgent project. Randall, the chief thinks it's a good idea for us to rekey all the locks here, in case whoever killed Clay has a key to the house."

"Does he have some reason for thinking that's likely?" Randall asked.

"Yes," I said. "Long story. I'll fill you in later. Just get those locks rekeyed as soon as you can."

"I'm on it."

I went back to the hall and looked for Ivy. She wasn't downstairs in the foyer. Or in the upstairs hall. I was opening the broom closet and peeking in, to see if she might be hiding there. No. Maybe in the basement—

"Meg?"

I started, and turned to find Ivy behind me.

"Do you need something?"

"Yes," I said. "You."

She looked startled.

"Look, I know you're very busy," I said. "I hate to interrupt your work, but could you do a quick sketch for me? It's really important."

"Of course," she said. "What do you want me to draw?"

"Remember Jessica, the young woman who was hanging around the house two days ago?"

"Interviewing us for the student paper," she said. "Yes."

"Could you do a good likeness of her?"

She nodded, and gestured for me to stand back so she could get into the closet. She took out a sketch pad, and a bunch of pencils, and went over to sit down on the hall stairs. She looked up at the ceiling, then closed her eyes and appeared to go inward for a few moments. Then she opened her eyes and began sketching.

I remembered Clay's sketchbook, still hidden in my tote. Should I take that to the chief as well? But getting a sketch of Jessica into the chief's hands seemed more important. When I delivered that, I'd mention the sketchbook.

"She was strange," Ivy said, absently, without looking up from her sketchbook.

"Strange how?"

"She kept going around tapping on the walls. She smeared some of the paint on my crèche mural. I don't like people touching my paintings."

More fodder for my theories. I watched over Ivy's shoulder as she sketched in the shape of a young woman's face.

At first it didn't look much like anyone. Then it started to look a little like Jessica, and then a little more, and eventually, after she'd added more details and tweaked others, a startling likeness emerged.

"That's it," I said.

"Just let me add a little color," she said, picking up her colored pencils. A few strokes with the red, orange, and brown pencils and Jessica's copper-red hair shone out. A touch of green to the eyes and a few strokes of flesh color to the face and it was done.

"Perfect," I said. "May I give it to the chief?"

"I'd be delighted if you did," she said.

And then, as if she'd used up her day's portion of human interaction, she smiled and fled upstairs.

I pulled out my phone, took a picture of her drawing, and e-mailed it to the chief. And then I called him.

"The sketch artist can't be here till tomorrow," he said. "I know it's irritating—"

"Call him off," I said. "And check your e-mail. I had Ivy do a sketch."

"Ivy?"

"One of the designers. The one doing all the paintings in the foyer and the upstairs hall."

"Hold on."

I heard random noises for a while. And then—

"This is Jessica?"

"Exactly," I said. "And the original sketch is even better."

"Can you bring that in?" he asked. "It could be a while before I can get anyone over there. Meanwhile, I'll get this photo out to my officers as a preliminary. We'll save the region-wide alert for the real thing."

"On my way."

Chapter 22

I was putting on my coat when I heard a crash, followed by a wail of distress.

"Oh, no!" It was Sarah's voice, coming from the study. I peeked in and saw her mourning over a green banker's lamp whose glass shade was now smashed into about a million pieces. "Damn—my foot caught on the cord."

"Oh, dear," I said. "Is it going to be hard to get a replacement?"

"I could drive down to Richmond and get one," she said. "But not by ten a.m. tomorrow morning."

"But the house doesn't open until—oh. The photographer."

"It just won't work without the lamp."

I tried to think of a way to suggest that while the room might not precisely match the vision in her head and in her sketches, the readers of the *Richmond Times-Dispatch* would still find it enchanting. But I'd figured out by now that the designers didn't find such suggestions the least bit comforting and that it was best to stick to practical assistance.

"We have a banker's lamp," I said. "In Michael's office. We could lend it to you."

Sarah looked dubious.

"There are banker's lamps and banker's lamps," she said. "They're not all the same."

"Yes, there are vintage originals and hideously expensive reproductions and cheap knockoffs," I said. "I think ours is a hideously expensive reproduction."

"Well." She sounded less dubious.

"Mother picked it out," I said. "To go with our Arts and Crafts décor in the library and Michael's office."

"Oh, well, then it should be fine. When can I get it?"

I checked my watch.

"I have to take something to town right now," I said. "I'll swing by the house and get it. I might have time to bring it here before Michael's show, and if not, I'll drop it off on my way home. How late will you be here?"

"Not much longer," she said. "Dinner with the boyfriend's family. But text me when it's here, and I'll drop by on my way home from that."

"Okay," I said.

"And when you pick it up, could you just send me a photo of it?" she asked. "It'll make me feel better, seeing it."

"Can do," I said. "Now I really have to run."

Of course, since I was in a hurry, I found myself behind one of the horse-drawn carriages Randall had organized to drive parties of tourists around the town. After a quick surge of impatience, I reminded myself that they weren't going all that much below the speed limit and focused on trying to see Caerphilly as the tourists were seeing it. Everyone, tourists and residents alike, waved as the carriages rolled past, with their hundreds of sleigh bells jingling and their red, green, and gold ribbons dancing in the breeze. And when two carriages passed, the drivers, well-bundled in their heavy Victorian greatcoats, stood and bowed to each other.

The boys would love this, I thought. Michael and I should take them. Maybe on Christmas eve, after the house was open.

Just then I noticed that one of the carriages was filled with people in Victorian costume. What was up with that, anyway? I'd thought the whole idea of the carriages was to charge the tourists a modest fee for the ride, not for parties of our costumed reenactors to ride around waving at the crowds.

But when I got a closer look, I realized that these weren't our costumed reenactors. They were tourists, dressed up in Victorian costume. Randall would be delighted to hear that people were joining in the fun, rather than simply watching it.

In fact, when I scanned the crowds lining the streets, I realized there were a lot more costumed people than there had been at the beginning of the season, and a lot of them were buying roasted chestnuts, drinking cider and cocoa, peering into shop windows, and hauling overflowing shopping bags, just like their more modernly dressed fellow tourists. Yes, Christmas in Caerphilly was booming.

I was smiling when I strolled into the police station, partly from the holiday cheer on the way over and partly because what I was bringing the chief was as good as a Christmas present.

As I anticipated, the chief was delighted to get the sketch.

"Not someone I've ever seen around town," he said, after studying it for a few moments. "You think it's a good likeness?"

"An awesome likeness."

"Sammy," he called. "Let's get this into the scanner and out over the wires."

"Have you found out anything about the family who used to live in the show house?" I asked.

"We have," the chief said. "Apparently Mr. Green was doing something risky and possibly illegal with mortgage-backed securities, and lost not only all of his money but a great deal of money belonging to a lot of other people. And the house sat empty for so long because a lot of his creditors were busy suing each other over who had first claim to it."

"And the Bank of Caerphilly ultimately prevailed?" I said. "Yay for the home team."

"Yes," the chief said. "By that time the house was in poor condition, so Randall's offer to fix it up so it could be used for the show house was a godsend to them. But none of this has brought us any closer to locating Ms. Green, and so far we've found no connection between her family and our victim, either in his Clay Smith days or as Claiborne Spottiswood."

"I bet he was simply in the wrong place at the wrong time," I said. "So what happened to the rest of the Greens? The parents and the brother?"

"Mr. Green was convicted of several dozen counts of fraud and has been in a federal prison for the last five years," the chief said. "Mrs. Green died of cancer four years ago. And young Zachary was convicted of vehicular manslaughter three years ago and is currently incarcerated in Red Onion State Prison."

"Red Onion?" I echoed. "Isn't that—"

"The Commonwealth of Virginia's highest security prison, yes," the chief said. "And usually you have to do something rather nastier than vehicular manslaughter to earn a place there, but apparently young Master Zachary has not been a model prisoner."

"Then where has Jessica been?" I asked. "Living with relatives? In foster care?"

"Still working on that." He sounded frustrated. "It's only been a couple of hours, you know. But I think we can safely say that she did not have a happy, normal childhood."

"Chief?" Sammy had returned and looked eager to talk to the chief.

"I'll get out from underfoot," I said.

As I was walking out to my car, Michael called.

"I'm at the house," he said. "Taking off in a few minutes—anything you want me to bring with me?"

"Yes!" I said. "The green banker's lamp from your office."

A short silence.

"Okay," he said. "I assume someone at the show house needs to borrow a banker's lamp. I was thinking more along the lines of a change of clothes. The boys are off sledding with Rob and your father, who are going to bring them directly to the theater for tonight's show, so I'm packing up presentable clothes for them—if you're not going to have time to get back here—"

"Perfect," I said. "The red velvet dress—nice and Christmassy, but not long enough that the hem will drag in the snow."

"Your wish is my command," he said. "And I will also pack suitable footwear and jewelry. See you at the theater."

I paused for a moment to feel thankful for having a husband who was not only capable of selecting suitable shoes and accessories but arguably had better taste than I did. And now I actually had a few minutes of breathing space. I decided to call Dad and see how the sledding was going.

"What's wrong?" he said, by way of a greeting.

"Nothing's wrong," I said. "Can't a girl call her dad to ask how he's doing and whether his grandchildren are enjoying the sledding?"

"They're having a blast," he said. "Hang on. Josh! Jamie! Let's send Mommy a picture. Come here! Smile!"

"Hi, Mommy!" Jamie called.

"Mommy, I sledded all the way all by myself!" Josh called.

My phone pinged to announce an arriving text, and I toggled over to look at the photo. The boys were smiling with delight. I could see the gap in Jamie's mouth where he'd lost his first baby tooth, while Josh's smile remained, to his consternation, unbroken.

"Come sledding, Mommy," Jamie said.

"Next time," I said.

And I meant it. As I chatted with Dad, and then with each of the boys, I vowed that I wouldn't even go near the show house next year.

"Mommy," Josh asked. "Do you like Nerf guns?"

"Not really," I said. "I'm not that fond of any kind of gun, not even Nerf guns."

"Oh." Evidently I'd squashed another present idea. He sounded so disappointed that I was almost tempted to take back my answer, but I reminded myself what would happen if we let Nerf guns into the house, and stood firm.

"I'll see you at the theater," I said finally.

My car seemed depressingly quiet after we hung up.

So I started the engine and headed over to the theater. There would be lights and people to talk to. People who didn't know passementerie from pizza and didn't care.

On the way over to the theater, it occurred to me that if I could find someone with a laptop and a connection to the college's wireless network, I could log into my e-mail and check out some of the information Boomer had sent. Not that I'd have much time.

By the time I found a parking space and rushed to the theater, Michael had arrived, and Dad with the boys, and I spent most of the time until the show started getting them and myself into presentable clothes.

I could log in and check Boomer's info when I got home. After all, it was beginning to look as if Clay's murder had more to do with the house's past than his own. But just in case any of Boomer's information was relevant, I took out my phone and forwarded his e-mail to the chief.

Dad and I took the boys out to the theater lobby, so they could watch all the people handing in their tickets to see their daddy's play. Josh had run into his nursery school teacher and was telling her his version of the entire plot of *A Christmas Carol.* Jamie had encountered a school friend who'd broken his arm while sledding and was now sporting a bright red cast. Fortunately, Dad recognized the early warning signs of cast envy, and was trying to nip it in the bud by interrogating the friend about how painful his broken arm had been and loudly sympathizing with him over all the exciting things he couldn't do until he got his cast off.

"Mission accomplished." I turned to see Randall standing behind me, holding out what looked like a small branch of plastic holly, complete with red berries. Upon closer inspection, I realized there was a bright red key attached.

"A nice, festive touch," I said as I took the key.

"The holly should make it harder to lose," he said.

"Or steal," I added.

"Exactly. Some of the designers have them, and I'll be there bright and early to distribute the rest. For the usual deposit, refundable upon return of key and holly."

With that he saluted and strolled off into the crowd.

"Meg?" someone said behind me. "I just wanted to say I'm sorry."

I turned to see Kate Banks, Sarah's partner, standing behind me.

"How are you?" I said. "And sorry about what?"

"Because maybe if I hadn't given Sarah my gun, you wouldn't have had someone murdered in your show house."

"Or maybe whoever killed him would have found some other weapon," I said. "We don't actually know that it was your gun. Why the gun, by the way?"

"I was scared of him," Kate said. "I thought Sarah should be. Have you ever seen him lose it?"

I shook my head.

"Be glad you never will," she said. "And the time he got mad at me—it was in a public place, at the Caerphilly Home and Garden Show, and I was still afraid he'd lose control and do something. And she was going to be in that house with him—maybe even alone with him. And he was an ex-con—did you know that?"

"I did," I said. "But did you have reason to think he had it in for Sarah?"

"He was stealing clients," she said. "Trying to, anyway. From us—from everyone. He pulled a real fast one on us. We did a proposal for a client, and the client wanted a bunch of changes. Somehow he got hold of our proposal and my notes for the changes the client wanted, and before you know it, we were down one client. 'He understands me soooo well,'" she cooed, obviously in imitation of the client. "'He knows what I want without my even having to tell him.'"

"Creep," I said. "But I don't see why that would make him mad at Sarah."

"She outed him to the client."

"Go Sarah!"

"And took a video with her iPhone of him making fun of the client and posted it on YouTube," Kate said. "So yeah, I think it's fair to assume he had it in for her. If she'd been the victim, I'd have said, look at Clay."

"So who do you think killed him?" I asked. "Most of the designers in the house are alibied."

"Not every designer who hated him is in the house," she said. "There's a few others in Caerphilly that he's had run-ins with. And a few in Tappahannock. And lots and lots in Richmond. Ask Martha—she knew him back when he was there. Ask her."

"I will," I said. Actually, I made a mental note to make sure the chief knew about Clay and Martha's pre-Caerphilly connection. Hunting down every designer in Virginia who might have a grudge against Clay was a job for the police.

"And don't forget all the other people he ticked off," she said. "Contractors, vendors, clients."

Definitely a police job.

"Anyway—I wanted to apologize," she said. "We'd better get our seats—they're dimming the lights."

I rejoined Dad and the boys and we trooped in to take our seats.

The boys seemed just as fascinated by the show as they had been the previous night. How lucky for us that they were still in that golden age when they idolized Michael and everything he did.

I would never admit as much to Michael, but I wasn't paying attention to the script tonight, only letting his voice and the words flow over me like a well-loved and utterly familiar piece of music. I could laugh when the crowd laughed and look solemn when they did, on autopilot, while my thoughts kept turning back to the house. Tomorrow I had to get there early enough to let in anyone who still needed a key. Supervise the photographer. Pick up the programs from the printer. Make sure the volunteer ticket takers and docents knew when to show up on Wednesday.

I'd almost forgotten—the banker's lamp. Probably a bad idea to pull out my notebook in the middle of the visit of the Ghost of Christmas Present, so I focused for a few moments on visualizing the banker's lamp sitting on top of my dashboard, in the hope that if I got into my car without it, the naked dashboard would remind me. And then I imagined myself pulling the lamp's gold chain to start the car. The idea made me smile, which would have looked odd in the middle of one of the show's sadder moments, but luckily just then Michael, in the small voice he used for Tiny Tim, had just cried out "God bless us, every one!" and the whole audience was smiling.

The show was a success, as always, and as always Michael's dressing room was filled with well-wishers. Michael's mother, who wanted to get an early start on her cooking, drafted Rob to take her and the boys home.

"Did you bring the lamp?" I asked Michael, when I could tear him away from one of Mother's cousins who wanted him to autograph her program.

"Of course," he said.

"Then I'm going to leave you to your fans," I said. "I can drop it by the house and probably still beat you home."

I fetched the lamp from the Twinmobile, which was parked right behind the theater, and carried it the three blocks to where I'd put my car. I kept a sharp lookout, but this time there didn't appear to be anyone following me. I was leaving earlier tonight, and I'd parked in a less isolated spot. I carefully stowed the lamp on the passenger-side floor and wedged it in with my purse before taking off for the house.

I passed stores that were closed or closing and restaurants whose last patrons were filing out into the cold, crisp air. When I'd first moved to Caerphilly, I found it annoying that the only things open all night were the gas station and the hospital. Now I found it soothing.

When I reached the show house, it was dark and a little

spooky looking. I wasn't thrilled to have to come back here by myself. But I was now convinced that Jessica had, indeed, taken Violet's key. And thanks to the rekeying, that key—along with any others the designers might have lost or given away—was useless. Only Randall and I and the remaining designers had access now.

In fact, it was possible that some of the designers had gone home before Randall had given out the new keys, so the subset of people who could get in was even smaller and mostly well alibied.

Of course, Jessica had probably also stolen Sarah and Kate's gun. And unlike the obsolete keys, that would be working just fine. So before parking in front of the house, I cruised past it so slowly my car almost stalled out, studying every pane of every window and every shadow on the lawn.

Nothing suspicious.

I parked my car right in front of the door. There were a few other cars up and down the street, but they looked like neighborhood cars.

I kept a close eye around me as I strode up the walk, and kept looking over my shoulder as I unlocked the door. I held the banker's lamp handy, ready to bash anyone who tried to sneak up on me. Sarah wouldn't be happy if I had to use it, but my life was at least slightly more important than her room.

The new key was a little stiff, but it worked. I was safely inside.

Safely inside a house that had already had one murder in it. I stood in the hallway for a few moments, listening.

Silence.

Then I walked quickly and quietly through the house and checked to make sure every door and window was closed and locked, and every closet empty. Fifteen windows and seven doors downstairs, counting the two garage doors. Thirteen windows upstairs. Nobody in the four upstairs closets, the five downstairs closets, or the basement.

Okay, now I could breathe more easily.

I went back down to the hall, where I'd left the banker's lamp, and took it into Sarah's study. I even plugged it in close to where I thought the old one had been. Of course, the minute Sarah walked in, she'd frown and arrange it to an ever-so-slightly different angle, following some logic understandable only to designers and inexplicable to mere mortals like me.

I turned the banker's light on. I could see why Sarah had wanted it. The room was a symphony in red fabric, muted golden bronze, and brown wood. Even the books were mostly in tones of red, gold, and brown. The green shade of the banker's lamp suddenly brought the room's whole focus on the elegant cherry desk and the bronze desk accessories on top of it. All it needed was a vintage typewriter and you could imagine *The Great Gatsby* being written here, or maybe *The Sound and the Fury.* I wanted more than ever to browse through the books—the real, identifiable, imperfect yet ever-so-beautiful books—and then plop down for nice long wallow in one of the red velvet chairs.

Maybe later. After the house had opened.

I took a picture of the lamp and e-mailed that to Sarah. Then I turned it off and went to check the rest of the house.

Mother's room was breathtaking. I stood in the middle of the floor and surveyed it. The tall tree, trimmed with so many sparkling ornaments that you had to take it on faith that there was green underneath. The rich red-and-gold brocade covers of the chairs and the sofa. The four red velvet Christmas stockings hanging from brass hangers on the mantel. The lovely contrast between the walls—painted in "Red Obsession," which didn't look nearly as overwhelming as I thought it would be—and the woodwork—painted in an off-white, whose name I had forgotten, and picked out with little touches of gold. The rich red draperies with their red-and-gold cords. The subtle colors and intricate designs of the elegantly faded red oriental rug. The cool contrasting touch of the blue-and-white porcelain. Yes, Mother had outdone herself. If there was any justice, she had a good shot at the prize.

I stopped long enough to take a few shots of the room. In fact, while I was at it, I took several dozen. In the morning, the *Times-Dispatch* photographer would probably get plenty of pictures—and better pictures. But I'd been in the habit of taking pictures every afternoon or evening, after the designers had finished for the day. I thought perhaps I'd do an album later. Or maybe an exhibit at the county museum. If we put my photos together with the ones Randall had taken of the repair work, we could show the whole history of the house, from wreck to palace. So I made sure to capture Mother's completed room from all angles.

Eustace's breakfast room was painted in off-whites and faded pinks that either matched or blended nicely with the woodwork in Mother's room. In spite of the room's name, the round, glass-topped table wasn't set for breakfast—a ruby-red punch bowl occupied the center, surrounded by ruby-red punch glasses, green-and-white Christmas napkins with a holly design, gold-plated flatware, a colorful fruit cake in a tall cut-glass cake stand, and several antique or vintage Christmas-themed cookie tins. I could imagine the guests attending a party in Mother's room and then stepping into this elegant little nook to refill their punch cups or grab something to nibble.

Was the fruitcake fake or edible? I lifted the top and poked it. Real, and therefore presumably as edible as any other fruitcake. Not that I wanted to try.

The kitchen itself, also done in carefully blended off-whites, was utterly impractical yet absolutely beautiful. Each cabinet contained half a dozen perfectly arranged bits of glass or china or pottery, mostly in soft shades of blue and turquoise. I only hoped all the people who fell in love with the look stopped to inventory the contents of their cabinets before investing in glass fronts. And as a nod to the Christmas theme, he'd placed a tray on the counter containing a large bowl of walnuts and an antique nut-cracker. Although clearly the walnuts weren't really meant to be eaten, since they'd all been painted gold.

I took a token peek into Martha's laundry room. It was clean, and sparkling white—evidently she and Eustace had agreed to disagree on the white/off-white issue. She'd hung pretty prints on the walls, pretty curtains at the window, pretty towels on the folding rack. But it was still just a laun-dry room. And not Christmassy at all—but then, who ever decorates a laundry room for Christmas?

Well, who apart from Mother?

Something startled me—a noise outside, like something being knocked over. It seemed to be coming from the back of the house—maybe on the terrace? I tiptoed across the hall and peered out through the glass panes in the terrace door. A little faint light spilled out through the dining room windows. Someone had shoveled the snow off the terrace. Maybe not such a good idea. It looked remarkably empty. Maybe we should put something out there. Or—

A movement startled me, and then a fat raccoon wad-dled across the terrace, raised his masked head to stare at me, and disappeared into the yard.

I had been holding my breath. I started breathing again, and continued my tour. I flicked the light on in the dining room.

Which was certainly . . . festive. I realized that Linda was probably aiming for the kind of luxuriant yet tasteful excess that Mother was so good at achieving. But Linda only managed the excess. She'd found at least a dozen different Christmas-themed chintz prints and used them to make angels, stars, wreaths, and garlands that now festooned the already busy walls.

Well, at least it was Christmassy.

I flicked the light off again, and realized that the room looked a lot better in the dim ambient light from the hallway. Maybe if I convinced Linda to use only candles, the room would show better.

I smiled again when I stepped out into the hall. Ivy had added a few bits of furniture—a chair here, a small side table there, just enough to justify the title of "designer" rather than "painter." But even if she hadn't, it wouldn't matter. Her murals were going to be the hit of the show house. They were ornate, intricate, and curiously reminiscent of early-twentieth-century children's book illustrations, like those by Kay Nielsen, Arthur Rackham, or Edmund Dulac. Was it disloyal of me to like them just a little bit more than even Mother's room?

"The Little Match Girl" and "Good King Wenceslas" flanked the front door—it rather looked as if the charitable monarch was about to rescue the shivering waif. On the long wall across from the stairs "I Saw Three Ships Come Sailing In" merged seamlessly into the harbor of Copenhagen, where the Little Mermaid peeked above the waves to welcome the arriving fleet. At the back of the hall, "The Friendly Beasts" and "The Ugly Duckling" flanked the

French doors to the terrace. "The Three Kings" marched up the wall beside the stairway.

"The Twelve Days of Christmas" took over the wall opposite the stairs in the upstairs hallway. On the other long wall, the Snow Queen in her elegant sleigh appeared to be heading for the manger, where a host of shepherds and animals surrounded a pensive Baby Jesus. "The Snow Queen" wasn't quite finished, but we could steer the photographer away from that. Perhaps toward my favorite, "The Nightingale," which filled the entire wall leading to Vermillion's room and appeared through the opening so it was also visible from Mother's room below.

And in addition to the large murals, smaller illustrations danced over every other square inch that could be painted. Was that "Thumbelina" standing to the left of the back window? "The Steadfast Tin Soldier" on the other side? "The Little Drummer Boy" performing near the basement door? "The Red Shoes" dancing above the sill of Clay's room?

Clay's room. I wanted to continue my tour of inspection to see what Vermillion, Violet, and the Quilt Ladies had done. But I doubted any of the decorators had spared a thought for the master bedroom. And even if the photographer really was coming to shoot the whole house, I suspected the room that was also a crime scene was a must-see on his list.

I stepped inside and looked around.

Not bad. Not bad at all. The glossy black furniture showed every speck of dust, so I grabbed a wad of tissue from the bathroom, dampened it, and gave all the wood surfaces a quick dusting. We'd have to make that a daily chore. I plumped the fat black pillows on the bed and made sure the curtains hung evenly.

The room was curiously quiet—the soft black curtains

and the thick red rug absorbed so much sound that the outside world felt curiously far away. I'd have hated sleeping in it, but I had to admit that if you liked the style, the room would probably be a soothing retreat.

One of Clay's paintings was not quite level. I was trying to straighten it when I heard a voice behind me.

"Wow, you guys really cleaned this place up."

I whirled around and saw Jessica standing in the doorway.

She was holding a gun.

Chapter 23

"Yes," I said. "We cleaned it up. You'd hardly know a murder happened here."

Jessica looked ill-kempt and scruffy, as if she'd been sleeping in the clothes she was wearing and not remembering to comb her hair. And I wondered if she was on something. The hand holding the gun was shaking slightly. And was it just because of the dim light, or were her pupils unnaturally dilated?

"How did you get in here, anyway?" I asked. "We changed the locks."

"Climbed a tree to get onto the roof," she said. "And broke a window in my room. My old room. The one that creepy witch has painted all black and red."

She must have done it after my tour of inspection, perhaps while I'd been busy taking photos. And maybe the noise I'd heard was her, not the raccoon on the deck.

"Downstairs," she said. She inched into the room, backed away from the door, and then jerked the gun slightly toward it. "Move."

She was motioning me toward the door. Well, that was a good thing, wasn't it? Here in the master suite there was only one way out, past her and the gun. Once I was out in the hall, there were the two stairways, which meant two escape routes. And downstairs would be even better.

"I said move," she snapped.

"I'm moving," I said. I made my way carefully to the door, not turning my back on her as I slid across the room and then backed out into the hall.

"Turn around," she said. "And walk downstairs. Slowly."

She was so wild-eyed and twitchy that I didn't like turning my back on her, but I figured it was more dangerous to disobey.

She followed me downstairs, far enough behind that there was no chance of turning around and jumping her.

"Into the living room," she said. "Far enough. Now kneel down."

I didn't like it.

"Look," I said. "There's no need to do this."

"Fat lot you know," she muttered from behind me. "Kneel down."

I turned slightly so I could see what she was doing, and crouched a little bit, as if to suggest I was about to obey her.

"Everyone knows Clay was a total jerk," I said. "I figure he must have tried to attack you or something. You'd get off on self-defense. Every designer in the house would—"

"I didn't kill him!"

She accompanied her shout with a hard punch to my stomach. I was frozen—only for a few seconds, but long enough for her to grab my arms and wrap something around them. By the time I could struggle again, my arms were tied behind me, and I was lying on my face on the living room rug.

"Stupid people," she muttered. "I didn't kill him."

"Then did you see who did?" I twisted slightly so I could see her.

"Of course not," she said. "He was dead when I came in."

"That's great," I said. "Then let's tell the police and everything will be okay."

"Yeah, right," she said. I heard a small clatter.

I wriggled a little more so I could see what she was doing. She had knocked the two middle stockings off the mantel, brass hooks and all, and was leaning into the fireplace and reaching up as if looking for something.

I decided to take a chance that some of my hypotheses were correct.

"Look," I said. "I know you used to live in this house. And you're looking for something you left behind. If I knew what it was, maybe I could help you."

She stopped and turned to look at me.

"I'm looking for the money," she said.

"You left money here?" I asked. "How much?"

"I don't know," she said. "But it's a lot. It was my parents' money."

"Well, where did they leave it?"

"If I knew that I'd have it by now," she said. "I thought it was in one of the secret compartments."

She sounded younger than eighteen. Did Emily, the neighbor, overestimate her age? No, she didn't just sound younger than eighteen. She sounded like a cranky child. I had a bad feeling about this.

"Have you looked in all of the secret compartments?" I asked.

"All I could find. My dad must have made some I didn't know about. He liked to do that—make secret compartments, and then he'd hide candy in them for me to find."

"Sounds nice," I said.

"But maybe he made some extra secret compartments for the money."

She was knocking on the mantelpiece, as if trying to find a hollow spot. I had managed to pull my arms far enough to the side that I could crane my head and look over my shoulder to see what she'd tied me up with.

It looked like a leftover bit of the black-and-red braided cord Mother had used to trim the couch and the chairs. I started picking at it with my nails, and casting my eyes around for something sharp I could rub it against. I vowed I was not going to die tied up with these little bits of string.

"Damned passementerie," I muttered.

"What?" Jessica said.

"I said, did your parents leave behind a lot of money?"

"Yes," she said. "We were rich. I had a pony, and I had ballet and piano lessons, and Daddy was building me a pool so I could practice a lot and make the swim team. And then the stupid bank took our house away."

Probably not a good idea to point out that people who really had a lot of money didn't usually have their houses foreclosed on.

Jessica had started knocking on the walls by the fireplace. She must have found something she liked the sound of. She walked out into the hall, putting the gun down on one of the end tables as she went.

I felt a little better now that she wasn't holding the gun.

Until she walked back into the room holding a large ax.

I redoubled my efforts to unravel the passementerie.

"The stupid bank *cheat*ed us." Jessica took a vicious hack at one of Mother's freshly painted walls. "They took away my *pony*." Another hack. "And then they took away our *house*. One day Mommy picked me up at school and told me we were leaving. And they wouldn't let my parents come back in to get their money."

"Are you sure they left it in the house?" I said. "And not

somewhere else? Because you've done a really good job of searching the house over the last six months."

"I know it's in the house," she said. "My mother must have said it a million times. 'You can't have a *pony*. You can't have *dance* lessons. We don't have any *money*. All our *money's* in the *house*.'"

I winced, and not because she'd just reduced fifteen or twenty square feet of Mother's "Red Obsession"–painted wall to wreckage. "All our money's in the house." I could remember saying those very words in those first few years after Michael and I had bought our house. The size of the mortgage payments had made us nervous in those early days, even before you factored in all the money we'd paid to the Shiffley Construction Company to make the house habitable. We'd had to economize a bit. All our money was in the house.

But not literally. We hadn't had Randall Shiffley's workmen build little hiding places in between the walls and under the floorboards to stash our meager post-down-payment savings in.

Maybe Jessica's parents had. But even if they had, what were the odds they'd left behind tons of cash when they moved away? However abrupt their departure might have seemed to eleven- or twelve-year-old Jessica, her parents would have had time to clean our their hiding places.

And did she really think the left-behind treasure would still be there after the house had been empty for six years, despoiled by vandals and squatters, and completely rebuilt by Randall and his workmen?

Yes, apparently she did. She was working on another wall now, alternately hacking out chunks and stopping to sift through the rubble she'd created. And she was getting more and more jittery and agitated. Was she on something?

Or suffering from some kind of mental illness? Either way, I needed to get untied and away from her, because she seemed to be spiraling down into some kind of frenzy.

She'd started muttering to herself. I caught a few words.

". . . be a lot easier if these damned creeps hadn't come in and messed up everything . . ."

She seemed to have forgotten I was there. Which was a good thing. But what if she glanced over, saw me, and remembered that I was one of the creeps who'd messed up everything?

Just then I spotted movement in the archway separating the living room from the breakfast room. Someone was standing there in the shadows.

I glanced over at Jessica, and then back at the figure. I shook my head, and then jerked it toward Jessica.

The figure took a step forward. It was Martha.

I couldn't remember when I'd been so glad to see a friendly face.

Chapter 24

I could see Martha peering out of the archway at Jessica. I tried to shake my head, ever-so-slightly, to suggest that stepping into the room was a really bad idea.

After watching Jessica for a moment or so, she glanced down at me, nodded, and withdrew back into the kitchen.

Make sure you're far enough away so she doesn't hear you when you call 9-1-1, I wanted to tell her. And get some kind of a weapon! But she's dangerous, so stay back and don't try anything—unless, of course, you see her about to shoot me or dismember me, in which case you should do something quick!

Martha was a cool customer, I reminded myself. She could handle this.

At least I hoped she could.

"Where is it?" Jessica again. "It's got to be here. It's *got* to!"

She seemed to be losing it. More of it than she'd already lost. She began flailing out wildly with the ax, shrieking inarticulately. She shattered the mirror above the fireplace. Knocked the legs out from under a delicate secretary desk. Chopped a couple of nasty holes in the carpet. Bounced around between the sofas and armchairs, shredding up the brocade cushions. I flinched when she came near me, but she sailed past and began trying to dismember the Christmas tree. Between her shrieks, the hatchet blows, and the smashing sounds as hundreds of ornaments fell to the floor and shattered to bits I could barely hear myself think.

Martha, bless her heart, began stealing into the room under cover of the tree surgery. She was heading for the table with the gun.

She had it.

I breathed a sigh of relief and gave my poor bruised fingers a rest—I'd made progress on unraveling the passe-menterie, but not enough. Not a problem, though—Martha could hold Jessica at bay until the police arrived. Or, if Jessica was so hysterical that she tried to attack her in spite of the gun—well, I suspected Martha had enough nerve to use it.

She lifted the gun in her right hand and steadied it with her left. She'd either used a gun before or had paid attention when watching TV and movie cops use them. Go Martha!

Then she fired, twice.

Jessica collapsed on the floor and fell silent.

I was stunned into silence myself for a few moments.

Martha walked over to take a closer look at Jessica.

"Did you have to shoot her?" I asked.

"She's not dead," Martha said.

"That's a relief," I said. "Can you come over and untie me?"

"Which means I'll just have to shoot her again," Martha said. "After bashing your head in with her ax, of course. It'll look as if you shot her just as she was hitting you with the ax. I'll let the chief of police decide who he wants to blame Clay's murder on."

I started working again on unraveling the passementerie.

"You killed Clay," I said. "Why?"

Not that I didn't have a pretty good idea why, between

their professional rivalry and their shattered romantic relationship. But it seemed a good idea to keep her talking.

"Oh, for heaven's sake, you know why," she snapped. "You've heard how he took me in. Let me set him up in the design business and then turned on me and took all my clients. I lost my business and had to go to work as a furniture store design consultant. Took me two years to save enough to start up again here in Caerphilly—it would have taken a lot longer to get started again in Richmond. And a year later, he moves here and thinks he can do it all again. No way. I told him—back off, leave my clients alone. But did he listen?"

"So it was all professional?" I asked. "Or am I imagining that the two of you also had a relationship?"

"The bastard," she muttered. "Turns out I imagined the relationship. He was just using me."

"So you killed him," I said.

"That wasn't actually the plan," she said. "I was just going to frame him."

"For what?"

"Possession of a firearm," she said. "In Virginia, a convicted felon who's caught with a gun can go to prison. I knew that from serving on a jury once. And when we were all trying to rescue Sarah's furniture, I dragged out this little end table, and suddenly the drawer pops open and a gun falls out. I kicked it under the sofa, and then picked it up later, with my cleaning gloves on. I wasn't sure what I was going to do with it, but I figured it would be good for something. And then I came up with the idea of leaving it in Clay's room and calling the cops to report it."

"So you took Violet out and got her plastered, so she'd tell everyone how sweet you were to take away her keys and let her stay in your guest room," I said.

"Yeah." She seemed to be enjoying the chance to brag about her cleverness. "I slipped her a Mickey to make sure she stayed out. I'm only six blocks from here, so I figured it would be a cinch to slip over here, plant the gun, and get back in before she noticed I was gone."

"All that trouble for an alibi for planting the gun?" I asked.

"I figured he'd blame me for planting it," she said. "He knew I had it in for him. So I wanted to make sure I could prove I hadn't done it. Lucky for me, isn't it? And bad luck for Clay, barging in when he did."

"And you struggled, and the gun went off," I said. "I'm sure you were devastated, but you were there to play a prank on him, not kill him. It was self-defense." I tried to put a sympathetic, concerned expression on my face, as if I really did believe she was innocent. "Completely understandable. Anyone who knew Clay would call it justifiable homicide."

"Nice try," she said. "But I'm not buying it. Wish your little nut job had wrecked a few other rooms. Wonder if I have the time to—no, probably better not."

"You won't get away with it," I said.

"I can sure try," she said. "And you know what? I may not have time to wreck everyone else's rooms, but I can hack Clay's stupid paintings to shreds."

"No," I said. The thought of her slashing those three paintings was curiously disturbing.

"It's going to be tough on your mother," she said. "When she comes over and sees you lying dead in the ruins of her room. I feel almost sorry for her, even though I know she had a hand in trying to cut me out of the house."

She didn't sound sorry. And she was dead wrong. Mother had much preferred her to Clay. It was only thanks to

Mother's intervention that she'd gotten the rooms she had. But she'd never believe it.

"Nothing I can do about that," Martha went on, as she headed for the archway that led to the hall. She stopped, looked back, and smiled at the devastation around us. "Before you know it—"

Something large, shiny, and metallic emerged from the shadows of the hallway and hit the top of her head. She stiffened and then slumped to the floor.

Ivy was standing in the doorway, holding the heavy bronze umbrella stand. She set the umbrella stand down, then bent over to take both the ax and the gun from Martha. Then she walked over, sat down on the floor beside me, and started untying my passementerie bonds.

"Thank God you stopped her," I said. "But where did you come from? I had no idea you were even here!"

"No one ever does," she said, with a faint smile, as she pulled away the last strands of passementerie.

Chapter 25

Ivy had quite sensibly called 9-1-1 before tackling Martha. By the time the police arrived, I had checked both Jessica and Martha and relayed their condition over the phone to Debbie Ann. Jessica was unconscious but breathing normally and I didn't find much blood. Maybe her wound was only minor, and it had hit her hard because of her agitated or even drugged state. A problem for the medics, when they arrived. Martha's head wasn't bleeding, but then, head wounds don't always, and she could easily have a concussion or even a subdural hematoma. I hoped the ambulance arrived soon. I wouldn't mourn too much if Martha died, but I suspected that killing someone, even to save a life, would hit Ivy hard. Then again, maybe I was underestimating Ivy. If she really had been the timid soul we all thought she was, I'd be dead by now.

Ivy had found a roll of duct tape and trussed up their ankles. We decided maybe binding their wrists was overkill, since both of them were still unconscious, and it might interfere with whatever the EMTs would want to do. Though just to be safe, we also taped their ankles to heavy things—Jessica's to what remained of the Christmas tree and Martha's to the more-intact of the two sofas.

Martha came around enough to start yelling just as the first police officer, Aida Butler, strode in the door, gun in hand.

"You bitch!" Martha roared, clapping her hands to her head.

"Not a really smart thing to say to a lady armed with forty-five-caliber semiautomatic weapon," Aida said.

"I think she means me," Ivy said, with a shy smile.

"She tried to kill me!" Martha roared, and she followed it up with a string of expletives.

"Please be quiet, ma'am," Aida said.

Martha continued her X-rated tirade.

"Ma'am," Aida said, stepping into Martha's field of vision. "Please be quiet, or I will be forced to arrest you for obstructing a police officer—"

Instead of shutting up, Martha increased her volume, and then she grabbed the umbrella stand Ivy had used to hit her and threw it at Aida. I winced, and mentally kicked myself for not moving it out of Martha's reach. But who knew she'd regain consciousness so quickly? The umbrella stand hit Aida's shin and then dropped down on her toe.

"Aiiieee!" Aida screamed. And then "Rainbows! Rainbows! Rainbows!"

For some reason, this seemed to unnerve Martha, and she finally shut up.

Just in time.

"What's going on here?"

Chief Burke had arrived.

Things happened fast. More officers arrived—almost every officer on the force—and the paramedics along with them. Chief Burke hustled Ivy into the dining room and me into Sarah's study, so I got to watch through the French doors while first Jessica and then Martha were hauled off to the ambulance.

Should I call Michael? I didn't want to wake him if he'd

dropped off to sleep. Or worry him by not calling if he was still waiting up. I pulled out my phone and texted him. "I'm OK. Coming home as soon as I can."

I lay back in the red-velvet armchair and worked on the deep breathing Rose Noire was always telling me I should do more of whenever I felt stressed. I really wanted to be somewhere else—anywhere else, thinking about anything other than crazy Jessica and murderous Martha. I'd have found it very comforting to pull out my notebook and start making lists, but I'd long ago figured out that most people looked at me oddly if they saw me busily making lists in the middle of a stressful situation—like almost being murdered. But still, it would be some comfort to work on a mental list of tasks I'd need to do to get the show house moving. Like calling to postpone the photographer. And finding out from the chief when we could have the house back. And coming up with a plan for Mother's room.

Mother's room.

I watched as Horace came in. He stood few minutes in the archway to the living room, obviously in shock, before plunging into the room to start his forensic work.

Part of me wanted to start dealing with Mother's room, and part of me just wanted to go home, check on the boys, curl up in bed beside Michael, and sleep for the next twelve hours.

I was not looking forward to being interviewed by the chief.

"Don't worry." It was Aida, coming through the front door. "She's fine."

"I want to see for myself." Michael followed Aida in.

I ran out into the hall and threw myself at him.

"Are you okay?" he whispered.

"I'm fine," I said. "And I am definitely not doing the show

house next year. If there even is a show house after this. Where are the boys?"

"Home with Mom," he said. "They'll be fine and—oh, my God. Your mother's room. It's a disaster."

"We need to find Dad, and make sure he's here when she sees it," I said.

Michael nodded.

The chief stepped into the room.

"Meg, I know you're pretty tired," he said. "But if I could just ask you a few questions . . ."

"I'll tell you all about it," I said.

It took a while, of course. And the whole while I was talking to him I could see people coming and going. Aida. Sammy. All the other town law enforcement officers. Randall. All of them, when they saw the great room for the first time, stopped dead in their tracks and stared for a few moments before shaking their heads.

"I think that should do it," the chief said finally, standing up.

Seeing that we were finishing, Randall Shiffley opened one French door and stepped in.

"Good news from the hospital," he said. "Both nut jobs will live to stand trial."

"That's good," the chief said.

"What now?" I asked.

"Now?" The chief looked startled. "Go home and get some sleep."

"I need to start doing something about that room as soon as you release it," I said.

"Meg," Michael began.

"I can't let Mother see it like that," I said. "Chief, promise me you won't let Mother in until we clean it up a little bit."

"As soon as the chief releases it, I'll be here with my

crew," Randall said. "I'll bring in as many cousins as it takes, and she won't see it like this."

"I'll send a deputy over to your parents' at first light, to break the news to her," the chief said. "And I won't let your mother into the crime scene until you're back to help her cope. But for now, you need to get some rest."

"I won't sleep a wink," I muttered to Michael as we walked out to the Twinmobile.

"Just close your eyes and rest then," he said.

I slept so soundly he almost couldn't wake me up when we got home.

And woke up well before dawn, already worrying.

Chapter 26

December 23

"It's not even seven," Michael mumbled as he watched me pull on my clothes.

"I have to get over there before Mother sees her room." I raced downstairs and into the kitchen to grab something to eat.

Michael followed me.

"And I need to figure out how to fix it," I said over my shoulder as I stuck a cup of water with a tea bag in it into the microwave.

"You've got Randall and his workmen," he said. "They can fix most of the damage."

"They can fix the walls and the woodwork." I rummaged through the fridge for a yogurt. "But I'm pretty sure they can't sew or do upholstery."

"You go over to the show house and help your mother through the shock of seeing the room," he said. "I think I can find you a few people to do a bit of sewing. Leave it to me."

"Thanks," I said. And then the microwave dinged, so I snagged my tea and the yogurt and dashed out the door.

There weren't quite as many police vehicles at the house when I got there. Only two patrol cars and the chief's blue sedan. That was a good sign, wasn't it? I also spotted three trucks from the Shiffley Construction Company parked in front and a Dumpster in the driveway. A dozen tall, lanky Shiffleys in boots, jeans, and heavy jackets leaned against the trucks with carryout coffee cups in their hands or stood in twos and threes on the sidewalk. Two shorter forms, heavily bundled, were barely recognizable as Tomás and Mateo. Eustace stood by them, blowing on his hands.

Randall ambled over to my car.

"Good," he said. "I was just debating whether to call you. Chief's going to release the house any minute now. And if it's okay with you, we'll start hauling off the trash and repairing the damage as soon as he does. Of course, all we can do is get the room back to where it was when your Mother started it. Decorating's not something we can do."

"We're working on some plans," I said. At least Michael was.

The front door opened. Chief Burke stepped out.

"All yours," he said.

Things started happening. Tomás and Mateo and the Shiffleys swarmed into the house. I followed, a little more slowly.

"Okay, boys," Randall said. "First thing we do is haul all this trash out. Meg, you want to take charge of rescuing stuff that can be reused?"

They were just getting started when one of the Shiffleys came running in.

"Meg? Your parents are here."

Mother followed close on his heels. She burst into the hallway, and when she saw me, she rushed over and gave me a fierce hug.

"I'm okay," I said.

"Yes," she said. "And as long as you're okay, everything else will be fine."

"Good," I said. "Because I'm afraid we're going to have a bit of work to do in your room."

"My room?" She turned and took a few steps toward the archway. We all froze. She didn't react for several long moments, and then she burst into tears.

"My room," she keened. "My beautiful room."

I must have heard every designer in the show house say the same thing at some time over the last few days, but never with so much cause.

Jessica had knocked over the giant Christmas tree. At least three quarters of the delicate glass ornaments had been broken, either in the fall or when she hacked the tree into dozens of pieces. Giant gouges marred the walls, where there were still walls—in some places Jessica had ripped away great stretches of wallboard. She had knocked over and broken lamps, end tables, and vases. She'd attacked chairs and sofas so fiercely that every one of them was missing at least one leg and cotton stuffing spilled out through gaping slashes in the upholstery. She'd smashed the mirror over the fireplace and several panes of glass. She'd even hacked great holes and tears in the beautiful oriental carpet.

"It's ruined," Mother said.

"We can fix it," I said.

"Not by tomorrow morning," Mother said. "It's taken me weeks."

"Darlin' you need to sit down." Eustace gently took Mother's arm and began steering her into the kitchen. "You come in here and have a cup of tea. Your family's going to fix your room up for you."

He was looking straight at me.

Why me? Didn't getting tied up and almost murdered entitle me to a little time off?

"It's beyond fixing," Mother moaned.

"No it's not," I said.

Mother stopped in the doorway and looked back at me. And suddenly I had the answer to "why me?" Because I might not be the only person who could get Mother's room fixed, but I was the only person she'd trust to do it. And also because every year I agonized over what to get her for Christmas, and always watched her face when she unwrapped her present, worrying that she was merely a consummate actress when she beamed and told me "I love it." If I could pull this off, I wouldn't have the slightest doubt when she proclaimed this "the best Christmas ever."

"We'll fix it," I said. "The best we can. We can't put it back the way it was. But we'll make it beautiful."

She smiled wanly and followed Eustace into the kitchen. I heard him fussing over her like a mother hen with a wayward chick.

"So, what do we do?" Dad asked.

He was also looking at me.

They all were.

Thank goodness Michael strode in just then. Rose Noire, Sarah, and Vermillion were on his heels.

"Okay, folks," I said. "We've got till ten a.m. tomorrow."

"And a lot of help is on the way," Michael added.

"Okay," I said. "Here goes. Unbroken stuff into the study—if that's okay with you, Sarah? There can't be that much."

She nodded.

"Broken stuff that might be repairable to the garage. All the other trash goes into the Dumpster. Someone find a box and collect the Christmas ornaments that aren't broken. More instructions later, but for now, let's clean up this room. Dad, hang on—I have a special mission for you."

"What is it?" He looked a little more cheerful, as I suspected he would at the thought of a special mission.

"There's a photographer coming at ten. Keep your eyes peeled; he might show up early. Your mission is to keep him from coming in. Send him back to Richmond if possible. Lie to him and tell him the show house has been relocated to the zoo if you like. Just keep him away from here until I tell you it's okay."

"You've got it!"

Sarah and Vermillion approached me.

"My room's in good shape," Sarah said. "I can help."

"Me, too," Vermillion said.

"Thanks," I said. "It would be nice if someone with some kind of decorating skill was involved in this."

The three of us retired to the kitchen to confer with Mother and Eustace while an ever-increasing crew of worker bees dismantled the damaged décor in the great room.

"We don't have the time to buy new furniture and have it delivered," Mother said. "Maybe we should do a theme room. Christmas in the bowling alley."

"Forget new furniture," I said. "What furniture can you think of in your house or ours that would work?"

"Now that's an idea," she said. "The chairs in your father's study might do in a pinch."

"What about those ratty sofas in the Trinity parish hall?" I said. "The ones you said have good bones and should be recovered? Let's call Robyn and see if we can borrow them and do it."

"Remember that pair of end tables I outbid you for at that estate sale last year?" Eustace said. "I could be persuaded to lend them."

I left them to it and went off to see how the cleanup was coming. And how Michael was coming on his phone calls.

By nine-thirty, the room was an empty shell. Tomás and Mateo were starting to replace the broken windowpanes. One crew of Shiffleys was going around the room installing new drywall while another crew followed behind, painting it in "Red Obsession."

"Meg, that photographer's here," Rose Noire stuck her head in the kitchen to say. "But don't worry—your dad seems to be coping."

"Coping how?" I asked.

"Well, last time I looked, he was taking the guy's blood pressure, and looking worried."

I strolled out to check on things.

"Oh, good," Dad said, seeing me. "Meg, this is Mr. Timmerman from the *Richmond Times-Dispatch*. I know you're expecting him to take some pictures, but I'm taking him down to the hospital. Don't worry," he said, turning back to Mr. Timmerman. "The heartburn could just be heartburn, and the shoulder pain could just be from hauling that heavy camera bag about. But even the possibility of a cardiac problem should be taken seriously. Let's just make sure, shall we? My car's over there. Just leave your equipment here; I'll bring you back when we're finished."

"Thanks," Timmerman said. He trudged back to his car and popped the trunk to put a suitcase-sized equipment bag in it.

"Dad," I said in an undertone. "I don't want to you commit malpractice for the show house."

"It's not for the show house, it's for your mother," he said. "And I'm not making up his symptoms. I was going to try that 'relocating to the zoo' idea, but then I saw him popping antiacids and rubbing his shoulder—that's how a cardiac problem presents sometimes. And his blood pressure's through the roof. I'd be astonished if a full cardiac workup doesn't show some symptoms, and I can keep him under observation as long as you need me to."

With that, he scampered off to his car, where Mr. Timmerman was waiting, looking a bit impatient.

I returned to the house.

As Dad drove off, Randall pulled up in a truck.

"Where do you want me to put the furniture?" he asked.

"In the garage for now."

Back in the kitchen, Mother, Sarah, Vermillion, and Eustace were nodding at each other over a large sheet of paper.

"Dear heart," Eustace said. "It won't be the room you wanted. But it's a room you can be proud of."

"Come here for a minute." I led her out to the garage, where Randall was unloading the furniture we'd arranged to borrow.

"They don't match," Mother said. "Each other or the room."

"We'll make slipcovers for them," I said.

"We?" Mother repeated. I could understand why—her sewing skills were even more rudimentary than mine. But before I could explain, the first of our worker bees came in through the garage door: Mrs. Tran, who along with Michael's mother ran a dress shop in my hometown of Yorktown, and three of her best seamstresses. They were followed by two graduate drama students I recognized as longtime costume shop volunteers.

"I think it's either the slipcovers or the curtains," one of the students said. "I'm not sure we'll have time for both."

"The heck we won't." Minerva Burke had arrived at the head of a contingent of a dozen ladies from the New Life Baptist Church Ladies' Auxiliary.

"Bring it on," said the Reverend Robyn, as she led in nearly the entire membership of Grace Episcopal's Guild of St. Clotilda, and even a couple of the ladies from the women's shelter.

"Our room's ready," one of the Quilt Ladies said, sticking her head into the study. "We can help. We've brought in extra sewing machines. What needs doing?"

Michael had also recruited some drama students with set-building experience. They got to work building canvas frames to replace the ruined artwork—frames that would cover a large portion of the walls and disguise any shortcomings in the hasty paint job. A lot of the volunteers had brought their children or grandchildren, so we set the kids and anyone who wasn't sewing to work painting holiday murals on the canvas. The Quilt Ladies, bless their hearts, borrowed several tarps from Randall, battened down or covered up everything in their room, and turned it into a children's art studio. Even Violet and Linda postponed the last minute primping they'd been planning to do in their rooms to pitch in.

And not long after we started, someone struck up the first verse of "Deck the Halls," and before long everyone, all through the house, was singing. Quite possibly the best caroling I'd heard outside the New Life Baptist Choir's annual concerts.

Someone brought in a bunch of cots and sleeping bags, and we set up Clay's room as a nap room for any kids—or grown-ups—who needed to take a break. Some of the Baptist women brought in supplies, took over Eustace's kitchen, and began turning out delectable soups, sandwiches, casseroles, cookies, and pies.

"Aren't you afraid they'll mess up your kitchen?" I asked Eustace at one point.

"Darlin', have you ever seen a church lady who didn't feel compelled to leave someone else's kitchen even cleaner than she found it?" Eustace said. "Those ladies just might be my secret weapon to winning the prize."

As the day wore on, more and more friends dropped by to help, bringing their kids, armloads of craft supplies, and boxes of decorations for the new tree Randall's cousins had gone off to find. Before long, Rose Noire showed up with a trunkload of dried flowers and other organic craft supplies, so when we had finished decorating all the canvas panels, we set the painting crew to work making homemade Christmas potpourri ornaments and stringing old-fashioned popcorn garlands. At first I was worried that we might be overboard with the ornaments, but when two of Randall's cousins showed up with the new tree, we began to worry about filling it all.

"More garlands!" I shouted. "More tinsel! More snow! More stars! More holly! More angels! More wise men!"

The children fell to work.

In the middle of all this, Dad called to update me on the photographer.

"The good news is that he wasn't actually having a heart attack," Dad said. "The bad news is that he's a heart attack waiting to happen. He's a lucky man. I'm in the process of turning him over to a cardiologist here at VCU—"

"VCU?" I echoed. "You're down in Richmond?"

"Yes, and I should be heading back in an hour or two."

"Does the *Times-Dispatch* know he's not up here taking pictures?" I asked.

"Oh, yes," Dad said. "But I don't know if they're going to send anyone to take his place."

Probably just as well, I decided. We still had a lot to do. The only halfway Christmassy fabric we'd found for making the slipcovers and curtains was a dull burgundy. It went nicely with the "Red Obsession" walls but it wasn't exactly an exciting choice. When we set the first slipcovered chair in the middle of the room, everyone stood back and studied the effect.

"Color's perfect with the walls," Sarah said.

"Nice slipcovering job," Randall said.

"But it needs a little something," Mother, Eustace, and Sarah said in unison.

"Yes, it does." Ivy appeared out of nowhere, as usual. "A little decoration. May I?"

Mother nodded. Ivy was holding several brushes and pots of paint. She quickly painted a little running decoration like a stylized vine along the back of the chair in gold paint with touches of green and black. It wasn't as intricately detailed as her own murals, but it was still magical.

"I like it," Mother said.

So as each table or chair emerged from the impromptu upholstery workshop, Ivy added in the vine. Tomás watched her for a few minutes, then said a few words to Mateo. The two of them grabbed pots of paint and tiny brushes and began working on the walls, adding in the same stylized vine here and there to the red-painted walls.

"Hiring those two just might turn out one of my smartest decisions ever," Randall said in a tone of great satisfaction. "And this place is shaping up."

"I thought we'd be working all night," I said. "But with all the help we've got, I think we're pretty close to done."

The curtains were finished and hung, the slipcovers completed and decorated by Ivy, Tomás, and Mateo. In fact, we'd finished every bit of sewing we could think of, so Mother hugged Mrs. Tran and each of her seamstresses, and they headed home to Yorktown. We ran out of ornament-making supplies about the time we ran out of room on the tree, so we thanked all the children, and their parents took them home. The students had one last hearty meal and headed back for the dorms, armed with generous doggy bags. The Baptist and Episcopal ladies stayed long enough to make sure every room in which our volunteers had worked was spotless. Most of Randall's workmen left. The Quilt Ladies thanked Randall for the tarps and began restoring their room to order.

Chief Burke stopped by to pick up his wife, and while Minerva was saying her good-byes to the rest of the Baptist and Episcopal ladies, he filled me in on what had been happening down at the police station.

"We're holding Martha Blaine for murdering Clay and attempting to murder you," he said.

"What about her so-called alibi?" I asked.

"Miss Violet is no longer quite so certain that Ms. Blaine was with her every minute of that night," he said. "And we'll be testing for the drug used to knock her out. Horace tells me that since it's been less than seventy-two hours, there's a chance the drug could still be in her system. Of course, disproving her alibi may not be quite as critical as it might have been. Ms. Blaine has been quite communicative since her arrest."

"Her lawyer will be displeased with her."

"Yes," the chief said. "Of course, what she'd already said to you when she was planning to kill you had already limited her lawyer's options to self-defense or insanity. And speaking of insanity, we're doing what we can to see that Jessica Green will be making her pilgrimage through the mental health system rather than the Department of Corrections."

"That's good," I said.

"Yes." He frowned and shook his head. "I don't think that poor girl has had many breaks in her life. Let's hope they can do something for her."

We fell silent for a few moments.

"And what about the Grangers?" I asked.

"Ah, yes. The Grangers." He grimaced. "Whose shenanigans proved such a dangerous distraction from the trail of the real culprit. Mrs. Granger has filed for divorce. And now that she's merely leaving him, and not leaving him for Mr. Spottiswood, Mr. Granger seems willing to accept the situation."

"Not exactly a happy ending," I said. "But probably for the best."

"And they do seem to be in agreement about one thing," he added. "Neither one of them wants their house—they both want to sell it and split up the proceeds. But the entire downstairs is only partially decorated, so they're looking for a designer who's neither dead nor in jail. Do you think any of the crew here would be interested?"

"I'll put the word out," I said. "Thanks."

"So will we see you at the Living Nativity tomorrow?" he asked.

"Wouldn't miss it for the world," I said. "Or the caroling in the town square."

"Till then," he said. "Merry Christmas!"

And he and Minerva hurried off—no doubt to buy a few more presents for their grandchildren.

Alice the Quilt Lady bustled up as they were leaving.

"By the way, Meg," she said. "I asked Randall this, and he said okay as long as it was okay with you. We're going to put prices on all our quilts. If anyone wants to buy one, they have to wait till the show house is over to take it home, of course."

"Sounds fine to me," I said. "And before we let any strangers in here, may I claim that tumbling block quilt?"

"Oh." She frowned. "I'm afraid that one's already spoken for."

I'm sure my face showed how disappointed I was.

"Don't worry," she said in a reassuring tone. She looked around to see if anyone else was listening, and then went on, in a lower tone. "Two young gentlemen who were here helping with the decorating saw it, and both thought it would be perfect to give their mother for Christmas. By an odd coincidence, the price we'd put on it was just a little bit less than what they had in their piggy banks. Seems they've been looking all over Caerphilly for days, searching for just the right present, and they think she'll like it almost as well as the pair of winter-white hamsters their daddy won't let them give her."

"Wonderful!" I exclaimed.

"Maybe I shouldn't have told you," she said. "But you looked so disappointed."

"Don't worry," I said. "I'm very good at pretending to be surprised."

She headed back to her room. In fact, all the designers were returning to their rooms to do a few bits of last-minute primping. Most of them were spinning their wheels, though, having raced to get everything ready and now finding nothing to do with themselves.

"Probably a good idea to leave now," Sarah said finally. "At this point, I'm more apt to mess things up than improve them. And they'll kick us out when the judges get here, right?"

One by one, the others made the same decision. Eventually, Mother and Ivy were the only designers left in the house. Ivy was upstairs, finishing her Snow Queen mural, and Mother was watching Tomás and Mateo doing something with strings of lights.

"Half an hour till the judges get here," I called out.

"I'll be ready," Ivy called back.

I strolled into the living room. Tomás and Mateo were dashing madly up and down their tall ladders. Whatever they were doing with the lights—more like a mesh of lights than a string—they had started on either side of the Christmas tree and were about to meet over the fireplace.

I could hear Randall's voice outside.

"Step this way, folks," he was saying.

"I'm just going to slip out the back," Ivy said. "I'm all paint-smeared and messy."

She looked fine, as usual. I gave her a quick hug. She seemed surprised, but not upset.

"We couldn't have done it without you," I said. "Any of it."

She smiled and left.

"No, the designers won't be watching you while you're judging," I heard Randall saying on the steps. "We'll just give them a minute or two to leave."

"*¡Fin!*" Tomás exclaimed.

Mateo scrambled down his ladder, raced over to the foot of the Christmas tree, and plugged something in.

The lights came on. Not just the conventional lights on the Christmas tree, but great swathes of tiny fairy lights, clustered thickly all along the ceiling and then thinning out to one or two lights halfway down the walls. And all the lights twinkled, and thanks to the metallic gold paint on all the curtains and furniture and the several tons of glitter the kids had used on all the canvas murals and the Christmas ornaments, the whole room twinkled along with it.

"It's beautiful." I said. I stopped myself from saying anything else, like "I know it's not the room you'd planned."

The room *was* beautiful. Full stop. And it looked like exactly what it was—a room decorated by a bunch of different people, some of them with a flair for design, and the rest with just a whole lot of love and Christmas spirit.

In fact, while I would never say this to Mother, I liked this room better. I found myself thinking of it as the real nightingale to the beautiful but artificial clockwork bird that was her original room.

Mother took a long, slow look around.

"Yes," she said. "It's beautiful. Let's go out through the garage."

As we hurried through the breakfast room, the kitchen, and the laundry room, we heard Randall's key in the front door.

"Step right in, ladies and gentlemen."

Mother and I stopped in the garage and took a deep breath.

"I need to get in here early tomorrow morning to tidy up," I said, looking around.

"Will people be coming in here?" Mother asked.

"Well, given that every shop in Caerphilly has been selling the tickets for weeks, probably not a lot of people," I said. "But we're going to have a ticket seller here, just in case."

"Then let's clean up tonight," Mother said. "It won't take long."

Normally, Mother's only involvement in cleaning was supervisory. But tonight she seemed to have been inspired by the events of the day and pitched in with a will. We swept, tidied, filled black plastic bags with garbage, stacked construction supplies for Randall to haul off in the morning, and arranged everything else neatly on the workbench.

But she still seemed pensive.

"A penny for them," I said.

"I was just wishing I had a picture of my room before that horrible girl attacked it," she said. "I was so tired when I left yesterday afternoon that I didn't take any—I was planning to ask someone to do it this morning."

"I have a few," I said.

"Oh, I knew you were taking them all along," she said. "And those will be lovely to have. But it finally came together yesterday afternoon, after you left."

"And I took a lot of pictures last night," I said. "When I first came in. Before Jessica arrived."

Her face lit up. I turned on my phone, opened up the picture album, and handed it to her.

I finished up the last few bits of tidying as she studied the photos.

"Yes," she said. "It was just the way I planned it."

"I'm sorry that no one else will get to see it," I said.

"I can show them the pictures," she replied. "You are going to send me those pictures, aren't you?"

"Of course."

"It doesn't bother me as much now," she said. "It's always silly to fall in love with a room—especially a show house room that you know from the start will only last a few weeks. But now that we have pictures, I don't feel nearly as bad."

"That's good," I said.

"We should get back to your house," she said. "Dahlia has a special dinner planned. She's cooking all the things she wanted to have on Christmas eve or Christmas day but didn't have room for."

"Well, that should be original," I said. "And after dinner—"

"And I have wonderful news," she added. "This afternoon Rob went up to fetch your grandmother Cordelia. She's coming, too."

"For tonight's dinner?"

"Yes, and for Christmas. Now that we've finally found her, it's about time we spent a lot more time with her."

"Grandfather won't like that," I said.

"Your grandfather will just have to cope," she said. "She's as much family as he is. And Christmas is a time for family, isn't it?"

"Absolutely." Suddenly I was eager to leave the show house and get home so I could really start enjoying Christmas. I glanced around to see how much more tidying we had to do. Not much. And with Mother pitching in, we'd be finished in no time.

"You were absolutely right, you know," she said.

Not words I often heard from Mother. Was I witnessing a small Christmas miracle?

"About what?" I asked aloud.

"About not having the show house at your house. It would have been a much better house, of course, but think of the disruption it would have caused."

"Yeah, murder does tend to be disrupting," I said.

"Not just the murder," she said. "Having peculiar things done to all your rooms, and then crowds of the people tramping through over the next few weeks. You were right to dig in your heels."

"Thank you."

"Next year, we'll just have to start looking for a house earlier," she said.

I decided not to say anything about my resolution to not to get involved next year.

"In January, I should think," Mother went on. "Perhaps not quite so large a house next time—after all, the design community's noticeably smaller than it was when we started this whole project."

Instead of answering, I hit the button to raise the garage door.

"We can sneak out this way," I said as the door slowly chugged up. "So we won't bother the judges."

"Look!" Mother pointed as the landscape outside. "More snow. How lovely!"

Yes, it was lovely. All you could see in the light spilling out of the garage door was snowflakes. Not the kind of big, sloppy, wet snowflakes that tended to melt as soon as they hit the ground. These were the tiny snowflakes you get when the air is really cold—serious, businesslike snowflakes, clearly intent on making a major contribution to our already record December snowfall totals.

"How many more inches are we expecting, anyway?" I asked.

"I haven't had time to listen to the weather," Mother said with a shrug. "But as long as we take off soon, we shouldn't have any trouble getting to your house."

No telling if she and Dad would be able to get home again afterward. But if this proved to be the snow that finally defeated the county snowplows—well, one more benefit of not holding the show house in our house was that Michael and I had enough spare rooms for everyone to stay over. The boys would love being snowbound with all their available grandparents and great-grandparents to spoil them.

"Let's not waste any more time," I said aloud. "And—"

"Mrs. Langslow."

It was Randall. He stepped into the garage. The six other members of the County Board filed in after him. They all looked solemn.

"Is something wrong?" I asked.

Instead of answering, Randall walked over to stand in front of Mother.

"Mrs. Langslow," Randall said. "I'm delighted to inform you that your room has been chosen as the winner of the best room contest for this year's Caerphilly Historical Society Decorator Show House."

The board members all broke into smiles, and a great deal of hugging and handshaking followed.

"The other rooms are all lovely, each and every one of them," one of the women said.

"In their own ways," chimed in one of the men.

"But your room is not only lovely, but it has a warmth and a sense of Christmas good cheer that we all loved."

"Thank you," Mother said. She was dabbing at her eyes. "I really couldn't have done it without so many people."

"Let's go home and make a list," I said. "So you can thank them all when you make your acceptance speech at the reception tomorrow. In the meantime, we have presents to wrap, and grandsons who are waiting for you to read them ''Twas the Night Before Christmas.'"

"Good advice, dear," Mother said. "Good night," she said, beaming one last time at the judges.

"Merry Christmas to all," I said. "And to all a good night."

Read on for an excerpt from

Lord of the Wings—

the next Meg Langslow mystery from Donna Andrews,
available soon in hardcover from Minotaur Books!

Chapter 1

"Someone's broken into the Haunted House!"

My cell phone almost vibrated from the excitement in
my brother's voice.

"Calm down, Rob," I said. I wanted to add, "And what
are you doing awake before eight a.m.?" but I suspected
he would take it as a slur on his character. I punched the
speaker button, set my phone on the kitchen table, and
went back to painting a goatee on my son Josh's chin.

"But Meg, the Haunted House—"

"Was anything taken?" I asked. "Or broken?"

"Not that we can tell," Rob said. "But Dr. Smoot is
upset."

"That's his normal state of mind these days," I said.
Then I winced, hoping the proprietor of the Haunted House
wasn't close enough to Rob's phone to hear me.

"If you can call anything about Smoot normal." Okay,
even Rob wouldn't have said that in front of the man.
"But definitely more upset than usual. The closer we get
to Halloween, the more hyper he gets."

Josh lifted up his piratical eye patch, twisted to look at
his reflection in the shiny chrome side of the toaster, and
frowned.

"I want to be more hairier," he said.

"Just hairier," I corrected. "I'm working on it. Did you report it to the police?" I added to Rob.

"Not yet," Rob said. "Dr. Smoot says Chief Burke never takes him seriously."

Dr. Smoot was probably right. Of course, it didn't help that while he was still serving as Caerphilly County's medical examiner, Dr. Smoot had taken to dressing as a vampire, complete with a long black cape and fake fangs, and collecting vampire-related paraphernalia. Chief Burke had been vastly relieved when Dr. Smoot had resigned his post to pursue this strange new hobby full time, complete with travels to such vampire meccas as Transylvania and New Orleans. The chief probably wasn't thrilled to have Dr. Smoot not only back in town but also running the Haunted House that played a central role in the town's ongoing Halloween festival.

"Never mind their past history," I said. "If there's any real evidence of a burglary, Chief Burke will want to investigate. In fact, he'll be pretty ticked off if he finds out you didn't call him right away."

"Dr. Smoot says since nothing was actually taken, he thought it was okay to call the Goblin Patrol instead."

"Rob," I began.

"Sorry," Rob said. "The Visitor Relations and Police Liaison Patrol. I still think Goblin Patrol's catchier. I'll call the chief. But Dr. Smoot's upset—he really wants to talk to you."

"I'm putting the boys into their costumes for school," I said. "And then Michael and I are going along as chaperones for today's school field trip to the zoo. And—"

"Great," Rob said. "The Haunted House is right on your way. You could just drop in for a few minutes—"

"After the field trip," I said. "Or if more than enough parents come to wrangle the kids, I might be able to break away once we've delivered our carload to the zoo. Call the police, and tell Dr. Smoot I'll be there as soon as I can."

"Roger," Rob said.

"Uncle Rob," Josh said. "I'm a pirate today."

"A pirate?" Rob echoed. "I thought you were a cowboy."

"A cowboy? Yuck. That was yesterday."

"Today he's a pirate," I said. "I've been trying to explain to the boys that when their teacher said they could wear costumes every day this week, it didn't mean a different costume every day."

"But it's more fun this way," Josh protested.

"Absolutely!" Rob said. "Goblin Patrol, over and out."

"Rob," I began, but he'd already hung up. "Josh, can you punch the button to turn off my phone? My hands are full."

He obliged, then turned back to me and lifted his chin as if silently demanding that I add another layer of painted beard.

"Mommy—look!" I turned to see Jamie, Josh's twin. "See my new costume! Isn't it cool?"

"Very cool!" I stopped myself before asking, "But what is it?" and studied his outfit for clues. Like most first graders he had only rudimentary costume-making skills, so at first glance, his new outfit looked exactly like Monday's dog costume, Tuesday's raccoon, and Wednesday's penguin. They all used as a base the same set of faded beige footed pajamas. Today he'd stuck tufts of fur rather than feathers to the flannel, so I deduced that he was a mammal rather than a bird. The catlike whiskers stuck on his cheeks with Scotch tape didn't help much, but then I noticed that the rope he'd tied around his waist, leaving one end trailing six or seven feet behind him, now bore a tuft of fur at the tip.

"So you're going as a lion today?" I guessed.

Jamie beamed.

"Look, Josh," he said. "Rowrrrr!"

Josh was studying himself again in the toaster.

"I guess it's okay," he said. "But I want a really cool costume for the real Halloween on Saturday."

"Josh," I said, "that's only two days away. I'm not sure we have time to make another costume. Can't you just go as a pirate or a cowboy or a space alien or a wizard? We can make some improvements to whichever one you choose."

"I want to be a robot," Josh said.

It could be worse, I decided. I could easily make him a robot suit with some cardboard boxes and tin foil.

"But not one of those lame robot costumes like Victor's mother made him out of cardboard boxes and tin foil," Josh said. "A *real* robot costume. It should be metal. And the eyes should light up when I get mad. And you should be able to open up my chest to see my motor."

"I'll think about it," I said. "No promises," I added. "You know I'm pretty busy with the Halloween festival."

"But I really want to be a robot!"

"No whining!" I exclaimed.

Josh recognized the wisdom of shutting up, and shifted tactics. He sighed and donned a look of patient, wistful longing—rather like Oliver Twist holding up the empty gruel bowl.

Maybe Michael could enlist some help in making a robot costume. An extra credit project for a couple of his drama department students with prop and costume shop experience. I could ask him.

And come to think of it, maybe Michael could drive the boys to school, pick up the other two kids we were supposed to transport, and take them to the zoo. Then I could drop by to soothe Dr. Smoot and still meet them there in time for the tour.

"Where's your daddy?" I asked the boys.

"In the backyard, chasing the llamas," Jamie said.

"Why is he chasing the llamas?" I asked. "Are they loose?"

Jamie shook his head.

"Then why—"

"Who's ready for waffles?" my cousin Rose Noire called out, as she sailed in, already dressed in her costume for the day, as Glinda, the Good Witch.

"Yay!" Jamie exclaimed

"Blueberry waffles?" Josh asked.

"*Organic* blueberry waffles," Rose Noire said. "With artisanal maple syrup."

The boys sat down and looked expectant. On mornings like this, I was profoundly grateful that Rose Noire still showed no signs of moving out of the third floor spare bedroom she'd occupied since before the boys were born.

I strolled outside to see why Michael was chasing the llamas.

Actually, he wasn't so much chasing them as being followed by them. He was jogging briskly around the perimeter of their pasture and the llamas, ever curious about human eccentricities, were loping along behind him.

I leaned over the fence and watched until he drew near, then climbed over the top rail and fell into step beside him.

"What's up?" I asked.

"An actor's body is his instrument," he puffed.

"That's nice," I said. "What does that have to do with your taking up jogging?" Then enlightenment struck. "You tried on your wizard costume last night, didn't you?" I asked.

Michael frowned and nodded.

"Too tight?"

"Not *too* tight," he said. "But a little tighter than it used to be. Tighter than it *should* be."

Not surprising, since it had been a few years since

Michael had donned the costume he'd once worn to play the evil wizard Mephisto on *Porfiria, Queen of the Jungle*, a long-canceled cult TV fantasy show. In fact, although die-hard fans kept inviting him to Porfiria fan conventions, he hadn't gone since before the twins were born, and they were six now.

"I could let your costume out a little," I suggested.

"No," he said, and picked up his pace a little. "I need to get down to my proper weight. An actor's body is his instrument."

"Okay," I said. "Carry on tuning your instrument. I'll figure out something healthy and low calorie for dinner."

"Thanks," he said. "And keep all that damned Halloween candy away from me."

"Roger," I said. "By the way, can you take the boys to school and pick up the other two kids we're taking to the field trip? I can meet you at the zoo—I have an errand I should run on my way."

"Goblin Patrol business?"

"Something like that." As I explained about Dr. Smoot, I considered whether I should stop fighting this Goblin Patrol thing. It was certainly catchier than Visitor Relations and Police Liaison Patrol. "If I hurry," I concluded. "I can deal with Smoot and still make the zoo tour."

"I don't envy you," he said. "And yes, I can take the boys."

We'd done nearly a complete circuit of the pasture now, so I decided I'd jogged enough.

"I'm going to peel off now and get ready for my busy day," I said.

"Not as busy as it would have been if Randall Shiffley hadn't hired Lydia," Michael called over his shoulder.

I made a noncommittal noise and headed back to the kitchen.

Yes, if Randall hadn't hired Lydia Van Meter to the

newly created post of Special Assistant to the Mayor, I would probably have been running the whole of Caerphilly's ten-day Halloween festival instead of merely heading up the Goblin Patrol. I definitely preferred my more limited role.

But that didn't mean I had to like Lydia.

Just thinking about her soured my mood. And it wasn't because she was doing a terrible job at organizing the Halloween Festival. Considering that it was her first major project, she was doing okay. Not perfectly—certainly not the way I'd have done it—but things were lurching along, and she was learning. She'd probably have an easier time with the much bigger Christmas in Caerphilly event that would start right after Thanksgiving, because we'd been doing that for several years now, and Randall and I had done a pretty good job of setting up procedures and training the townspeople in them. By summer, when it was time for the Un-Fair, the statewide agricultural exposition Caerphilly hosted every year, she should be in fine shape—again, thanks to all the ground work Randall and I had done on past Un-Fairs.

Since, in the long run, she was going to make my life easier, it was probably ungracious of me to dislike her. Maybe I was the only one who minded her constant griping about how hard she was working and how impossible the job was. I couldn't count the times I'd had to bite my tongue to keep from saying, "You think you've got it bad—I used to do all that and more, as a volunteer." And was it just my imagination, or was she developing an annoying tendency to ask me how I would handle something and then do exactly the opposite?

"Chill," I muttered. After all, Lydia was making it possible for me to spend more time with Michael and the boys, doing things like today's field trip to the Caerphilly Zoo.

And accompanying the boys to the zoo was definitely

important, and not just because I wanted to see their reaction to the brand-new Creatures of the Night exhibit. As the zoo's proud owner, my grandfather was planning on conducting the tour himself, and I knew better than to expect common sense from him. What if he gave in to some first grader's pleas to be allowed to pet the arctic wolves? Or began explaining the curious mating habits of the greater short-nosed fruit bat, as he had a few weeks ago when giving a preview tour to the Baptist Ladies' Altar Guild?

I ran upstairs to throw on the last few bits of my costume—a modified version of the red satin and black leather swordswoman's outfit I wore whenever I exhibited my blacksmithing work at a Renaissance festival. I added the festive black-and-orange armband that marked me as a member of the Goblin Patrol and headed for town.

The first few miles of my journey lay through farmlands—pastures dotted with grazing cows or sheep, fields filled with late crops or post-harvest stubble, and orchards picked clean of all but the latest fruits. Closer to town, I began to see Halloween and harvest decorations on the gates and fences. I particularly admired the farmer who'd used a collection of scarecrows to simulate a zombie attack on his cow pasture. The contrast between the bloodstained shambling figures clawing at the outside of the fence and the Guernsey cows calmly chewing their cuds inside never failed to amuse me.

I was nearing town when my phone rang. Lydia. I considered letting it go to voice mail. Then I sighed, and pulled over to answer it. She was probably calling about something she considered important. Her definition of important rarely coincided with mine, but I'd already figured out that the best way to keep her calm and off my back was to talk to her. She seemed to resent having to leave a voice mail.

"Thank goodness I caught you!" she exclaimed as soon as I answered. "Can you drop by to see me as soon as possible? Something important's come up. Festival business! Thanks!"

"I'm already on my way to take care of festival business," I began. But before I could make the case for discussing whatever had come up over the phone instead of face to face, I realized she'd hung up.

"Damn the woman," I muttered as I punched the button to call her back. But her phone line was already busy.

So I muttered a few words I didn't usually let myself say, for fear the boys would pick them up, and pulled out onto the road again. Dr. Smoot's burglar would have to wait while I tackled whatever crisis Lydia had to offer.

Chapter 2

Even Lydia couldn't spoil my enjoyment of the Halloween scenery. Closer to town the farmlands gave way to houses whose yards almost universally contained some kind of decorations. Strings of orange pumpkin- or skeleton-shaped lights festooned at least half of the fences. Most of the steps bore jack-o-lanterns. Some yards contained miniature graveyards, with or without skeletons or vampires digging their way out of the earth, and I lost count of the number of witches that appeared to have slammed into trees.

In the outskirts of town I passed by the left turn onto the Clay County road that would have taken me to Dr. Smoot's Haunted House and then on to the zoo. Instead I continued on toward the town square.

The official town decorations, though attractive, were somewhat more sedate, reflecting a harvest theme rather than a Halloween one. The streetlights had been enclosed in plastic covers to make them look like pumpkins—just pumpkins, not jack-o-lanterns. Graceful black, brown, and orange garlands hung between the lampposts, and all the trash cans and benches and other public fixtures were festooned with gourds and sheaves of dried grass and flowers. "It's the Caerphilly Garden Club," Randall Shiffley had said in a slightly apologetic tone when he showed me the design. "They always like to err on the side of good taste, and I don't think most of them really like Halloween all that much."

They probably didn't—but they were clearly in the minority. Most of the shops and houses contained enough jack-o-lanterns, faux skeletons, black cat window decals, bat garlands, and rubber rats to make up for any excess of good taste on the part of the Garden Club.

It was early enough that I had no trouble finding a parking spot near the courthouse. As I climbed the long marble steps up to the front portico, I could see that the two small groups of protesters were already on duty. I turned to study them for a moment. To the right were a small group of people who objected to our Halloween festival on the grounds that it was a godless pagan holiday that a respectable town shouldn't be celebrating. To the left was a group of about the same number of devout pagans who were protesting our commercialization of what was for them an important religious holiday and our use of decorations that perpetuated society's negative stereotype of witches.

Neither group had started picketing yet, only milling around as if waiting for something. The arrival of the first tourists, perhaps.

If I'd been in charge, I'd have long ago sent a couple of local ministers out to placate the Halloween haters and tasked Rose Noire with figuring out what we could do to calm down the pagans.

Then I saw them all perk up as two figures approached. It was Muriel, owner of the local diner, and one of her waitresses, both carrying trays laden with doughnuts and carryout cups of coffee. Muriel began serving the pagans while the waitress continued on toward the Halloween haters.

"You were right," said a voice from over my shoulder.

I looked up to see Randall standing at the top of the steps, gazing down at the protesters. His buckskin costume already looked wrinkled, and his Davy Crockett-style coonskin hat was askew.

"I usually am right," I said, as I made my way up the

rest of the steps. "What in particular am I right about today?"

"We never should have tried to chase them off," he said, nodding at the protesters. "Should have killed them with kindness from the start."

I refrained from saying that it was Lydia who tried to order the protesters away, and demanded that the police step in when her efforts failed. Fortunately Chief Burke had a cool head and a strong respect for the First Amendment.

"I see you're taking my idea about the refreshments," I said.

"Yup." Randall smiled with satisfaction. "Coffee and doughnuts every morning from Muriel, and tea and cookies every afternoon from one of the churches. If the forecast calls for rain, we put up those little canvas shelters for them, and they know they're always welcome to use the courthouse bathroom."

"You're spoiling them," I said.

"And we're down to about a third of the number we had last week this time," he said. "Clearly it's no fun protesting people who seem perfectly happy to have you stay around. What brings you downtown? I'd have thought you'd be out at the zoo with the first graders today."

"I will be," I said. "As soon as I talk to Lydia and find out what's so important that she had to drag me all the way downtown."

Randall winced, and I felt slightly guilty for venting at him.

"Sorry," he said. "She means well, and she's learning."

Not learning fast enough to suit me, but I refrained from saying so aloud. I just nodded, went inside the courthouse, and took the elevator up to the third floor where Lydia had her office, a few doors down from Randall's office.

As usual, Lydia was on the phone. Not just on the phone,

but switching back and forth between the two lines on her desk phone while texting something on her cell phone with her right hand and clicking something on her computer keyboard with the left. She nodded and smiled when she saw me, and held up two fingers, like a peace sign. Her intent, of course, was to say that she'd be with me in two minutes. I knew better by now.

I sat down in one of her desk chairs and resigned myself to wait. If I were a snarkier person, I'd have brought along a thick book—*War and Peace*, perhaps—and made a show of settling down to read it while she talked. Instead, I pulled out my notebook-that-tells-me-when-to-breathe, as I call my giant to-do list, and made productive use of my time.

Other people rarely understood how comforting I found it to spend time with my notebook. Knowing that everything on my plate was captured between its covers cleared my brain to concentrate on whatever I was doing. Since the boys' arrival, life had grown even more complicated than before, and I'd traded in my original spiral notebooks for a small three-ring binder, but apart from that my system was the same. My notebook gave me peace of mind, and all it asked in return was that I tend it for a few minutes here and there. I marked a few tasks as done and added a few new ones.

"Yeah, yeah," Lydia was saying. "I'll take care of it."

I glanced up to see that she was scribbling something on a yellow sticky note.

She stuck the sticky on the left side of her computer monitor, where it was largely indistinguishable from the hundred other yellow sticky notes that clung to the monitor, gradually encroaching on the viewing space. Her calendar and the wall it hung on were similarly encrusted. As I watched, one lonely yellow square gave up hope of ever being read and let itself fall to the floor.

By contrast, her desk contained only a few sticky notes, hidden here and there among the books, folders, paper stacks and yellow legal pads that covered every inch of horizontal space and in some places had begun to slide off onto the floor.

Every time I walked into her office, my fingers itched to start organizing it all.

Not for the first time I wondered where Randall had found her, and how in the world she had convinced him that she was good at organizing.

"Chill," I murmured under my breath. Lydia's organizing skills might be overrated, the festival might not be running the way I'd like to have seen it run, but it was limping along adequately without me doing anything other than organizing and running the volunteer security force. I reminded myself to be grateful for that.

"Sorry." She hung up and turned to me with a perky little smile that didn't really reach her eyes. "There's just so much going on."

"Understandable," I said. "What did you need to see me about?"

"Oh!" She began scanning the sticky notes on the left side of her monitor and plucked one off. "Here it is. Dr. Smoot called. He seems to think someone broke into the museum very early this morning. Could you check to see if it's something the police should handle or if he's just being hyper again?"

"You could have told me about it over the phone," I said. "As it happens, one of my volunteers already told me about the break-in, and I was on my way over there when you called. If you'd told me that was why you were calling, I'd be there by now, dealing with it."

"Oh, sorry," she said. "But it's only a little detour, after all."

"Only ten miles." My smile probably didn't reach my

eyes, either. In fact, it was probably more of a grimace. But since Lydia had already half turned away to dial another number on her phone, she probably didn't notice.

I closed my eyes and counted to ten. Then I stood up and left her office, ignoring her cheerful goodbye wave.

Luckily Randall wasn't still at the top of the courthouse steps, so I was spared the temptation to tell him what I thought of his assistant.

The protesters had finished their morning coffee break and were marching up and down their assigned sides of the sidewalk. The anti-Halloween crew carried signs with slogans like "Halloween Is the Devil's Nite." The pagans' signs all had a picture of a spectacularly ugly cartoon witch riding a broomstick. The witch was in a circle with a line through it, reminiscent of a no-smoking sign. During the first few days they hadn't had any slogans on them, giving some of the tourists the erroneous impression that they were against witches, or possibly declaring the town a no-fly zone for broomstick riders. So they'd added slogans like "No Stereotyping" and "Caerphilly Unfair to Witches."

The protesters were all remarkably well-behaved, especially considering the fact that each group probably considered the other its arch-enemy.

Behind them, in the town square, the farmers and craftspeople and other merchants were starting to set up for the farmer's market. I could see merchants and volunteers performing a few last-minute tasks, finishing up the job of switching things over from the Night Side, our evening mode, into the family-friendly Day Side.

In the daytime, we insisted that none of the festival attractions display any excessively graphic or scary decorations, and we discouraged overly gory or provocative costumes. We had no control over what the owners did on private property, of course, but most of them voluntarily complied with the daytime guidelines. Then, an hour after sunset, dozens of volunteers throughout the festival rushed to transform everything. Smiling pumpkin heads turned into evilly grinning ones. Fluffy black cats gave way to snarling wolves. Instead of "Ghostbusters" and "Monster Mash" on the loudspeakers we played "Night on Bald Mountain" and Bach's "Toccata and Fugue in D Minor" and, as the night wore on, truly sinister-sounding mood music. Welcome to the Night Side.

Most of the volunteers found it easier to switch things back before going home, so there was less to do in the morning, but as long as the switch was complete before the tourists streamed in we were okay with it. Members of the Goblin Patrol checked every morning to make sure the switch was complete by eight a.m. That was probably why Rob had been out at Caerphilly Haunted House so early, since the Haunted House and its environs were a hot spot for inappropriate decorations.

My route out of town passed by Caerphilly Elementary and I could see that the children were lined up on the curb in groups of four, being given their marching orders by Mrs. Velma Shiffley, their teacher. I spotted Michael easily. At six-four he towered over all the children—and for that matter, all the adults. He looked very impressive in today's costume—a Union general's uniform that he'd originally acquired for participating in the town's Civil War celebrations. Probably more suitable for a school outing than the over-tight evil wizard costume.

On impulse, I made a U-turn and pulled into the school parking lot. Lydia be damned. Dr. Smoot could wait. I was going to the zoo with my boys.